"The gunshot startles sleeping birds that rise from their nests and go squawking into the night."

Published by Mary Marchese

ISBN: 978-1-54392-258-5

Cover design, illustration & interior formatting:
Mark Thomas / Coverness.com

WHAT REALLY HAPPENED TO STEVE NATHAN

MARY MARCHESE

MARYMARCHESE.COM

Our lives are a story
shaped by circumstance,
twisted by Fate,
And ultimately judged
by how we reacted.

PART 1 – NATE AND LINDSEY

CHAPTER 1

Lindsey

I stare at the faded Polaroid of my mother in the arms of a tall, blond stranger, who looks vaguely familiar. Both of them are turned toward the camera with happiness from newly ignited love glowing from their faces and every nuanced curve of their entwined bodies. My opinion of love, since my divorce, is that when the passion burns out, nothing's left but cold ashes. I frown and glance at the bottom white edge of the photo where I read my mother's perfect handwriting. "The happiest day of my life. June 24, 1974."

Who is this man? Where is he now? I don't remember her ever talking about him.

I toss the photo onto the bed among the rest of the clutter I dumped from my mother's top bureau drawer. It's a jumbled mess of stuff from her life that she no longer remembers—stuff I'm attempting to sort through as I clean out her house before putting it on the market.

Because of my mother's worsening dementia, I'm the one who has to do this. She, like me, is all alone since Dad died of a sudden heart attack two years ago, and other than my brother Jonathan, who has a family and isn't as available, there's nobody else who cares.

I sigh. It's hard making decisions for a parent who is no longer able to. She deteriorated so quickly, I haven't had time to adjust to the role reversal.

I pick up the photo again. Behind the happy couple is what looks like a picnic table and the remains of lunch. My mother is wearing a long orange, green, black, and white geometric design halter dress that shows lots of cleavage. Her long dark hair, in a Cleopatra cut, frames enormous dark eyes—eyes that I have inherited. The man, the stranger, is tall and rangy with a young Robert Redford look and a killer smile.

Hmmm. So Mom had a serious boyfriend before Dad—a handsome, blond man. I wonder what happened to him?

I look at the date again, written on the bottom of the Polaroid. June 24, 1974.

I was born March 21, 1975.

A jolt of realization takes my breath away. The stranger looks like a male version of me!

I sit down quickly on the bed amid the clutter, my mind scrambling to make sense of this.

The father I grew up with was a large, quiet man with dark, perfectly combed hair and hazel eyes that usually looked past me when he spoke to me. His face was too white and puffy, and when he smiled, which wasn't often, you saw that he had very crooked bottom teeth.

Every evening when he arrived home from work, he would say to me, "Hi there, Poppet," in a deliberate sort of way before he gave my mom a kiss. After he changed out of his suit, he would sit in the living room, watching the news on TV until supper was ready. At least that's what he did until my brother

Jonathan was born.

Right before my brother was born, while he was safely tucked inside my mom's swelling belly, she let me listen to his drumbeat heart and watch the ripple of a knee or elbow go across her belly that was stretched so tight I thought a pin prick would burst it open and that's how the doctors would get him out.

He came out—not the way I had imagined—as 8.4 pounds of squalling, wrinkly redness. I had pictured him as a live baby doll, something pink and placid that I could push in my doll carriage. That, he was not.

But it wasn't just my disappointment in the reality of my baby brother—the reality of runny yellow poop and bouts of inconsolable crying. What set my mind firmly against my little brother Jonathan, at least when he was small, was the way my father acted around him.

The day after Jonathan came home from the hospital, my father became a different person.

"How's my little man?" he'd say, dancing around the room, holding Jonathan, a grub in footed pajamas.

As Jonathan grew from grub to a slightly more complex creature, my father became ecstatic over a smile, a new tooth visible through the drool, and often remarked about the thick head of fine dark hair, unlike mine, that was Jonathan's signature from day one. My straight blonde hair, which I have put into a ponytail while I'm working, is different from every other member of the family.

I blow out the breath I had been holding and take in a fresh one.

Now I understand why there was a barrier between my father and me! I could never make him look at me the way he looked at

Jonathan, no matter how hard I tried. Although it makes sense now, I still feel in my heart the failure from all the frustrated efforts on my part to connect with him. If it hadn't been for my loving mother...

I close my eyes, my mind unable to make sense of this new information and collate it into the memories that were my reality up until now.

So—now what?

There is more sorting to do, yet my world as I knew it has just exploded. I can do nothing more today, physically or mentally. I'll go home, pour myself a glass of Pinot Grigio, and try to rearrange the pieces of my life.

As I leave the bedroom, I tuck the Polaroid into my purse.

*

I'm on my second glass of wine when I remember the portable metal box that holds my mother's legal papers. It was the first thing I brought to my condo for safe keeping and has her birth certificate, marriage license, insurance information—all the important papers that she can no longer be responsible for.

Hurriedly I gulp the last swig of wine and go to the closet where I stashed her box behind my ski boots. My hands shake as I lift it out. What will I find?

My mother, like me, is not the most organized person, so all the papers are mixed together. I carefully remove them and examine each one. There's a speeding ticket—who would have guessed that my demure mother would exceed the speed limit?—an expired mortgage agreement for the house I grew up in, and yes—a marriage license!

The license is dated October 6, 1976. I was a year and a half old. Behind the license and attached with a rusted paper clip is another document—adoption papers showing that Joe adopted me as his child.

The impact of the discovery freezes my mind momentarily. This is proof of what I suspected and feared. Joe Casselton is *not* my father. My mother was knocked up by a good-looking blond man, whom she never told me about, and I was the result. Why didn't she tell me? Who is he? Where is he?

*

It isn't until the next weekend that I have the time and the courage to return to my mother's brown cedar-shake home a block from the ocean. It's a cozy, quaint little house with nooks and crannies, and it used to be my grandparents' home. I can't walk in the door without remembering the delicious terror from Poppy's bear hugs and recalling the taste of Grammy's walnut brownies fresh from the oven. After Grammy and Poppy died, my mom and Joe moved there. I was busy with my new married life and came only for holidays. At one time, I thought I'd like to move in after my mom had to go to the nursing home, but it would have meant a long, miserable commute through heavy interstate traffic. So I live an hour away in my condo, the one I bought after my divorce.

I return to my mother's house with firm resolve to find out everything I can about the man in the Polaroid photograph. I have told no one about my find, not even Sue Ellen, my best friend from college who's like a sister to me.

It has snowed since I was here last weekend, and because no

one is living in the house, I've stopped the shoveling service. I go up the front steps sideways for more traction in the two-inch accumulation of snow. Gripping the metal railing, I feel its coldness through my glove.

As I open the front door, I wonder, *What else will I find here today?*

The living room with its rounded stone fireplace has been cleared of personal items. Jonathan and I have civilly sorted through the books and knickknacks, taking what we wanted and boxing the rest to give away. We did the same with the dining room and kitchen. All that is left to be cleared are the attic and my mother's bedroom, where she slept alone for the last year she was here. I agreed to deal with my mother's things in her bedroom as Jonathan dealt with our father's personal belongings when he died. Neither of us has been in the attic since we played there on rainy days as children.

I walk into the bedroom and glance at the bed covered with dresser drawer clutter. Might there be more Polaroids? Or a memento from the mystery man?

Half of me wishes the photo had never shown up—that my life would continue running in well-worn grooves of predictability. The other half of me is intrigued and wants to learn the truth, even though it might leave me vulnerable and unconnected to the family safety net I thought I had.

I rifle through the scattered pile of tangled jewelry, scarves, empty perfume bottles, little ceramic dishes with hand-painted flowers. There are no more photographs. Rather than sort through what is spread on the bed, I open up another dresser drawer full of underwear, nylon stockings, wool socks, pajamas, and feel into their soft depths for paper or something solid.

Nothing.

The next two drawers again yield nothing of interest. I walk to the clothes closet, remembering how less than a year ago I had selected clothes from this closet that I thought my mother would wear in her new life in the Alzheimer's unit. It had not been easy then, and it wasn't easy now realizing that all those clothes so carefully chosen are no longer worn. My mom stays in bed all day now, and when I visit, she often has no idea who I am.

I stop to let the feeling of sadness flow over and past me, a common sensation I'm learning to live with. When it passes, I look up at the top shelf to a row of boxes labeled with dates. The leftmost one says "2000–2005." I pull it down and find folders with old receipts. I want a box with records from 1974, but the oldest box is "1980–1985." My father Joe was an accountant and kept meticulous records, a quality I did not, and apparently could not, inherit from him.

The attic. It's the only place left that might contain a clue.

*

The attic is accessed through a small door off the upstairs hallway. Whatever is there probably hasn't been touched for years. My retired parents were not very agile, and the stairs have a narrow tread and curve sharply.

Entombed cold air with the scent of cedar assaults my nose. Surprisingly, the attic looks empty. Then I remember my mother's obsession when her parents died about getting the house ready for renters. She hired people to clean all her parents' clutter out of the attic, the clutter of old magazines and comic books, empty milk bottles, even an old spinning wheel. I look around in the dim light coming from the dusty window, nostalgic for what used to be there. It appears that the only thing in the attic is a steamer trunk that looks too new to have been my grandmother's. It's big and I can't carry it down the stairs by myself. I'll have to open it up here and get Jonathan to carry it down later.

Fortunately, the trunk is not locked and I'm able to open the snap fasteners holding it closed. As the top rises, I see clothing. Old dresses, hats, and purses from the seventies. There's even the orange, green, and black geometric dress from the Polaroid. I groan with disappointment. I was hoping for letters and documents.

"Mom!" I say like I did when I was a teenager. "What were you thinking?"

I'm about to let the top crash down to punctuate my dashed hopes when I see a red clutch leather purse. Very retro. I could use something like that with the red heels I bought on sale last month.

I take the purse out and let the trunk top fall with a satisfying crash. I don't bother to re-attach the snap fasteners.

So much for more information about my real father. Best to let the whole matter go and get on with my life.

I retrace my steps down the narrow curved stairwell. Back in my mother's bedroom, I get down to business, sorting and boxing everything. It's dark when I finally leave the house with my head full of what must be done next—call a Realtor, get the house appraised, perhaps paint the living room a more appealing color, get estimates for updating the kitchen and bathrooms and see if it makes sense in terms of raising the value of the house.

It isn't until bedtime that I remember the red purse. I bring it to my closet to see if it matches my shoes, and it does. Perfectly!

It's well made, but I can't find the label. I open it, hoping to find the name brand inside. The cream colored satin lining is in good shape, but I still don't see a label. A zippered compartment on one side bulges. I unzip it. Inside is a folded piece of letter paper that is worn on the edges. I open it slowly.

June 25, 1974

Dear Alice,

My tired body is here in the barracks after a 5-mile run, but my mind is floating with memories of our recent two days together. Mind blowing days!

Speaking of floating, I'm glad I decided to "float" on your dad's fishing boat. I saw you selling tickets and I was "sold". It was the start of the best thing that's happened to me in years! I haven't been this happy since my college basketball team won the division title!

Tomorrow I have to go to Vietnam for a year. Major bummer! The good news is that the war is as good as over and I can see the light at the end of my tunnel. The bad news is that I've been assigned to the transition team and security will be tight. You can't call me and I can't make calls either.

You are a beautiful dream and one that I will treasure until I can wake up with you in my arms again.

Please don't forget me.

Love,

Steve Nathan

After reading it through twice, my shaking hands fold the letter and put it back into the zippered compartment where it was probably kept for over 40 years.

I wonder how many times my mother read the letter. Hundreds? Thousands? I imagine the joy she felt when she read it the first time and maybe even the first twenty times. Did she write him? Did he write her back, and if so, where are his other letters?

My thoughts move from my mother to me and what I want to do next. Do I want to find out about this Steve Nathan? It seems that he is my father, and he obviously loved her. Or was it more of a "Wham, bam, thank you, ma'am?" What kind of a man was he? What have I inherited from him?

The questions flow into thoughts of my grandfather, who used his fishing boat for guided tours in the summer. My mom, who helped out during college breaks and afterwards while she was teaching elementary school, was an accomplished fisherwoman. She caught the record swordfish one of those summers. In spite of my heritage, I don't have the patience for fishing, and rough waters make me nauseous.

My mind drifts back to what I now know about this Steve Nathan, probably my father. He was athletic. He ran five miles and was a basketball player. A good basketball player. He was a smooth talker. "You are a beautiful dream and one that I will treasure until I can wake up with you in my arms again."

And either he really couldn't be reached by phone after he went to Vietnam, or he knew how to tell a damn good lie.

I start to feel anger rise within me. How dare he use my mother the way he did! How cavalier and irresponsible! Just who did he think he was? God's gift to women? Or—and this thought puts a freeze on my anger—maybe he died.

How I wish my mother could tell me more. Why didn't she tell me when she could? Who can tell me more? I remember that my mother has a younger brother, my Uncle Bob, who lives in Minneapolis. Apparently Uncle Bob left home right after high school and married a woman who refused to leave Minnesota to meet his family. I only met him once when he came to my grandmother's funeral. And my impression of him was that he was loud and drank too much of our booze.

I search my phone contacts to see if I have a number for Uncle Bob. I don't. My mother's old Rolodex is in one of the boxes I've stored for her. I rifle through one box then another and finally find it. Robert Groton.

I dial his number. It rings three times, and I do a mental check to see if it's a respectable time for calling someone in Minnesota. It's one hour earlier than here in New England, so yes, even though he's old, he should be awake.

"Hello," a male voice says.

"Uncle Bob? This is Lindsey. Your niece."

"Lindsey? Alice's daughter? Is she…"

"Oh, my mother is fine. Well, as fine as possible." I hesitate. I can't just jump right in demanding answers. That would be rude. "How are you doing, Uncle Bob?"

"Passably well, I think."

There's an uncomfortable pause during which I hear what sounds like the pop top of a beer can. I decide to stop playing etiquette games. "Uncle Bob. I know this call is unexpected, and I hope you don't mind that I'm calling you, but you are the only person I can think of who might be able to answer some of my questions. You see, while going through my mom's things at the house, I came across a photograph and then a letter."

Uncle Bob says, "I was wondering when I'd get a call like this."

"You did? You mean…"

"Yes. Go on. Tell me what you found."

"A Polaroid photograph of my mother with a tall, blond stranger, dated nine months before I was born, and then a letter from someone named Steve Nathan to my mother."

"That would be the one."

"The one? What do you mean?"

"His name was mud in our house for a good many months! Not sure how much detail you want me to lay on you, but he sure was one unpopular guy." Uncle Bob seems to relish telling me this as if he had been holding in the secret for decades and finally was permitted to talk about it. "Let me tell you, you almost weren't born! Your mom fought daily with our parents over whether to have an abortion, give you up for adoption, or keep you until the golden boy returned from 'Nam."

The idea that I might not have been born hits me with sudden force, and I tune out of the rest of the conversation until I hear Uncle Bob say, "Then she contacted the military and found out that Steve Nathan was killed. Right at the end of the war."

I had thought it was a possibility earlier, but really, he was killed? Steve Nathan was killed?

"Your mom could be stubborn, as I'm sure you know, so in spite of pissing off our parents, she decided to keep you, saying you were the only thing she had left from the love of her life— this Steve Nathan guy. Of course, then she met Joe Casselton when you were a baby and you know the rest."

I am numb. My dad was killed? I'll never get to know him?

Uncle Bob stops talking, and I am unable to say anything for several moments. Finally, I say, "Thank you," but I'm not really thankful at all, only confused.

"Any time," Uncle Bob says. "Oh, and give my regards to your mother."

"Thank you," I say again like a robot.

CHAPTER 2

Nate

The first time Nate asked about his absent father was in 1979. He was four years old. He had recently enrolled in a Head Start program two blocks from their second floor walk-up apartment that was just inside the invisible wall around Little Saigon in San Jose.

"Ma," he said. "Tran has a papa. Kim has a papa. Miguel and Maria have the same papa. Where's my papa?"

His mother Mai stopped washing the rice and shook excess water from her hands over the sink full of fresh, wrinkled greens.

"My baby Nate," she said, enfolding him in her arms and touching his bowl-cut black hair with her still wet hands. "Your papa is with the ancestors. But he watches you every day."

This made no sense to Nate and, in fact, frightened him.

"Does he see me now? Why can't I see him?"

His mother sucked in her breath and was silent as she crouched, rocking him slowly. Finally, Nate wriggled out of her arms, and when he looked at her, he saw her cheeks were even wetter than her hands had been.

"I want to see him. Now!"

His mother stood slowly. "Come." She walked to the small

windowless bedroom they shared and opened the highest dresser drawer, the one Nate couldn't yet reach. Whatever she wanted was right on top.

She sat on the bed and patted the space next to her. "Sit."

She held a photograph in her hands and wouldn't let him touch it. "Just look," she said. "There's your papa."

Nate saw a man dressed in baggy camouflage, like the GI Joe doll Miguel always brought to school. The man stood next to his mother who came up to the middle of his arm. His mother had a big smile that showed all her teeth. Her hair was long and shiny and hung down to her waist, not tied up in a bun like it was now. The man had his arm around her and looked at her with just a little smile. On his chest pocket was a word that Nate didn't yet know how to read, but it started with the first three letters of his name, NAT.

"Oh." Nate slid off the bed and went looking for the red fire truck he liked to push around the apartment and pretend he was the tiny little driver sitting inside.

*

The next time Nate and his mother spoke of his father was several years later. Nate was going to public school now and on this particular day when he came home, he let the screen door slam behind him, something his mother hated. He set his school backpack onto the kitchen table, another thing she strongly disliked. Rather than start his homework immediately as he usually did, Nate sat staring at the red plastic flowers in the middle of the table next to the cruet of nuoc mam.

From the stove where she was already making his dinner

so she could leave for work, Mai said, "What?" She said it in Vietnamese, the language they spoke at home.

Nate pushed his backpack. It bumped the flowers and made them wobble. His mother moved a sizzling pan off the burner and came to stand in front of him, arms crossed.

"What?" she said again.

Finally, Nate looked up at her. "Am I a bui doi?"

Mai sighed and pulled out a chair to sit next to her son. "Bui doi, children of the dust, is an old term for unloved children of the streets. You are not that."

"But," Nate looked up at her finally, a glistening of tears blurring his vision, "Jimmy said because of my light eyes, my father was an American who left me..."

"Your father died saving your life and mine!" Mai hissed. "He..." She couldn't speak for a moment. "He loved you even though he never saw you."

"What happened?"

Mai pulled a handkerchief out of her pocket and wiped her eyes. "It's time you knew."

She stared at the worn linoleum floor, apparently seeing something else. Finally, she said, "Your father was one of the last Americans in Vietnam. I worked for him as a translator at the American Embassy. He was doing secret work for the government that had to do with the Russians and Chinese. It was dangerous work. He was a very smart man and brave."

Nate looked at his mother. *Smart? Brave? Dangerous work? Could this be bullshit like the story she used to tell him when he was a baby? The story about the fierce and wondrous dragon who gave her a baby and told her that this baby was the most precious gift she would ever receive. He used to picture the dragon with slimy green scales and nostrils blowing fire as it handed him over. He could almost feel the dragon claws curled around his small body.*

"Ma!" he said. "Tell me the truth! I don't want another dragon story."

His barb hit right on target, and he saw her wince before she regained her composure. "You *are* the most precious gift I have ever received. That part of the dragon story is true. And this, too, is true. Your father was very smart. He was brave. He died helping me and you, not yet born, get to freedom. And that's all you need to know."

"How did he die?"

She closed her eyes and didn't say anything for a long time. "Someday I will tell you, but not now."

"Ma, tell me. Now!"

His mother turned to him with a look he knew well—the look that meant nothing he could say or do would change her mind.

Nate stood up and, after kicking the chair leg once, walked to the windowsill where his mother kept his blue plastic glass and poured himself some green tea from the pitcher his mother kept full for him.

He had a smart and brave father who loved him. Loved him so much he died so his mother and he could come to America. Actually, it was pretty cool. None of his friends could claim that. Especially the ones with living fathers.

Nate slowly drank the tea that his mother said made his heart strong and kept his brain smart. When he had drained the glass, he returned to the table, opened his backpack, and took out his homework. After his mother went back to cooking, he put the backpack on the floor where it belonged.

*

By the time Nate was a senior in high school, he was 6'2" and played guard on his high school basketball team. Things were going well. He had been accepted at UC Berkeley, and in spite of his mother's objections, he and Rosy Gonzales were an item.

"What? Are you prejudiced?" he asked his mother. "So what if Rosy is part Spanish and part Indian. I'm part Vietnamese and part Anglo Saxon. Maybe Nordic. Our children could be honorary members of the UN."

His mother looked pained, as she always did when he argued with her. "You have good life ahead of you," she said in English. And finally as she looked away, "Don't make her pregnant."

Mai was working full-time at a nearby Vietnamese restaurant known for its authentic cuisine. She was head chef and worked long hours, leaving Nate to organize his life as he saw fit. He was a responsible teenager and organized his life well. Between studying for his AP courses and playing sports, he had little time to get into trouble. His teachers loved him. His coaches loved him, citing him player of the year twice in a row. He was on a partial basketball scholarship to UC Berkeley.

Life was rosy, Nate thought and smiled at the pun. Rosy, the most popular cheerleader at the high school, was not his life, but she made it sweeter, for sure. She wanted to become a world-renowned fashion designer and was going to the Fashion Institute of Technology (FIT) in New York City in the fall. Nate was realistic enough to know that their paths would diverge and they'd find other partners. But for now, he was at the top of his world, and his future looked "rosy." That word again.

It hadn't always been that way. The bad times began in junior high school when a division formed between the purebred Vietnamese and the Amerasian Vietnamese. Nate was obviously Amerasian with his green eyes and unusually tall frame. Gangs of both varieties recruited young teens, and Nate, because of his height and athleticism, was especially desirable.

Mai cut back her work hours during those years to spend more time with Nate. Once she stood blocking the apartment door with a kitchen knife in her hand when Nate said he was going out that evening to "hang out" with some new friends. He could easily have overpowered his small mother, but her fierce love, the love he had experienced his entire life, won.

In the hallways of the junior high school, the purebreds hissed, "Half breed!" to Nate. The bolder ones said, "Your mother's a whore!"

One evening when Nate was despondent, Mai got him to talk about the insults he was hearing at school. To hide the tears that threatened to fall, he put his head on crossed arms at the kitchen table as he mumbled his woes.

When he finished, Mai stared thoughtfully into space before she said, "My mother told me a story a long time ago. It's about a one-legged duck. It's a story told to young children, but it has a truth in it for people of all ages.

"After Heaven completed the creation of the world, there was a duck with one leg. He could only hop, and it was very difficult to get around. He became discouraged when he saw how easily other birds and animals moved about on two or more legs.

"He decided to complain to Heaven but didn't know where it was. He asked a rooster who knew everything, and the rooster told him that Heaven was a long distance away, too far for the duck to get to, but there was a nearby temple with a god who could convey a petition to Heaven.

"The duck eagerly hopped behind the rooster to the local temple. As they entered, they heard a loud voice asking why the temple's incense burner had five legs instead of four and demanding that the extra leg be removed at once.

"The rooster, speaking for the duck, said, 'Your lordship, I have come here because this duck has only one leg. He feels that Heaven has not treated him fairly, and he would like to send a petition.'

"The god roared, 'What Heaven gives at creation is final. A petition won't change anything.'

"The rooster turned to leave the temple, but the duck was desperate. In a trembling voice he said, 'Your lordship, you said something as we entered the temple about removing a leg from your incense burner...'

"The god roared with laughter. Then he became silent. Finally, he said, 'Heaven approves of those who help themselves. If you can remove the extra leg from the burner, you may have it. But it is made of pure gold and is very valuable. Guard it carefully.'

"So the duck, with the rooster's help, removed the extra leg from the incense burner and attached the gold leg to his body. Soon, with practice, he was able to move about like the other creatures. But at night when he went to sleep, he pulled the leg up so nobody could steal it. Other ducks and birds who saw him assumed that was the proper way to sleep, so they imitated him and now they all sleep by standing on one leg."

CHAPTER 3

Lindsey

After a sleepless night where I imagine my newly found father getting killed in a hundred different ways, I realize I can't go to work the next morning. I have vacation days the company owes me, plus the latest version of software is in beta test. My job as a software interface designer is in sleep mode until we get feedback from customers.

Maybe I'll take the whole week off.

Wearing my oldest sweats from college and cradling a cup of dark roast in my cold hands, I stare out my kitchen window, seeing and promptly forgetting the gray sky and the token trees planted at predictable intervals around the condo parking lot.

How did my mother feel when she learned my father was dead? She was pregnant with his child. She had hoped he was coming back to her.

Slowly I begin to understand how brave my mother was and how much she must have loved my father—and me. She could have aborted me. I exist because of my mother's stubbornness against my grandparents who wanted to have me aborted. I understand their reasoning and don't hold it against them, but if my mother hadn't been so strong, I might not be here. The thought makes me wonder if she actually had the abortion and I'm merely a figment of my imagination. I touch myself to make sure I'm not a ghost and immediately feel silly.

My mother also could have given me up for adoption. If so, I'd have a different name, I would have grown up someplace else, met different people, experienced other life situations—not be me as I am now. I briefly entertain the idea of multiple versions of myself and decide that the one I am now is all I can handle for the moment.

Why didn't she tell me about my real father? Was it loyalty to Joe, who bailed her out and adopted me at age one and a half? Was she ashamed of her summer fling with a stranger?

We all make mistakes in love. Ten years with Drew was mine. Yet if someone had taken a picture of Drew and me after we first met, we'd have looked as awash with love as my mother and father did. That makes me wonder if my father had lived and returned to my mother, and if they had married, could they have survived the day-in and day-out of unromantic reality? The reality of morning breath and burnt pot roasts, and the daily stresses that stretch good humor to the snapping point so that soon the number of blow-ups exceeds the tender moments, and the only truce is numb detachment?

In retrospect, I blame Drew's career in part for the failure of our marriage.

Drew was a pilot. Not a Navy pilot like his father who flew an F-4 over North Vietnam and bragged about "blowing up thousands of Gooks," but an airline pilot, which meant we were apart most of the week. In the beginning of our marriage, we acted like honeymooners when he came home from crisscrossing the country. I'd make a fancy candlelight dinner, which, more often than not, was left to be eaten cold, the candles burning down to weak flames in pools of melted wax blobs.

After a year or two, we settled down to the stereotypical peck on the cheek upon his return and a less urgent trip to the bedroom. I still made him dinner, but there were no candles.

I'm not sure when I noticed the change. I probably sensed it subconsciously first and chose not to acknowledge it. By then I was busy with my career and not as emotionally dependent on my role as wife.

Eventually, even my blinders couldn't hide me from the fact that Drew was cheating on me. I confronted him. He was defensive and blamed me for letting our marriage deteriorate. We spiraled to murkier depths of hurt and accusation until it was a relief when he no longer came home. We divorced soon afterwards.

My mother's reaction to Drew and me splitting apart was odd. At least I thought so at the time. She said, "Romantic love is a unicorn that must be fed by both parties in equal measure to keep it alive. It's far easier to be happy in a relationship if the unicorn never existed."

She and Joe must not have been deluded by unicorns, and from what I saw of their marriage, it was a sturdy, no-nonsense relationship based on respect and friendship.

What if I had been raised by my real father? Would I be different? Would he have nurtured my technical side and praised me when I won first place in the science robotics competition— something that seemed to embarrass Joe. He was more encouraging when I went to the Senior Prom with the captain of the football team.

What was my father like? How can I find out more about him?

I open up my laptop and search under National Archives. I type in "Steve Nathan" and get the message:

Sorry no results found for "Steve Nathan." Try entering fewer or broader query terms.

I then try "Steve AND Nathan" and get the same results.

Frustration sets in until the answer becomes obvious. He was a Vietnam War veteran. His name would be on the Vietnam War Memorial Wall.

I find the site for the Vietnam Veterans Memorial through the US National Park Service and click on it. When I enter the name "Steve Nathan," I see:

STEPHEN C. NATHAN
2LT-O1
Age: 25
Race: Caucasian
Sex: Male
Date of Birth: 9/15/1950
From: Ridgewood, NJ
Religion: Protestant
Marital Status: Single
STEPHEN C. NATHAN INFO PAGE

The last line is a link to more information. I hold my breath and click on it. Another page displays:

STEPHEN C. NATHAN
2LT – O1 – Army – Reserve
His tour began on June 26, 1974
Casualty was on Apr 29, 1975

In HO CHI MINH CITY, DISTRICT 1
HOSTILE, Died while missing
Personal Comments or Pictures Click Here

He died when I was just a month old. I stand and pace up and down my living room, back and forth behind my sofa. What does it mean? What should I do? My step is to the beat of my thoughts. What does it mean? What should I do?

Finally, a thought overrides the others. What do I *want* to do? I could end all this angst and go on with my life as if it never happened. Or...

I've always been curious. It's what got me through high school and beyond because I wanted to understand how things worked and why. So I can't walk away from learning the truth about my father. I need to know who he was, what he did, and how he died.

I click on the Personal Comments or Pictures Click Here link.

The result takes my breath away. On the left is a headshot of the man from the Polaroid I found in my mother's dresser drawer. He's wearing a dress uniform and has a slight smile, as if he has the world on a string and is about to reel it in like a yo-yo.

Underneath is a heading called Remembrances with messages left from various people.

POSTED ON 11/2//08 - BY TOM CLARKSON
TOMMYBOY@GMAIL.COM
Hey, man you were voted "Most likely to succeed" in high school. I still can't believe you're not coming back.

POSTED ON 7/2//03 - BY WILLI HENDERSON
My name should be on the wall. Not yours.

POSTED ON 5/31/99 - BY SHELLEY J. NATHAN
SNATHAN@YAHOO.COM
I never got to meet you, but from all the stories I heard about you, I wish I had. From your sad niece, Shelley. God's will be done.

Now what do I do? I can try to locate relatives in Ridgewood, NJ. Perhaps his sad niece, my newly discovered cousin, still lives there, and if not, other family members may be there who can tell me about my father. Or I can go to Washington, DC, and look up his name on the Wall. See what other information is available about him.

Somehow interacting with my newly discovered relatives is too personal for me to deal with right now. I'm still getting used to my new identity. I'd rather go to Washington, DC. I'll call work and say I'm taking the week off. Then I'll get a train ticket, book a hotel room, and do a little detective work.

But first, I need to try to talk to my mother.

CHAPTER 4

Nate

Rosy left for New York City in September and soon afterwards sent Nate a letter saying that as much as she loved him, trying to maintain a relationship across 2,500 miles was more difficult than she had imagined. She wished him "the best."

Nate wasn't surprised, but he wished he had written that to her first. What did surprise him was the finality of her letter. There was no "Let's get together when I come home for Christmas."

Nate soon recovered from Rosy's ding to his pride. Berkeley was a new exciting world for him to explore, and where before he was the exceptional student in his high school classes, now he was merely one of many exceptional students. In other words, he was average, other than his unusual physical appearance. There were not many Vietnamese students in his classes. Most people thought he was Chinese until they looked into his startling green eyes.

He met Janet his second year, when he no longer sat on the bench during basketball games. She was a blonde, bubbly freshman and had a habit of saying "like" in almost every sentence.

"Nate, my family is, like, having an extra big turkey this

Thanksgiving, so, like, if you want to join us, like, for dinner and the weekend, my mom says you can fit in."

He wondered briefly about her use of the words "fit in" and whether he would or not, but Janet was charming, and he hadn't experienced a traditional American Thanksgiving turkey dinner before. His mother usually made duck.

So Nate agreed to go to Marin County with Janet Eberly for Thanksgiving break. She drove them there in her little red sports car that "Daddy, like, gave me when I, like, graduated from high school."

Janet turned her little car into a long driveway that led to an elaborate Spanish-style hacienda. As she stopped in front of the house, the massive oak front door opened.

"Janny baby, you're here!" A heavier, older version of Janet in a loose pink outfit floated down the stairs and took Janet into her arms.

"Mom. This is Nate. You know, who I told you about."

Mrs. Eberly looked at him with no expression. Then she put out her hand, and Nate shook it. Her hand felt like a bunch of overcooked asparagus. Her eyes were a cold blue, and as she swept ahead of them into the tiled foyer, Nate caught a whiff of a flowery perfume.

Inside, the house continued the Spanish motif with heavy leather furniture, wrought iron window treatments, and hand-painted pottery accented in cobalt blue.

Nate found it curious that Rosy's parents, who were Spanish, decorated their house with secondhand Early American, and his mother was happy with any piece of furniture, preferably free, that was sturdy. Nate's bed, Rosy told him, was French provincial, something usually chosen for a young girl's bedroom. Rosy had taken great pains to educate Nate on décor. Perhaps he could use that knowledge as a talking point with Janet's mother.

"Let me show you your room." Janet motioned Nate to the stairs.

"Janny, honey," her mother took Janet's arm and moved her away from the stairs, "Uncle Roger and his new wife are coming and might stay over. I've decided to put Nate in our downstairs guest room."

Janet looked baffled. "What downstairs guest room?"

It was so obvious that Nate was not welcome, yet Janet didn't get it.

They walked past the huge kitchen with decorative tile countertops and dozens of pots and pans hanging from a central iron rack suspended from the ceiling. Nate thought about his mother's tiny kitchen, essentially one wall of the main room, from which she made miraculous stir-fries, delicately wrapped spring rolls, fragrant soups with glistening noodles, and his favorite—roast pork strips. Rice in the well-worn rice cooker was a constant.

At the far end of the house, next to the door that led to the swimming pool, Janet's mother opened a door into a small room with a sofa and a large open closet that held folded deck chairs, beach towels, and large containers of pool chlorine.

Janet turned to her mother and was about to say something, but her mother spoke first. "Nate, this is rather primitive and I'm sorry, but we had a last-minute confirmation that my brother, whom I haven't seen in years, is coming. I'm sure you're the rugged type, being a basketball player and all. The sofa pulls out and I'll bring you some sheets. There are plenty of towels. Just help yourself."

Before Nate had a chance to respond, she pulled Janet with her and closed the door on him.

Nate took a deep breath and sat on the sofa. It was brown leather and much nicer than the one they had at home, blue fake suede with shiny patches from butts and backs.

Now what?

This was not the first time Nate had experienced prejudice, and he knew it wouldn't be the last. He had learned from his mother and from observation that life wasn't fair. One of his mother's favorite sayings was, "If you don't have beef, learn to like chicken." On the other hand, in history class just last week, he'd read a quote from John F. Kennedy that resonated with him. "We choose to go to the Moon in this decade and do the other things, not because they are easy, but because they are hard."

It would be easy to make up a story about not feeling well and have Janet drive him to the closest bus, if there were buses here in Marin County. Much harder would be to stay and be respectful. To rise above their pettiness. To show them that he was as intelligent as they were and tougher than they expected.

Could he do it? He took another breath. He'd prefer a physical contest against a 6'7' center who trash-talked and knew how to knee him in the nuts without the ref noticing.

*

When Nate finally gathered his resolve to leave the little room that now felt strangely like a sanctuary, he followed his nose to the good smells coming from the kitchen. Something was roasting that smelled almost as good as his mother's crispy-skinned duck.

Mrs. Eberly was the only person there. She didn't see him

approach as she chopped an onion with great vigor and almost as quickly as his mother did. A ten-pound bag of potatoes was next to the sink.

"May I help you?" Nate asked.

Mrs. Eberly, visibly startled, said, "Oh, Nate. You crept up on me!"

"Sorry," he said, not too convincingly. "I can peel potatoes or whatever you need doing."

"Oh, Janet can do that when she comes down later."

He waited a minute or two and then said as pleasantly as he could, "My mother's a chef and she's taught me a few things."

"A chef?" Mrs. Eberly scraped the chopped onions into a dish. "What kind of chef?"

"Well, right now she's the chef at Coriander's in San Jose. Before that she worked at a French restaurant."

"Coriander's. Is that a Vietnamese restaurant?"

"Yes." Nate neglected to add that it recently won Best New Restaurant in Northern California. What he did say was, "When I was too small to be left alone at home, she would take me with her, and I helped her do whatever she was doing in the kitchen. As a result, I'm a decent sous chef."

He was rewarded with a small smile from Mrs. Eberly. "All right, Nate. Show me what you can do to those potatoes over there."

"Peeled, then quartered for mashing?" he guessed.

"Exactly."

Nate took it upon himself to select a large pot from the ones hanging from the ceiling and fill it with cold water. Then he expertly wielded a potato peeler he found in a drawer next to the sink and started dropping naked potatoes into the cold water at a remarkable rate.

By the time Janet showed up an hour later, Nate had prepped all the vegetables and was helping Mrs. Eberly take the company china from the large buffet in the dining room and set it on the newly extended table.

Janet raised her eyebrows at Nate. "You are, like, full of surprises!"

*

The next two days passed pleasantly enough for Nate, in spite of the difficult beginning. Janet's father and Uncle Roger were big golfers and spent most of the time, when they weren't eating, out on the golf course. After an initial handshake with Nate, they basically ignored him. Evenings, they drank too much and loudly traded stories of their accomplishments, each trying to outdo the other.

Janet drove him to the beach one day, where they walked for hours. Another day they went to a concert. Nate liked Janet, but there was no depth to her. It could have been that she was merely young, but he suspected she would become her mother at some point, and although he and Mrs. Eberly had an unwritten truce, he didn't trust her.

That distrust proved valid on his last evening at the Eberlys'.

After yet another turkey sandwich with cranberry sauce, Nate excused himself for the evening, saying he'd like to "hit the sack" early. The truth was, he was uncomfortably saturated with the Eberly lifestyle and needed time to himself.

As soon as he reached his room, he realized that he had nothing to do for the several hours before he could sleep. He remembered a bookcase of books, mostly paperbacks in an alcove off the kitchen. He retraced his steps back to the main part of the house and was scanning the book titles when he heard Janet and her mother talking at the kitchen table.

"Isn't Nate great!" Janet said.

"He's a responsible young man."

"But, I mean, he's, like, so cool and nice."

"Janet," her mother's voice had a quality to it that made Nate stop cold. "It's time you grew up a little and understood something." She paused and took a deep breath. "You need to realize that Nate's mother was most likely a bar girl in Vietnam. Most of the mothers of half Vietnamese children were. So, how would you explain to your children that their Vietnamese grandmother was a whore?"

Nate didn't remember the walk back to his room. He gradually became aware of his breathing as he sat on the pulled-out sofa bed with his arms crossed, his hands in fists.

What had his mother told him about her previous life? That she was a translator at the American Embassy. Her English was better than most Vietnamese mothers he knew. But was it good enough to be a translator at the American Embassy?

Suddenly, Nate knew he had to leave the Eberly house immediately. He stuffed his clothes into his backpack and opened the side door that led to the swimming pool. From there he went around the side of the house and down the long curved driveway. He would hitch a ride to where he could find public transportation, and if nobody picked him up, he'd walk.

The night air was cold and seemed to wake up his mind. He breathed deeply, and gradually the stale air in his lungs was replaced with fresh. It was pleasant outside. He took another deep breath and noticed the stars, glittery points of light in the clear sky. There was a slice of moon, the thinnest possible slice. A new moon. Brand new. He recalled a children's book in his elementary school library that had a picture of a man's profile on a slice of moon. He was a smiling man with thick lips, a big nose, and a pointy forehead and chin. Nate used to think it was stupid to put a face on the moon. Everybody knew the moon wasn't human.

A dog from a large house on a hill sensed him walking by and began to bark. Nate kept a steady pace, his non-thoughts flowing in rhythm to his steps.

Time passed. It could have been a half hour or two hours, but by the time he reached a gas station with a pay phone, Nate realized that it didn't matter to him what his mother had had to do to survive in Vietnam.

CHAPTER 5

Lindsey

I visit my mom at least once a week and always approach the single story, gray Alzheimer's unit with trepidation. In the beginning, I was anxious about whether she was having a good day or a bad day. Regardless, she would recognize me and smile her gratitude at my coming to see her. Lately my anxiety is whether she will know who I am through the delusional film that clouds her mind. Often her eyes will light up when she sees me, but she doesn't seem to know why she's happy I came.

Today I bring daffodils, which were probably flown in from South America. They are my mother's favorite spring flower. She had mounds of them in our back yard, planted randomly at the edge of the lawn bordering the woods. There were classic daffodils with long tubular trumpets, pale narcissus with blunt orange ruffled centers, miniature daffodils, even an unusual pink one she found in the seed catalog and had to have. Growing up, I loved the subtle scent of those flowers she brought inside and arranged in a blue glass pitcher.

My mother's eyes are closed when I enter her room. "Hi, Mom," I say. She is motionless. I busy myself getting a vase to put the flowers in and find a clear glass, run-of-the-mill one that came free with a flower delivery.

I set the vase on the table next to her bed. "I brought you some daffodils, Mom."

Her eyelids quiver and then open. She smiles when she sees the flowers. I bring the vase close to her face so she can smell them. Her smile widens.

"Good." She says the one word.

Normally that response would make me consider the visit a success. But I want more. I sit next to her bed and take her hand. "Mom," I say. "Do you remember somebody from a long time ago named Steve Nathan?"

She wrinkles her forehead as if concentrating on an answer. But soon the wrinkles disappear and she smiles at me. I bring the flowers to her nose again, and she happily breathes in the scent of daffodils.

I brought the Polaroid photograph with me, and now I remove it from my purse and hold it in front of her face. She frowns and blinks her eyes as if she can't focus. Then she shakes her head and points to the vase of flowers.

Again, I bring the flowers to her nose, and she ecstatically sniffs them.

I feel conflicted. I'm happy that I can give my mother the simple pleasure of smelling flowers yet sad that she isn't able to go beyond it. She is reduced from a complex, intelligent woman to a simple, almost childlike being.

I wipe away my tears as I reach down to give her a kiss. I smooth the thin white hair away from her face and look at her a long time. "I love you, Mom."

"I loved him," she says clearly with a look in her eyes that is different from a moment ago.

"What did you say?" I ask, even though I heard her.

It's gone. She looks at me with the same blank expression she had before, as if the sudden brief connection of memories to prompts from the present never happened.

*

The next morning, earlier than I am normally at work, I sit in the padded high-backed seat of the Amtrak train, feeling the unique sensation of being roughly propelled forward at the same time that I'm being jerked side to side.

Eight hours of this, I think. What possessed me to take the train? And the breakfast I purchased in the café car was barely edible.

Because I didn't have time to stand in the long line to buy breakfast at one of the restaurants in South Station, I'd had to settle for a train-purchased sausage, cheese, and egg sandwich on a warm and spongy English muffin. It was beyond disgusting, but I'll make up for it tonight at a restaurant in DC.

The door between cars slides open, letting in a blast of cold air. I shiver and look out the window at the lightly falling snow. It highlights every silhouetted tree branch and reminds me of the powdered sugar my mom used to sprinkle on my favorite dense chocolate cake. For special occasions, she'd lay a doily over the top before sprinkling the sugar, making a sweet, lacy design.

My mother. I think back to my visit yesterday. She said, "I loved him." She said it clearly. Past tense. Soon after hearing his name and seeing his photograph. I have no choice but to think she was referring to Steve Nathan.

I feel no jealousy that she spoke of loving him after I told her that I loved her. I've never questioned that she loved me. More so now that I've learned she had to fight against her family's wishes to keep me.

I miss her. I hate not being able to communicate. Even if I weren't on a mission to discover her connection and mine to a tall, mysterious stranger, I miss having a lucid conversation, any kind of conversation, with the loving, wise woman who was always there for me.

What would she tell me, if she could? Would she hold back information because of embarrassment about her poor judgment? Did she sanctify the incident and store it in a holy structure that no one but she could enter? Or did she suspect that Steve would not return to her even if he had lived?

Perhaps she entertained all of those thoughts and chose to keep them to herself as she dealt with her reality—Steve who was dead, me, Jonathan, and her steady but not-very-exciting husband Joe.

I'm drawn away from speculation back to the present when larger flakes of snow fly horizontally past the train window. We're heading south into warmer weather where the snow isn't accumulating. As if hypnotized, I stare through the snow at fleeting glimpses of people's back yards with winter-abandoned grills, some covered, some not, and windows of every size and shape, a few with slatted blinds askew.

Eventually, the sky brightens and the snow ends, and I feel a surge of anticipation mixed with apprehension for what awaits me.

*

After settling into the hotel I picked because of its proximity to the Vietnam Memorial, I walk two long city blocks toward the Wall. The sky is overcast, and I have limited daylight left, just enough to be introduced to the memorial. Tomorrow I'll come back and spend more time.

Ahead of me is the Washington Mall, its long expanse of winter-bleached grass stretching from the Lincoln Memorial to the Capital with the Washington Monument in the middle, pointing heavenward. The miles of open space offer no resistance to wind that penetrates my down coat and forces me to pull my wool hat lower over my ears until it almost covers my eyes.

The Wall could easily be missed by a casual observer. It first appears as a black angled gash that drops suddenly from the lawn. Its two outstretched wings start from pointy tips and meet, fully formed, in the center at about a 120-degree angle.

I look for the building associated with the memorial. There's only a closed kiosk that sells drinks and snacks during the summer. How am I supposed to find more information about Steve Nathan? I assumed there would be a building with computer terminals linked to databases full of information about each name. Obviously, I assumed incorrectly.

Discouraged, I start to walk away, feeling my trip to Washington is a wasted effort. Eight hours jerking along in a train for nothing better than slightly warmer weather than New England. I pass a clear stand with a shelf containing what looks like a phone book attached by a thin chain. The names. It must contain the names on the Wall. Steve Nathan should be in that book.

I go back to the stand with the book and, with gloved hands, attempt to locate Steve Nathan's name. Eventually, I remove one glove and continue flipping the pages with increasingly numb fingers. There it is. Stephen C. Nathan 1W, 121.

What do the numbers mean? What does the W mean?

I decide to walk down the paved path along the Wall. This memorial was designed for the average citizen, so it shouldn't be rocket science to decipher the numbers. The tip has just a few names on it and as the sections increase in size, they hold more lines of names. In the bottom corner of each section, I see a number that decreases as the section increases in height. 70W...68W...65W. I appear to be going in the right direction if I'm looking for 1W. Soon the Wall is taller than I am, and I have to look up to see the top names. 30W...27W...22W. I see a single carnation at the foot of various sections—a gift to the memories of loved ones. Little American flags dot the base of other sections. 15W...12W...11W. Now the Wall is so tall I have to crane my neck to see the top names. At the point where the two wings meet, I finally see section 1W.

Now for 121. It can't be name number 121. That would be cruel to expect people to count each name among the thousands on the panel to find the 121st.

I sigh. My warm, condensed breath floats like a cloud before me. The low sun behind me projects my silhouette onto the shiny surface of the Wall, an outline of a living human being filled with the names of the dead.

It's time to go. Tomorrow I will decipher the Wall. Now, I want warmth and a decent meal with at least one glass of wine.

CHAPTER 6

Nate

The call from the hospital came while Nate was working on a paper for his Market Research Data and Analysis class. He was in his first year at the Berkeley Haas School of Business, getting his MBA.

"Is this Nate Huong?" the voice asked.

"Yes," he said, wondering how the person had gotten his unlisted number.

"I'm calling about your mother, Mai Huong, who is currently hospitalized with us. She is in the ICU with a critical, unknown illness. We thought you would want to know."

"May I talk to her?" Nate said quickly.

"I'm afraid she is unable to speak due to her condition."

Mai was never sick. Nate couldn't remember her ever staying in bed during the day or even relaxing in a chair for any length of time. She was always doing something in her deliberate, unhurried way—chopping food, cleaning up, or sitting at their table, calculating expenses with an abacus, sliding the beads first one way and then the other.

The caller gave Nate his mother's room number at the ICU, and Nate left, not bothering to do more than write a quick note to his roommate.

Unknown illness, he thought. The uncertainty of what it was and how to deal with it made him anxious.

By the time he arrived at the hospital, he had imagined every possible cause of illness from a rare poisonous spider bite to a bad case of the flu—from bacterial meningitis to a collapse from exhaustion and overwork. She was working ridiculously long hours, and the last time he was home, she'd mentioned that her boss had no understanding of all that she did as head chef. He was a businessman, not a chef, and although he appreciated her expertise, he didn't credit her for the rave reviews Cilantro got from most food critics.

That was most likely the reason for her illness, Nate thought. *Exhaustion and overwork.*

He parked his beat-up red Datsun in the visitor parking lot of the hospital and walked to the reception area. It was evening, and most of the visitors had gone home. The receptionist looked up at Nate over her reading glasses, surveying him with eyes the same shade of gray as her hair. "May I help you?"

"Yes. How do I get to Room I-362?"

"Go down the hall and take a left. You'll see a bank of elevators. Take one to the third floor."

Nate didn't like hospitals. Not that he'd spent much time in one, except the week he brought homework to a basketball teammate who broke his kneecap during a game. There was something about the artificially clean smell that made him wonder what foul and abhorrent odors it replaced. His imagination took him places he didn't want to go.

He managed to put a check on his imagination as to what he was about to find in room I-362. No sense continuing the baseless speculation he had indulged in on the drive to the hospital.

Outside his mother's room, there was a sign and a bin of surgical apparel. The sign said all people entering the room must put on a gown, mask, and gloves. As he was standing there deliberating, a nurse approached him.

"Are you family?" she asked.

"Yes."

She began to put on the paraphernalia. "I'll go in with you," she said.

Nate struggled with a gown that was meant for a much smaller human being and ended up having it cover the front of him, much like a poorly cut bib that left his back exposed. All the while, his panic grew. In a way, it was beneficial, because by the time the nurse opened the door and he saw his mother lying very still with machines looming over her, he didn't see anything that he hadn't already expected.

The nurse guided him over and said in a low voice. "She's not in a classic coma because she speaks. Not conversationally, but rather as if she's talking in her sleep."

"How long has she been here?" Nate expressed one of the thousands of questions circulating in his head.

"One day. Are you her son?"

Nate nodded and felt the mask slide further up his nose, pressing uncomfortably under his eyes.

"The doctor will make her rounds in the next hour or so. You can ask her more questions."

"Do I have to wear this mask?"

"It's to protect her from outside bacteria and protect you from whatever it is that she has. So yes, keep the mask on."

The nurse pointed to a chair next to the bed and left.

Nate settled his mask further down his nose with a gloved hand and let out a breath that filled the mask with warm air.

Mai's hair was loose onto the pillow and framed her face, making it look small and vulnerable. She began to moan and roll her head back and forth with her eyes tightly shut.

"No!" she said. "Steve! NO!"

Then she began speaking rapid Vietnamese, obviously agitated. Nate could only make out a few words that sounded strangely like "purple dragon."

He put his gloved hand on her arms gently. "Ma," he said softly. "I'm here. It's going to be all right."

She quieted down for a few moments and then spoke again with force, "No! Steve, what did they do to you? This can't happen!"

Nate again spoke soothingly to his mother as he had before. His voice seemed to calm her, so he continued talking. "Ma, I came here from school to see you. I'm with you now. There's nothing to be afraid of. The doctor will be here soon, and we'll take care of you. Just rest for now."

*

When the doctor eventually came into the room, covered with gown, gloves, and mask, she nodded to Nate and said in a muffled voice, "Let me examine her, and we'll talk outside later."

Nate took it as a dismissal from his mother's bedside and reluctantly left the room. During the hour or so that he had sat by her, his mother had talked more nonsense. Once she mentioned his name in connection with a stern reprimand to always keep his promises. "A man is only as good as his word," she said in

Vietnamese. Apparently it was a Vietnamese quote as well as the American one Nate had heard.

Taking advantage of the time away from her room, Nate grabbed a soda and some pretzels from a vending machine. He settled into an orange plastic chair in the waiting lounge down the hall from his mother's room. He hadn't realized how hungry he was. His mother wouldn't have approved of the soda. When he was growing up, she always kept a pitcher of green tea for him in the refrigerator because it was cheaper and healthier than soda.

The woman doctor found him a few minutes later and sat in a chair across from him, looking at him intently as if to gauge how to say what needed to be said. Nate remained silent and looked at her, waiting.

"Your mother," she said finally, crossing her legs and jiggling the one on top, "has an undefined illness. I'm inclined to think it's a rare tropical fever. Your mother did *not* grow up in this country, did she?"

"That's right. She grew up in Vietnam."

"There are viruses that can remain dormant in people for decades and suddenly, for no apparent reason, come to life. Perhaps it's because of stress or a weakened immune system. This is out of my realm of expertise, so I'm consulting with a tropical medical expert who should be here tomorrow. He's attending a conference in San Jose this week and agreed to see your mother."

"Good," Nate said, "but in the meantime, will she be all right?"

"We're giving her fluids and keeping her fever down. Other than that, we'll have to wait until the expert arrives." She looked intently at Nate again. "I don't advise staying in her room for more than a few minutes at a time. I have no idea how contagious this virus is, if it even is a virus."

"I'll take the chance." Nate stood abruptly to end the conversation. All the questions in his head had vanished.

CHAPTER 7

Lindsey

The young man at the Washington hotel's front desk recommends an Italian restaurant that has been receiving rave reviews. It's a Tuesday evening, so I figure I don't need a reservation. My cab drops me off in front of a nondescript façade, but the minute I open the door to the restaurant, I'm greeted with aromas of roasted meats, herbs, and something yeasty with a touch of garlic. Walls of wine bottles with fancy labels partition the room into intimate dining areas. I'm ready, more than ready, for this meal.

The maître d', in a suit and tie, greets me. "Good evening, ma'am. Do you have a reservation?"

"No."

"Well, I'm sorry, but we are all booked for tonight."

"You are?" I say stupidly, not wanting to believe it. Back home, most restaurants are empty on a Tuesday night.

"Yes. We're usually booked two days in advance. Would you like to make a reservation for this weekend?"

"I won't be here this weekend," I say, turning to leave as I try to remember other restaurants I saw on the way here. Wasn't there a burger joint down the block?

"Excuse me, miss," a woman's voice says behind me. The voice is husky and comes from a woman about my mother's age, perhaps a little older, with spiky white hair and dozens of gold bracelets that jangle together as she waves at me.

"Yes?" I say.

"You're welcome to join me at my table."

I hesitate. One of my lifetime rules is—don't start a conversation with a stranger unless you can easily escape. I learned this lesson after exchanging pleasantries with a chatterbox seated next to me on a nonstop flight from New York to San Francisco. Now when I fly, I bury myself in a book and only nod when spoken to.

But tonight I'm famished, and a stranger is offering me a place at her table. "Thank you!" I say. "That's very kind of you."

The maître d' pulls out a chair for me at her table and nods rather curtly.

"I'm Lindsey." I put out my hand.

"Vivian." She takes my hand in a firm grip, and I feel the presence of multiple rings on her fingers—rings that, when she drops my hand, I see are unusually intricate, some with large stones.

"You have no idea how grateful I am for this," I say. "I haven't had a bite to eat since breakfast, and I could eat this napkin right about now!"

"Well, my dear, I hope you don't do that. I'm happy to share my table with you. I've already ordered, so let me get my waiter and have him put your order in right away. I recommend the crab cake, as we are in crab country. I had it last night, and it was delectable—pure, moist crabmeat with a crunchy top. All their pastas are handmade, so you can't go wrong with any of them. I'm trying pappardelle with rabbit tonight. Last night I had fettuccine with asparagus and prosciutto in a creamy sauce. Delicious."

She lifts her bangled hand with a slight wave, and the waiter comes over immediately. "Give this beautiful young lady a menu and hold my order to come out with hers, please."

Although this woman might be my mother's age, she is as different from my mother as anyone could be. Confident. Cosmopolitan. Pushy?

I mentally chastise myself for looking a gift horse in the mouth, so to speak.

"Now, what are you doing in Washington?" she asks.

The menu is in front of my face, but I lower it to say, "Sightseeing."

"Most people chose to sightsee in the warmer months, but Washington can be beautiful any time of year. The fabulous museums are just as fabulous in the winter as they are in the summer."

"And why are you in Washington?" I ask to be polite.

"It's my wedding anniversary to my husband whose name is on the Vietnam Memorial Wall," she says. "I've come here every year since the Wall was built to look at his name."

I set the menu down and look at her.

"That's why I'm here!" I say. "Not to see my husband's name, but my father's. And I haven't found it yet. Not the name, nor my father." I realize I'm not making any sense. I take a deep breath and mentally kick myself for opening my mouth to this bejeweled stranger with the puffy eyes and the "look-at-me" spiky hair.

"Very interesting," Vivian says. "We have all evening to talk, and it sounds as if you have an interesting story. Are you ready to order?"

Really pushy! I think, *like my ex.* Yet my stomach tells me I'm more than ready to order, so I let it go and return my gaze to the menu. *She isn't really like my ex.* Crab cakes are not my favorite. Homemade pasta, however, sounds wonderful.

A few minutes later, I tell the hovering waiter that I'll have the fried squash blossoms filled with goat cheese and prosciutto as an appetizer and a thick homemade fettucine with wild boar ragu, aged parmesan cheese, and shaved artichokes as my entree.

"Sorry if I rushed you," Vivian says. "I'm so used to being alone that I forget that everybody isn't in my time zone."

I gaze at her, amazed at her seeming ability to read my mind and stunned by her unabashed ego.

She continues, "I ordered a bottle of Prosecco. I hope you'll share it with me. That's another tradition I keep when I come to Washington, even when I don't have someone to share it with."

"Tell me about your husband," I say, hoping to distract her from asking me personal questions I'm not ready to answer.

"Ah, Robert. My beautiful, impetuous husband. We were married less than a year. Sometimes I think that because we were together for such a short time, our relationship didn't have time to sour. He was going to Vietnam, we were in love, so we married. I still think of him as the perfect man, and no man since has been as perfect."

'Did you have children?" I ask.

"No, and because I never fell out of love with him all these years, I never remarried." She uses her napkin to dab at her eyes, leaving a smudge of mascara on the crisp, white cloth. "As soon as the Wall was completed, I began this tradition of coming to Washington to see his name. Robert was a POW who was never accounted for."

"So he may still be alive?"

"I entertained that thought for many years. I wrote letters to my congressman, even hired someone to go to Vietnam and look for him. The reports were inconclusive and not encouraging. Finally, I had to accept the inevitable. Next to his name on the wall is a plus sign, unlike most of the other names with a tiny diamond shape that means their deaths were confirmed. If someone missing is found alive, the plus next to his name is circled. I've heard it's never happened—yet."

The Prosecco arrives, and our waiter pours us each a glass of the bubbly pale amber liquid.

"To Robert," I say as I hold up my glass.

"And to your mysterious father," she says, holding up her glass to touch mine. She takes a sip then begins to talk, looking me straight in the eye. "I was disappointed when I first came to the Wall to reconnect with memories of Robert. I expected more. It was sterile—beautiful in a shiny, technical way, but impersonal. There was a man about my age who was standing next to me. I watched him locate the name of a loved one or friend—maybe somebody he fought next to. The man stared at the name with a hard look on his face in the beginning. His gaze softened. Then he clenched his fists and started to walk away. In less than a minute, he was back. He rested his forehead on the stone and sobbed."

Vivian takes another sip of Prosecco. I can think of nothing to say.

"So," she continues, "I've learned over my years at the Wall that its power is subtle but strong. You need to open yourself to the reality of that bloody, useless war and let out all your anger, your sadness, your feelings of personal betrayal by God or Fate.

And when you are empty of feeling, then you can absorb the fact that there are more than 58,000 names etched before you, and each of the names was loved by someone who also has a hole in his or her heart. You are not alone."

*

The next morning when I open the heavy curtains in my hotel room, the sun pours in unfiltered by clouds. This is the day I will locate my father's name on the Wall. Unlike Vivian and most visitors to the Wall, I won't have memories of the man whose name I find, so there should be no emotional catharsis like Vivian described in the restaurant last night. I will view it simply as one name among thousands on a block of polished black stone—a name that is most likely my father's. I might feel a tinge of regret that I never knew him, but that's all.

I dawdle over coffee in the hotel's breakfast room. There's no rush. My train leaves at 2:00 pm. Vivian had wanted me to stay another day in Washington so she could show me her favorite sites, but when I tried to extend my stay by another night at the hotel, it was fully booked. Just like the restaurant.

As I stir cream into my third cup of coffee, I realize that Vivian both fascinates me and frightens me. Last night at the restaurant, she loosened me up, so I told her everything. In spite of my resolve to keep silent about my story, her commanding presence turned me to jelly. To be fair, she was forthcoming about the fact that she is a well-known artist, and she spoke about her shows, but I'm unclear about what she does. The frightening thing about her is that she's the kind of person who could suck me into her sphere like an insect into a Venus flytrap. Unlike the flytrap, she isn't malicious—I hope—but I fear I would lose my identity. We plan to keep in touch, however, and perhaps meet in New York, where she has an apartment.

Back in my room, I gather my personal items and throw them into the overnight bag. I'll pick it up after my walk to the Wall.

The sun warms the morning air, and without gusts of wind, it is a much more pleasant walk than it was the evening before. I go straight to the clear plastic stand with the book. Perhaps it will have directions on how to locate a name. Before the alphabetically listed names are a few pages of introductory information, and among the paragraphs, I find a sentence that explains the numbers. I was right that the "1W" refers to the first of the western panels. The "121" is the location on the panel of Steve Nathan's name. It's the 121st row where every ten rows are marked by a dot on the left in front of a block of ten lines of five names each.

I also notice an explanation about the markings that Vivian told me about last night. Most names are followed by a small diamond that indicates they are confirmed dead. A person who is missing and assumed dead has a small "+" after the name. If that person were to be found alive, the "+" would be encircled, symbolizing the circle of life. Apparently no one with a "+" has been found.

Walking down the paved path along the Wall on this sunny day feels different from the day before. A young boy, ignored by adults busily locating a name, swings on a section of draped white chain that hangs between posts separating the path from an expanse of grass. His foot almost knocks over a red, white, and blue wreath. A woman my age holds an older man's arm and says as they pass, "Are you all right, Dad?"

I arrive at the juncture of the west and east wings of the wall where I stood last evening. I count down twelve dots and one row. The glare of the sun reflects skeletal trees, sky, and drifting clouds off the mirrored black surface. I see it at last. STEPHEN C. NATHAN +.

I can't breathe for a moment. Missing? My father is missing, assumed dead.

CHAPTER 8

Nate

Three months after Nate first visited his mother in the ICU, she was back at home, jobless and too weak to work. Her unsympathetic boss, after sending a bouquet of chrysanthemums to her hospital room, had told her that he was hiring a young Vietnamese man trained in France to be head chef. But she was always welcome. They'd find a position for her—somewhere.

When the rare tropical virus ran its course, it left Mai an emaciated shell of her former self. Nate attempted to finish his semester at Berkeley, but between the distractions of worrying about his mother's health and their dwindling finances, he decided one morning to simply walk away from the MBA he had dreamed of getting. He was a natural businessman. He didn't need an MBA to succeed.

"Ma," he said the afternoon after he told his advisor that he was through, "we're going to open a restaurant—you and me."

"How?" Mai was sitting on their blue suede sofa with a cup of green tea cradled between her cold hands.

"You'll do the cooking and I'll be the manager."

"But how? We can't afford."

"That's the kind of thing I've been learning at grad school.

You have a proven track record as a chef, I'll get the funding, and we'll make it work." He sat down next to her, careful not to jostle her tea. "Our first order of business is to get you strong again."

Nate suspected that part of his mother's weakness was due to depression and a sense of failure. He was confident that he and his mother could run a successful restaurant, but he also knew that she needed to believe in something that would give her hope, something that would spark the will to go forward with her life.

"What shall we name the restaurant?" he asked, hoping to get her involved in the process. "The Golden Phoenix, to symbolize our rebirth out of the ashes? Or perhaps something with turtle in the name—the Jade Turtle! You've always liked them. Remember the turtle I found that you let me keep when I was kid—until it crawled out of the tank and we couldn't find it? I wonder what happened to it?"

Mai said, "I put it in irrigation ditch on my way to work."

"You what?"

"It unhappy."

Nate looked at his mother in amazement. "Okay. So we can name the restaurant after that turtle that you freed. Maybe the Happy Turtle."

"No," Mai said. "My restaurant name be Rice."

"What?"

"Rice is life. This restaurant be my new life."

And mine, Nate thought with a momentary twinge of regret at the turn his life had taken.

*

Over the next few months, Nate wrote a business plan and

presented it to local banks. The first bank manager listened respectfully and, without looking at the plan, stated that they were not in a position to finance any new small businesses in the near future. Other bank managers were not as polite.

Nate decided to mail his business plan to the same banks he had visited. Fifty percent of them responded favorably and invited him to come in person to discuss it further. When he showed up, most of them managed to find an excuse why they couldn't fund him, except for one. She listened intently and asked pertinent questions.

Eventually, she said, "Nate, this is a fantastic business plan. You've addressed all the angles, and your mother is obviously a known commodity in the restaurant world. I think we may be able to do something for you."

After several more meetings with the bank and a lawyer that Nate had to hire, the deal was done. The nice bank manager further helped them by connecting them with the owner of an available 40s bungalow-turned-restaurant with living quarters in the rear.

It was almost as if Fate had flicked a switch in Nate's life. After hitting bottom, he and his mother were on the way up again. They moved into the apartment at the rear of the bungalow, which was far more pleasant that the two-bedroom basement apartment they had rented since Nate was in elementary school. The restaurant, however, needed work.

One day soon after their move, Nate was standing bewildered in front of a display of paint colors in a hardware store when someone punched him lightly in the arm. "Hey, how's it going?"

He turned to see Rosy. She looked exactly as he remembered except her hair was pulled back into a soft bun at the nape of her neck. A few stray tendrils of dark hair framed her face. Seated in her shopping cart was a small child, a miniature version of Rosy.

"Rosy!" *She looks great*, he thought, *but who is the child? Hers? A niece?*

"This is Sophie," she said nodding toward the child who had a pink bow in her head of dark curls. "She's mine."

"Hi, Sophie," Nate leaned down to be closer to the little girl, whose large dark eyes were like her mother's, only softer. She backed away shyly from him. Nate's eyes strayed to Rosy's left hand. She wasn't wearing a ring.

Over a cup of coffee, Nate learned that Rosy didn't graduate from FIT. She got pregnant instead and had a brief marriage to Mario, a fellow student. After the marriage dissolved, she came home and moved in with her parents, who watched Sophie evenings while Rosy worked as a cocktail waitress.

When Nate told her about his new venture opening a Vietnamese restaurant, Rosy offered to be a design consultant. For free.

Her first comment upon entering the bungalow was, "It's dark in here. You need to lighten it up!" Her second comment was, "So you want it Asian-like, with bamboo and stuff?"

Nate agreed to everything Rosy suggested, mainly because he didn't have an eye for that kind of thing and also because he was in love with Sophie. When she turned her big eyes on him, Nate's insides became pudding. She started calling him Uncle Nate.

After Rosy transformed the dark interior into a bright space of pale yellow accented with graceful lime green bamboo, the restaurant opened. Mai shopped for ingredients every morning and bought only what passed her rigorous inspection. The menu at Rice was simple, and prices were reasonable. Lunch used the same menu as dinner with slightly smaller portions and prices. When Nate contacted the local newspaper and invited a reporter to come to the restaurant for a free meal, they received a positive review, and Rice's clientele grew.

In six months, the restaurant began making a profit, and Nate, Rosy, and Sophie found an apartment within walking distance of the restaurant. In a few more months, Rosy quit her job as a cocktail waitress and began serving tables with Nate at Rice. Sophie, who was a docile child, fell asleep each night in Mai's apartment, connected by a baby monitor to the kitchen where Gramma Mai kept a sharp ear out for what was rivaling Rice as the most important thing in her life.

CHAPTER 9

Lindsey

It isn't until the train is halfway to Boston that my mind can function. Up until then, the sounds of people talking and moving about fill my brain. Every seat is taken, and the man next to me sleeps with his mouth open. Every once in a while, he snorts and wakes himself up. It takes so much of my energy to cope with external stimulation on the train that I can avoid dealing with my inner turmoil. I pretend to sleep because real sleep escapes me.

After people leave the train in Philadelphia and New York and I'm alone in the seat, I feel I can be myself again. I look outside the window and absorb the sight of brittle, yellow salt marshes with snow, white between the stalks. Beyond is rippled gray water. As the train slows down through a coastal town, I see icicles hanging from the low scallops of rusted corrugated tin roofs. It's bleak yet beautiful.

Finally, my mind opens itself to the issue of Steve Nathan, missing and not confirmed dead.

The word my mother must have received when she inquired in 1975 was that he was dead. That's what Uncle Bob said happened to Steve, and most likely Mom told Uncle Bob. Perhaps she didn't hear or wasn't told that Steve was missing, presumed dead. Or, she might have heard it and chosen not to hope. The hope that he would return to her even if he were alive was an uncertain one, so maybe she was realistic enough to forget double-damned hope and go on with her life—her life of raising me, her love child with Steve. And then she met Joe and didn't fall in love, but recognized him as an older, reliable person with whom she could share a life.

It's time to move from the seat I've felt glued to for over five hours. I take my laptop and walk with lurching steps to the dining car, where I open it on one of the tables. Trying several sites, I search for people with the last name of Nathan in the town of Ridgewood, New Jersey. I find two people of interest—one a 75-year old woman, Sarah Nathan, who might be an unmarried sister or a sister-in-law. Another is George Nathan, a 45-year old man, who could be a nephew or cousin. And then there is the sad niece, Shelley, who left her email with her comment on the Vietnam Wall website. I quickly return to that page and jot down her information, along with that of a person who apparently went to high school with Steve, Tom Clarkson.

I could go the route of cold calling and emailing these contacts. Or I could try to learn more background by checking out Ridgewood websites to see if I can obtain records of residents. On the Village of Ridgewood website, a well-constructed one with photos of neatly kept parks and municipal buildings, I see an option for obtaining marriage, birth, and death certificates. When I select it, one of the requirements is that you need proof of relationship.

I sigh.

Going to a blank Word doc, I decide to compose sentences I

might use as openers when I contact potential family.

After a half hour, I've written six possibilities, and as I reread them, I grade them on a scale of one to ten for acceptability, ten being the best.

"Hi, my name is Lindsey and I might be related to you." (One)

"Hi, my name is Lindsey. I'm sorry to bother you, but I'm looking for someone who might know a person who fought in the Vietnam War named Steve Nathan. Because your last name is Nathan, I thought you may be related." (Seven)

"Hello. My name is Lindsey and I'm calling on behalf of the Vietnam War Veterans. I understand you have a family member who fought in the Vietnam War." (Two)

"Hi. My mother got knocked up by someone named Steve Nathan and I'm the result. Do you know anything about him?" (Zero)

"Hi, my name is Lindsey. You don't know me and I apologize for intruding. You see, I just discovered that my father, who probably died in the Vietnam War, was Steve Nathan from Ridgewood, NJ. Are you by any chance related to him?" (Three)

"Hi, my name is Lindsey and this might be one of the strangest calls you are ever likely to get. I really don't know how to start. You see, the other day when I was going through my mother's things, I found..." (One)

I like the second one the best, and although it isn't perfect, I feel more confident as I dial the number of George Nathan.

"Hey," a male voice says.

"Oh, uh, hello. My name is Lindsey, and I'm looking for information about someone who died in the Vietnam War named Steve Nathan."

"Never heard of him."

I hear the click as he hangs up on me.

Fifty percent of my phone options are gone. Maybe I'll have more success emailing Steve's high school buddy, Tom, and niece Shelley.

I spend another half hour on the emails and end up with:

My name is Lindsey and I'm looking for people who knew a person who fought in the Vietnam War named Steve Nathan. I found your email on the communication page for Steve Nathan and hope you will respond to my inquiry.

I appreciate any information you can give me. Thanks.

Lindsey

The instant I send the email to Shelley, a message is returned that says:

Address not found

The email to Tom appears to be successfully sent.

While waiting for a reply from Tom, I dial the phone number for 75-year-old Sarah Nathan.

"Hello?" A voice answers. It's hard to tell from the one word just how old the person is and, more importantly, how receptive she will be.

"Hi. My name is Lindsey. Is this Sarah Nathan?"

"What do you want? I don't donate over the phone."

"Oh, I'm not soliciting anything. Really. I'm just looking for someone who might know a Steve Nathan, and your last name is Nathan, so I thought perhaps you could help me."

"Steve's dead."

"I know. I just saw his name on the Vietnam Memorial Wall. Are you related?"

"By marriage."

"Is your husband available?"

"He died last year. Heart attack. Fell over—bam—and he was gone. He was Steve's cousin."

"I'm so sorry. And I'm really sorry to call you out of the blue like this, but," I pause. "You see, I might be related to the Nathans. I know it sounds bizarre, but I think Steve Nathan was my father."

"When were you born?"

"March of 1975."

"Steve left for Vietnam in the summer of '74. So, yeah, the dates work. Why do you think he was your father?"

I summarize my story, and she listens without interruption. The other end of the line is so quiet, I suspect she may have hung up. But when I finish talking, she says, "That sounds like Steve."

"What do you mean?"

"He was popular with the girls."

Hmmm. "Mrs. Nathan," I begin. "Do you mind if I come see you so we can talk some more?"

"I guess I don't mind. Not much to do these days. But my husband was just his cousin."

"That's fine. You knew him."

I arrange to go to Sarah Nathan's home in Ridgewood the next afternoon. I'll have time to unpack, sleep in my own bed for one night, and then drive to New Jersey.

CHAPTER 10

Nate

Rice, because of its reasonable prices, excellent food quality, and authentic flavors, soon became a very popular restaurant. Most evenings, a line formed outside the door. Nate suggested they require reservations, but Mai disagreed.

"People cancel last minute. Some people no show. Empty tables no earn money. We do take-out."

"Take-out? That puts us in the same category as every chop suey strip mall joint. Is that what you want?"

"Maybe," she said. "If our chop suey joint make money like McDonald's."

"No!" Nate rarely raised his voice, but he did now. "Don't even think about it! That would put us into a clichéd lower class of restaurant. You would lose the joy of preparing exceptional food and begin cranking out poor quality, low-class junk food. Is that what you want? Really?"

"I no cook junk food! It never be junk food."

"But if you have to prepare ten times the amount of food you do now, you'd have to streamline the process and hire help who wouldn't do as good a job as you, and soon it would be junk food!"

Mai turned to the chopping board and whacked a clove of garlic with the side of her cleaver. Then she took another clove and another and whacked them one at a time until the board was covered with flat irregular disks surrounded by papery skin, and the kitchen became filled with their odor. Nate watched her and frowned. He knew it was senseless to continue the discussion, so he left the kitchen and walked to his apartment. Sophie would be home from school soon. He stood outside their apartment building and waited for her, kicking at a crack in the sidewalk.

By the time Sophie's bus arrived, Nate had calmed himself to the point where he wasn't cursing his mother's stubbornness, that same unyielding quality that had guided him through his teenage years and into adulthood unscathed. It was a positive trait except when it blocked what he wanted. From experience, he knew he could not change Mai's mind when she clamped down hard on something. He tried to imagine a Rice chain of fast food Vietnamese restaurants. There would be the benefits of selling franchises, yet even though the money might be good, it was not something he could be proud of. The perfection of his mother's cooking would be lost, watered down by poor imitators and tired minimum-wage workers.

"Uncle Nate, Uncle Nate!" Sophie saw him first as she stepped off the bus that stopped with a shudder of squealing brakes in front of him. "Look what I brought you!" She waved a paper in front of her, Barney lunchbox rattling as she ran, dark curls bouncing.

Nate, as usual when he saw Sophie, felt himself melt, and when she handed him the paper, he was unable to stop tears from welling up. She had drawn three stick figures, one large, one medium, one small, and under them in uneven letters she had written, "Daddy,

Mommy, Sophie." The daddy had green eyes.

*

That evening after all the diners had gone and the newly hired dishwasher had finished cleaning up, Mai motioned Nate to follow her to the living quarters behind the restaurant. Rosy had already taken Sophie home to her own bed, so the two of them were alone.

"Sit." She pointed to a wooden chair that had been retired from the restaurant because of peeling paint.

Nate sat, bracing himself for what was coming. His mother busied herself in the corner of the room for a moment, then brought over two small glasses of a dark amber liquid.

"I bring this from Vietnam before you born," she said. "I save for special occasion. My father and brother make it."

Nate brought the glass to his nose. It was alcohol of a kind he had never encountered. It was pungent and strong and not altogether pleasant.

"This rice wine from very special rice," his mother said. "This rice not in United States. In Vietnam, many, many kinds of rice." She paused. "Try it."

Nate took a sip and made a face. He looked his mother in the eye. "What's the special occasion?"

Mai took a sip from her glass before she spoke. "Special occasion because you go Vietnam meet my family."

Nate knew enough not to react openly against being told what to do by his mother. She seemed to forget sometimes that he was a grown man with a lot more education than she, and they were in a culture she was not entirely familiar with. On the other hand, to be fair, she was a tough survivor of things he could only imagine.

"Tell me about your brother," he said at last, not recalling that she had ever mentioned a brother. She had told him about her mother and father, who were killed by an American bomb as they plowed their rice field with a water buffalo, and a younger sister who wrote letters and sent photographs of his pureblood Vietnamese cousin.

"Brother name Tran. Older brother. Very smart man. He now important man because he know farming. You go Vietnam ask him for rice. Bring rice here for restaurant. Special rice make us famous. Make restaurant famous."

So this was how his mother was conceding to him. Not directly, of course. That would be humiliating for her and make her lose face. But Nate was American, so he said, "Does that mean you want Rice to be a fine dining experience instead of a fast food chain?"

"I want Rice give American people rice. All kinds of rice."

CHAPTER 11

Lindsey

Mrs. Sarah Nathan lives in a mustard yellow Victorian on a side street off Main Street. As I walk onto the wraparound porch, I notice patches of peeling paint around the windows behind which are lace curtains.

When I ring the doorbell, I hear barking that gets closer and closer until it's accompanied by scratching on the other side of the door. "Down, Buster!" a woman's voice says. A key turns in the lock, and the door swings open to reveal a gray-haired woman in a blue print dress, holding a tousled black terrier. I get a mental flash of Toto and Auntie Em. Am I about to go to the Land of Oz? It has been a wild ride up to this point, for sure!

"Lindsey Casselton," I say, putting out my hand. She stares at me, almost rudely, and eventually, without taking my hand, opens the door wider so I can enter, then she closes it behind me, shutting out most of the light. I smell freshly baked cookies.

After a long silence, she says, "I'm Sarah Nathan, as you probably guessed, and this is Buster." She sets him down. He approaches me cautiously, then sniffs my shoes. "Well, ah..." she seems to be debating about what to do next.

We stand in the gloom of the entryway with only the sound

of Buster's sniffing.

"Coffee?" She points to a door behind her. "I made some cookies."

"You didn't need to fuss," I say, "but the cookies smell wonderful, and coffee sounds great."

She leads me into a living room with somewhat shabby furniture with antimacassars on the arms, just like at my grandmother's, and with a bay window full of African violets. Sarah is a generation younger than my grandmother but must be one of those people who chose to stay in the time warp of her mother. I sit down in a worn green overstuffed chair. She goes into what must be the kitchen, and I hear water running. Buster sidles over and looks me up and down. He has amber eyes partially covered by fringes of black fur that move when he blinks. I put my hand out for him to sniff. His muzzle is wet, and soon my hand is being damply tickled, then licked.

Buster and I are just becoming friends when she comes back for me. I follow her into a large, old-fashioned kitchen that also reminds me of my grandmother's. The cream-colored linoleum on the floor is worn gray by the sink that's positioned in front of a window framed in red checked curtains. She seats me at a wooden farmers table and brings me a steaming yellow mug of coffee and cookies still warm to the touch.

"Thank you! These cookies are delicious! I love it when the chocolate chips are still gooey."

She sits next to me. Her mug has a quote in curlicue letters— "World's Best Cook."

After staring at my face, she says, "You have brown eyes."

"Yes." Then I get it. "My mother has brown eyes."

"Steve had green eyes. But you're tall like Steve was, and your hair is blond like his. And there's something about your smile. Yes, that's it! You have Steve's smile."

She stands suddenly. "I have to make a phone call." She walks to a landline phone on the wall, and I hear the singsong tones of a number being punched.

"Yes," Sarah's voice says, "she's here." Pause. "Yes, I'm pretty sure of it." Pause. "Okay."

Weird. And rude. Who did she call, and what's happening?

She returns to me at the table and announces, "I've invited Steve's brother to come over. He'll be here in a few minutes."

Steve's brother! I abruptly set down my coffee mug. Am I ready for this? He's my uncle! As close a family member on my father's side as I may ever meet. I wish I had been prepared. She should have asked me first. Will he look like my father?

Sarah says, "I called Mark after I spoke to you yesterday. He said he wanted to meet you if I thought you were the real deal."

Mark. Mark and Steve were brothers. "Is Mark younger or older?"

"Younger, by four years. He adored his older brother. You know how it is with the younger ones. He copied everything Steve did, except go to Vietnam, of course."

"Does Mark look like his brother?"

"Yes. All the Nathans are good-looking. I was so jealous when I went to family reunions. I felt like an ugly duckling, except my husband told me I had better legs than any of the women, and I was a better cook."

Two stellar qualities in a woman. I glance at Sarah's veined legs and try to imagine them young and svelte. Based on the cookies I've eaten, I'd say she can still cook. I feel a momentary softening toward this woman, who based her self-esteem on what men thought of her rather than internal self-worth. She seems to be from Mom's generation when women had fewer choices. But enough ruminating. I need to get more information before Uncle Mark shows up.

"Does Mark live in Ridgewood?" I ask, wondering why I didn't find his name in my Internet search.

"No, he lives a few towns over. He and his wife. They have three children, all grown now, of course."

"Is one of their children named Shelley?"

"Yes. She married suddenly, if you know what I mean, and moved to Colorado."

"Did Steve have any siblings besides Mark?"

"No. There were only the two boys."

"You said over the phone that Steve was popular with the girls. What did you mean by that?"

"Well, he was a good-looking young man and could date any girl he wanted. I was dating his cousin around the time Steve was in college. He brought home a different girl every time he came home. Couldn't seem to find one to settle down with. But then, it's good he didn't because he went off to Vietnam and all."

Too late, she seems to realize she might have said something wrong. We are both saved by the doorbell.

Buster goes through his protective ritual of barking when the doorbell rings, and even though he obviously knows Mark, who calls to him through the door, he continues until Sarah picks him up. It provides enough of a distraction to help me hide my feelings of awkwardness. Still, seeing an aged version of the photographed man, who I was now accepting as my father, is a shock.

It seems to be emotional for Uncle Mark, as well, because he does a double take, then covers his face with both hands. He manages to sit down in the green chair I had occupied earlier, and when he looks up, there are tears in his eyes. He shakes his head slowly and says, "Well, praise the Lord! You are most definitely a Nathan. You could be my daughter Shelley's sister."

Sad niece Shelley.

He continues, "So, how did you figure out that your father was Steve?"

I sit opposite him on the burgundy sofa with matching pillows and a multi-colored afghan on the back and start to tell him my story.

"You say the photograph was taken in June of 1974 in New England?" Uncle Mark asks.

"Yes."

"Steve called me the end of June. It was the last time I ever spoke to him. He said he met the girl of his dreams in some little fishing village in New England."

I grab a pillow next to me and hug it hard, unable to speak for several minutes.

I finally manage to say, "She never forgot him, and I believe she still loves him."

Sarah gets up at that point and brings Mark a cup of coffee and the cookies. I take another one, and we eat in silence. Eventually, I continue my story.

When I get to the part about my trip to Washington to visit the Vietnam Memorial Wall, and finding the "+" next to Steve's name, Mark says, "That plus sign is cruel. It gives false hope to people who would be better off accepting the death of their loved one." Mark sighs. "First we were told Steve was dead. Then six months later, we received another call that said he was missing, presumed dead. My mother and father were beyond ecstatic. It was as if he had risen from the dead. My father sent inquiries and pursued every avenue possible, but because Steve was working with the CIA and his job was highly classified, nobody could tell us anything. To access his file required a high-level security clearance."

Uncle Mark shakes his head and continues. "I know my mother believed until she died that Steve would suddenly show up at the door one day. My father may have been more realistic, but that hope kept them from properly mourning my brother and getting on with their lives. It was cruel."

I say, almost to myself, "And because my mother never heard that he was missing, she mourned his death and then went on with her life."

The afternoon continues with stories of Steve. I learn that as a young child, he gave his favorite well-worn stuffed rabbit to his little brother, slipping it into his crib one night when Mark was crying. A year later, he gave his little brother a black eye. When he was an adolescent, he risked his life, saving a dog that fell through the ice. Steve had a partial basketball scholarship to the University of North Carolina and was in ROTC. Mark noted that Steve always pretended to be on top of the world even when he wasn't, like he was trying to fool himself as well as everybody else.

Sarah invites me to stay for dinner, which I'm sure would have been delicious, but I am emotionally drained. I need to go somewhere quiet to process my newly acquired information.

As I say goodbye, Uncle Mark shakes my hand and says, "Welcome to the family, and please stay in touch. I'll be praying for you."

CHAPTER 12

Nate

Nate's first trip to Ho Chi Minh City was in the spring. Mai had written to her brother Tran, explaining what she wanted, and when he agreed to meet with Nate and introduce him to various agricultural products unique to Vietnam, she wrote to her sister, Kim, asking if Nate could visit the family. Nate was to pretend to be a representative of an American corporation that was looking to import rice and other goods into the United States. The careful planning and subterfuge made Nate suspicious. Could his Uncle Tran be an official in the Vietnamese Communist government? If so, that meant Uncle Tran had had nothing to do with the Americans during the war. Anyone associated with Americans was ostracized, at best, after the war and certainly not given a government position. In fact, Uncle Tran may have fought against the Americans.

His mother's final words to him as he left for the airport were, "Nate, you do what uncle say. You hear me? No be crazy American."

Nate's suspicions increased when he was met at Tan Son Nhut airport by a uniformed official who greeted him and escorted him to a waiting Russian-made car. Because it was midnight

Vietnam time, the car took him directly to a hotel. The driver wished him a good night in Vietnamese, and Nate, who spoke adequate Vietnamese, wished him the same. Then the driver said in English, "Eight o'clock." And with that, he drove off.

Ho Chi Minh City was more modern than Nate expected. He found his room in the seven-story hotel to be clean and comfortable—especially after spending 20-plus hours jackknifed into a seat designed for someone eight inches shorter than he.

In San Jose, it was nine hours earlier, and inexplicably, Nate's internal clock woke him up at exactly 7:00 a.m. local time, which was 10:00 p.m. back home. He showered, dressed, and went looking for coffee. Even though Nate hadn't learned to read Vietnamese, the words on the signs were phonetic enough that he could guess the spoken words and followed the signs and his nose to a dining room. He sat at a small table with a glass top that covered a red tablecloth. It was one of a dozen in the room, most of which were unoccupied except for two tables with white men of unknown origins.

A waiter handed him a menu written in both Vietnamese and French. Nate glanced at the nearest occupied table and saw one of the men eating an omelet. He said to the waiter in Vietnamese, "Coffee and eggs served like that," pointing to the omelet with his chin. He didn't know the Vietnamese word for omelet.

The waiter nodded and soon appeared with the best coffee Nate had ever tasted. It was rich and complex, and not at all acidic. The omelet was okay, a little dry, and Nate realized he was turning into a food snob. *I guess my priorities have changed,* he thought. *A few years ago, I wouldn't have noticed whether an omelet was moist or dry. And coffee was coffee—something to wake me up after a night of studying or partying.*

Nate was finishing his third cup of coffee when the driver from the night before appeared and motioned him to come. "Get your luggage," he said in Vietnamese. He followed Nate to the room and watched as Nate packed.

Big Brother is watching, Nate thought, not at all comfortable with the situation.

A half hour later, after weaving through erratic swarms of bicycles and motor scooters, cars that used horns instead of brakes, and buses that spewed noxious fumes, they arrived at a squat gray office building. The driver led him up a flight of stairs to one of a dozen doors that lined a dim hallway. He knocked loudly and said, "Your guest is here."

A voice responded with muffled words that Nate didn't understand.

Nate's uncle stood as they entered, a small man with a broad forehead like his mother's. A mole on his chin sprouted 4-inch hairs that he apparently cultivated. Prominently positioned on the wall behind his desk was a colored picture of a gaunt-looking Ho Chi Minh with a sparse beard and mustache and a red Communist Vietnamese flag in the background.

"Good morning," Uncle Tran said in formal Vietnamese and nodded his head. Then he dismissed the driver with a wave of his hand.

Nate put out his hand as he repeated, "Good morning," but Uncle Tran did not shake it. Instead, he motioned Nate to the one chair in the room. Nate sat.

Without any recognition of family ties, Uncle Tran began to talk in rapid Vietnamese about agriculture. Nate could only understand about half of what he said. There were facts about rice yield and the need to export, some history of how, after the war, rice production was down, which, Nate guessed from the words he understood, was because of communal farming, something imposed by the government and not well received by the farmers. But now, his uncle was happy to report, with new incentives for the farmers, there were thousands of varieties of rice grown in the Mekong alone, not counting other areas of the country. He became particularly excited about a variety called floating rice that grew several foot-long stems to keep it alive above floodwaters.

The speech ended as abruptly as it began. Uncle Tran handed Nate a sheaf of papers with Vietnamese writing that apparently listed agricultural products available for export and dozens of other pages to fill out before the government would allow anything to leave the country. He nodded again, and at that moment, the door opened and the driver stood in the doorway.

This is beyond weird, Nate thought, as he followed the driver down the stairs, back to the little gray Russian-made Volga that hopefully still held his suitcase. Nate knew enough not to part with his backpack that had his passport and everything else essential.

Once again the driver maneuvered within the chaotic traffic until it began to thin and they were driving unimpeded on a two-lane paved road. The sun was midway in the sky and beat down with an intensity Nate was not used to. That and the humid air made the car feel like an oven. Nate rolled down his window and rolled up the sleeves of his light blue dress shirt.

They drove through small towns separated by rice fields of such an intense spring green they seemed to glow. Air from the open window smelled of damp dirt, fish fertilizer, and other unidentifiable scents. Nate settled himself as comfortably as possible in the back seat and dozed off.

*

What woke Nate was the feel of the car rocking and pitching as it slowed to a crawl going down a rough dirt road. There was only green ahead and on both sides like a sun-dappled cocoon formed by low growing bamboo, over-arching palm trees, and glimpses of shining rice paddies between the tree trunks.

They emerged into a dirt-packed clearing with a one-story rambling cement house. Its orange terra cotta roof contrasted with the predominantly brown and green surroundings. The driver honked his horn, which brought people running from the house and the edges of the property. The first to reach the car was a slight teenage boy. Nate recognized his cousin from photographs he had seen. Behind him was a younger version of Mai, who slowed as she approached the car as though uncertain what to do, especially as Nate unfolded his tall frame from the back seat. When his eyes met hers, she audibly drew in her breath.

Finally, she said, "Welcome, Nate. How is your mother?"

"My mother is well." Nate felt comfortable with this level of interchange in Vietnamese. "Thank you for having me to your home. And is this my cousin Binh?" Nate put out his hand to the teenager.

The boy took a step forward and shook Nate's hand. "Good day," he said in English. "How are you?"

Nate had to smile at the formality and answered in English, "I'm great, man. How are you doing?"

After a brief look of confusion, Binh gave him a big smile.

CHAPTER 13

Lindsey

My first day back from New Jersey, I stay in bed all day, and when the phone rings, I bury my head under the covers. The second day, I get up and make myself tea and toast—the easiest food to make that requires the least amount of effort. It isn't until the third day that I feel strong enough to deal with my situation. Because the sun is out and the temperature is above freezing, I decide to take a walk along a wooded trail near my condo. Walking often fuels my brain cells.

There is a thin skim of ice trapping bubbles in shallow puddles on the asphalt. The crisp air invigorates me, and I begin to sift and sort through facts and feelings.

Like most everyone I know, I grew up with a mother and a father and learned about life from them. I learned gradually, little by little, and that knowledge shaped me into the person I am. But now I find out that I'm not who I thought I was. Two weeks ago, I learned that I have a different father than the one I grew up with. How does that change me? Who am I? What kind of a man was my real father? I'm trying to reprogram the wiring in my brain and piece together bits of facts to replace a lifetime of assumptions. My brain is tired. It needs to be rebooted.

By the time I finish the two-mile loop and return home, I conclude that I'm still who I was—the product of my mother and stepfather's upbringing. But I have a key that allows me to open a previously unknown door that will answer questions I didn't know I had.

This conclusion leaves me with an even greater desire to find out more about my father. How did he die? What did he do in the intelligence world? Why did he die at the end of the war when there were very few American casualties?

I open my laptop and notice that I still haven't heard from my father's high school friend Tom, whom I emailed several days ago. It was a long shot anyway.

On a search screen, I enter "CIA Vietnam War" and am inundated with books and papers written by former veterans and officers who attempted to understand what went wrong in the "unwinnable war." I learn that the CIA started in Vietnam as the Saigon Military Mission (SMM) in 1954 to stabilize the government after the Viet Minh defeated the French. Some CIA officers thought that the war against Ho Chi Minh and the Viet Minh was a political and ideological war, not one to be fought with military weapons. They, however, were later overridden by the militarists.

It's surprising to see that much of the information is newly declassified. I look through papers with some sections removed or marked out in black, but they are now available to the public, where before they were top secret. Much of the newly declassified information is about efforts before the Paris Peace Accord of January 15, 1973, a treaty signed by North Vietnam, South Vietnam, and the United States. The peace accord specified that US troops had 60 days to withdraw, all war prisoners were to be released, and North and South Vietnam were to be reunified through peaceful means.

In the spring of 1975, North Vietnamese forces captured Saigon and ended the 30-year war. *So much for the peace accord,* I thought. And what piques my interest is that intelligence and every other branch of the US military were winding down after 1973, so what was my father doing that caused him to become missing and presumed dead?

I find a timeline of the last few months of the war and most likely the last few months of my father's life. Apparently, early in 1975, the North Vietnamese Army (NVA) started a major offensive against the Army of the Republic of Vietnam (ARVN) and began attacking and gaining ground. Civilians abandoned their besieged towns in a mass exodus, clogging roads, while the NVA shelled the retreating masses. Victories increased the NVA's motivation, and they accelerated their advances. The ARVN was nearing collapse, and as the NVA inched closer to Saigon, overtaking cities along the way, the ARVN soldiers surrendered or fled.

By April 20, 1975, nine days before my father supposedly died, US Ambassador Graham Martin urged President Thieu to resign. The next day, President Thieu gave a 90-minute resignation speech in which he blamed everybody for his problems—the Paris Peace Accords, Henry Kissinger, and the US for not fulfilling its promise to protect the South Vietnamese. Then the CIA took him to Taiwan, where he was put into exile.

On April 23, 100,000 NVA soldiers marched on Saigon, which was full of refugees. President Ford, in a speech at Tulane University, stated that the war in Vietnam "is finished, as far as America is concerned."

April 27 – Saigon was surrounded, and although there were 30,000 South Vietnamese soldiers within, they were leaderless. The NVA fired rockets into the downtown civilian areas, and there was chaos and widespread looting.

April 28 – A "neutral" general, "Big" Minh became the new president of South Vietnam and requested a cease-fire. He was ignored.

April 29 – The NVA attacked Tan Son Nhut air base and killed two US Marines at the compound gate, supposedly the last two Americans killed in the war. President Ford ordered Operation Frequent Wind, the helicopter evacuation of 7000 Americans and South Vietnamese from Saigon, using a radio broadcast of "White Christmas" sung by Bing Crosby as the signal to begin the evacuation. Frantic Vietnamese civilians swarmed the helicopters, so the evacuation was moved to the enclosed American embassy. There, too, thousands of desperate civilians sought to enter the compound and were warded off by US Marines in full combat gear.

I try to picture Steve Nathan in all of this chaos. Where was he? If he was one of the Americans who made it onto a helicopter that flew to the aircraft carriers waiting off the coast of Vietnam, he would still be alive. So did he die in the terrible confusion of rockets and rampaging Vietnamese who had aligned themselves with Americans during the war and now felt abandoned? The confusion spread to the supposed safe havens of the waiting aircraft carriers where $250,000 choppers were tossed into the South China Sea to make room for incoming choppers with the luckier refugees.

Now that I have a general picture in my mind of what was happening in the days before my father's disappearance, I'm even more curious about his circumstances. I open my laptop and go to the National Archives site. There I find out that depending on the discharge date, some records are open to the public and some are not. Records older than 62 years are open to the public. Otherwise, one must be the military veteran or the next of kin (un-remarried widow or widower, son, daughter, father, mother, brother, or sister.) And if you are the next of kin of a deceased military veteran, you must provide proof of death: either a death certificate, letter from a funeral home, or a published obituary.

I print the three-page Request Pertaining to Military Records just to see what is required. For starters, I need Steve Nathan's service number, social security number, and proof of death. And the two types of records that would be available to me are a proof of military service in order to get benefits, and the veteran's medical and hospital history. Although accessing medical and hospital information might give me clues, it wouldn't necessarily explain how he died and why.

My ex-husband used to call me pigheaded and other even less flattering names because of my stubborn independence. Rather than ask for help, I prefer to do things myself, even if it takes more time and I risk doing a botch job. At least it's *my* botch job, and I usually learn something in the process. But no matter what I try to do in this situation, it doesn't look like I can access my father's files on my own. And do I want to access the files available from this website even if I could?

I make myself tea and toast again, this time with honey. As I swallow the last lukewarm sip of tea, it becomes obvious what I must do. I take out my cell phone and call the number Uncle Mark gave me three days ago.

"Hello," he says.

"Hi, this is Lindsey, your newly discovered niece."

"Lindsey! I've been thinking about you. My daughter Shelley would like to meet you. I called her the other day and told her about our visit at Cousin Sarah's. You two are about the same age. How are you?"

"Fine," I say. "Well, actually I'm confused. I'm trying to sort out my new identity and becoming more and more curious about my father. I tried to access his military records online and hit a brick wall."

"Well, that's no surprise. My mother spent years trying to find out what really happened to Steve. Everything was classified, classified, classified. She wrote down everything she found out and the names of people she talked to."

"She did?" She would be my grandmother. She sounds a little bit like me in her pig-headedness. "Do you have the information she wrote down?"

"It's probably around here somewhere. Sue!" Uncle Mark says to someone in the room with him. "Do you know where that box of notebooks is that my mother kept on Steve? We didn't throw it out, did we?"

I hold my breath, waiting for Sue's response, which I can't hear. Eventually, Uncle Mark says, "We can't put our hands on it, but we'll look for it, and if we find it, I'll let you know."

"Thank you," I say, not at all assured that they will find anything because I know about cleaning out your mother's papers.

*

A week later, after a particularly stressful day at work, I come home to find a shoebox-sized package in my mailbox. The return address is from Mark Nathan in Paramus, New Jersey. Inside, a note says, "We found my mother's notebooks and you are welcome to copy whatever you want. Please send them back when you are finished. Good luck and God bless! Uncle Mark. P.S. Shelley is coming home for our family reunion this July at our lake house. You are welcome to join us. More later."

Lake house? July? It might be nice by then to meet the rest of my new, ready-made family. But right now, I'm a little shaky about meeting any more strangers who are related to me.

I reach into the box and pick up the first of six identical black notebooks filled with broken phrases in a scrawling handwriting. Usually there's a date at the top of a page and a phone number. Sometimes there's an abbreviation and the name of the person or persons spoken to. The most common phrase is "No further information at this time." In July of 1979, I see a list of names, addresses, and phone numbers. It's unlikely the addresses and phone numbers are still viable, but the pages that follow record my grandmother's calls to those people.

A call to Darrell revealed that Steve was "a decent human being" and "a loyal friend." Jeb said, "Your son Steve saved my hide more than once. May God rest his soul." But it is someone named Tom who said something that really catches my interest. He said, "Being a purple dragon in 'Nam was an elite position. And it was dangerous work sometimes. We were targeted more than other Americans, especially at the end."

Purple dragon? Was it a code name for some covert operation?

A quick search on my laptop brings up a scanned document with a black-and-white image of a contorted dragon. The words

"Top Secret" are crossed out and below them are "Purple Dragon: United States Cryptologic History."

So my father was involved in sending and intercepting secret codes at the end of the Vietnam War. From reading what isn't blanked out, I learn that the enemy in Vietnam was being forewarned about US operations, and it was the mission of Purple Dragon to find out how the enemy was getting the information and to stop the leak. It sounds dangerous to me—and likely involved Vietnamese double agents whose allegiance was questionable.

I go back to the black notebooks my grandmother kept and decide to cheat and go to the last entry in the last book. It was the end of her search, and I'm curious about what she discovered that would make her stop looking.

The writing on the last page appears to be written hurriedly and slopes down to the right. The date is September 1994. The call was apparently to someone in the government, because she had underlined the words Official Last Word. Below that, I read:

Files declassified now. They can tell us. Steve last seen leaving Saigon on April 25. Borrowed civilian car from Vietnamese co-worker—drove out of the city into the North Vietnamese army. Never seen again. Group field office in Phan Thiet, hours away. Getting something important from office? Chance of survival—none.

CHAPTER 14

Nate

When roosters began crowing the next morning, no light penetrated the green thicket around the rambling house. Nate closed his eyes again and turned over on his wooden shelf of a bed with a thin straw mat for a mattress. He heard rustling in the room and reopened his eyes to see Binh hurriedly pulling on clothes. Binh had slept on a heap of bags filled with seed of some sort.

"Where are you going?" Nate asked.

"To school."

"This early?"

"I must prepare for the yearly exams," Binh said. "I want to be selected for university. Only 2% are selected."

"What?" Nate sat up slowly, his internal clock protesting that it was far too early to be having this conversation.

Binh said some words in Vietnamese about the educational process that Nate didn't understand. Whatever. He'd ask him about it when he woke up. "See you later," he said in English as he settled back down on the hard bed.

"Goodbye," Binh said carefully in English, then, hesitantly, he copied his American cousin. "See you later."

*

The next time Nate awoke, the sun had penetrated the green foliage cocoon surrounding the farm, and he smelled charcoal smoke and heard sounds of activity around him. He lay still for a minute, reviewing what he had learned the day before about where he was. The center of this house was the original farmhouse where his mother grew up. Her parents were killed by American bombs during the war, so the three siblings—Tran, Mai, and Kim—lived there for the duration of the war. Mai obviously left for the United States, and Tran moved to Ho Chi Minh City. Kim stayed at the house, and over the years, Uncle Tran, who did well in his government job, built a wing off the original house for himself and his family. When Aunt Kim married Danh, they built another wing on the other side. That's where he was now, in Binh's room, which was also a tool shed of sorts with pointed sticks and wooden yokes, presumably for water buffalo, against the wall.

Nate's stomach growled. It, too, was on San Jose time and protested, in spite of the sumptuous feast last night. Aunt Kim was almost as good a cook as his mother and prepared similar dishes to ones Nate had eaten growing up, plus some that were new to him. The rice was more aromatic than what he was used to. He'd have to find out what variety it was and get it for the restaurant.

The agenda for the day was to show Nate around the farm, according to Nate's cousin Lieu, Uncle Tran's eldest son, who obviously was the boss of this family compound. Lieu and his family dominated Uncle Tran's more elaborate wing of the house. Nate was just beginning to put names to faces and understand which of the several small children belonged to which branch of the family.

"Good morning, Aunt Kim," he said a few minutes later when he walked into the lean-to kitchen off the central room of the house. She was stirring a pot of rice congee over a charcoal fire and had boiling water puffing steam on a separate cook stove.

"Good morning, Nephew Nate," she said. "Would you like some coffee? I hear Americans prefer it to tea."

"Yes, most Americans do. Your Vietnamese coffee is very good. Where does it come from?"

"The highlands," she said. "Maybe we take you there."

"And your rice is very good. What kind of rice did we eat last night?"

"Ordinary rice. White rice. Later I will cook you special rice. Your mother's favorite."

Mai had given Nate gifts from America to give to the family. He wasn't sure of the proper time and place to present gifts, especially because he wasn't sure he had enough for everyone. He and Kim were alone in the kitchen, so he said. "My mother sent gifts to the family, but I don't know how to present them. Shall I bring them to you now?"

Kim was squatting, her heels flat on the ground, fanning the charcoal fire, and she rose to her full height, which was the middle of Nate's chest. "We invite you to our home, not for American gifts but because we love your mother. We don't need gifts."

"But," Nate said to the top of her head, "I brought them, and my mother, who also loves you, wants you to have them. I will get them now."

He went back to his shared bedroom/tool shed and located

the bulky bag that had taken up most of the space in his suitcase. His mother hadn't been clear as to what to do with it.

When Kim saw the bag of gifts, before looking at them, she seated Nate at a small wooden table at the far side of the lean-to and handed him a bowl of congee topped with a brown powdery substance that smelled like dried fish. Then she poured him a hot cup of coffee. "Eat," she said.

He did. After she was sure he was taken care of, she turned to the bag and opened it carefully. Nothing was wrapped. She brought out handfuls of colorful dishtowels, aluminum flashlights with spare batteries, plastic Fisher Price toys for preschoolers, a bottle of Jack Daniels Black Label well-padded in bubble wrap, T-shirts of every color in many sizes, and blue jeans.

She turned to him with a big smile. "Good!" she said. "There is something for everyone. I will bring it out tonight after we eat."

Nate was on his second helping of congee and whatever the stuff was that was sprinkled on top, when Lieu came to the kitchen. "Good morning, Cousin Nate," he said, helping himself to a bowl. He was taller than his father and thicker through the chest. Perhaps it was due to physical labor and better food than his father had had during the war.

"Good morning, Cousin Lieu."

Lieu ate his bowl of congee standing up and held the bowl at his chin as he spooned its contents into his mouth. When it was almost gone, he tipped the remains into his mouth and then set the empty bowl down with finality.

"Come," he said to Nate.

*

They walked a narrow dirt path that separated two rice paddies. Lieu pointed to the field on his left. "This is white rice, the kind that people eat every day."

Nate looked closely at the field, similar to hundreds he had seen yesterday. "I didn't realize there is so much rice here, but that's all I saw on my ride, rice fields and more rice fields."

"Vietnam is the fifth largest producer of rice in the world. And this," Lieu pointed to the field on his right, "is Forbidden Rice, the black rice. Emperors ate it because it is very healthy and gives longevity. It is difficult to grow."

"How many types of rice do you grow here?" Nate asked.

"Many, many types. We try all kinds and then tell the people which are the best to grow."

So they are an experimental farm, Nate thought. He wanted to ask about the government and how it factored into this farm, but he didn't have the Vietnamese vocabulary to do so, and his better judgment told him it was too early to ask such politically-charged questions.

The farmhouse was surrounded by rice paddies, some of which were tended by neighboring farmers who were allowed to take a percent of the harvest. In their tour of the farm, Nate saw several farmers walking in muddy rice paddies behind water buffalo.

"See those mountains?" Lieu pointed to a series of purple peaks on the horizon. "That's where the highlands begin. We have a coffee plantation there where we try many ways to grow coffee. The soil is different in the mountains. It is red and the climate is cold. We can't grow rice there, but we can grow many other things. My brother runs the farm in the highlands."

This was the first that Nate had learned about Tran's other

son. He wondered how many children Tran had and whether they were all managers for their father. By the time Nate and Lieu returned to the house, his esteem of Uncle Tran and his mother's family had greatly increased. He was impressed with the scope of his uncle's farm and with Lieu's knowledge. Vietnam was not the poor country torn by war that his mother had described.

Lunch was served to the family on a table out under the trees in the back yard. Chickens scratched in the dirt, and a couple of small yellow dogs sniffed under the table, hoping for a stray bit of food. It appeared that Kim was the head chef of the compound, and she, with the help of the other women, served several dishes of sautéed vegetables each mixed with a meat, pork or chicken or fish. In the center of the table was the ubiquitous rice, a different variety from the night before. Kim said it was jasmine rice, a more expensive kind. Although Nate had eaten jasmine rice most of his life, it tasted nothing like the rice he had that day for lunch.

After the table was cleared and people left for a siesta, Nate chose to remain at the table outside in the shade where a slight breeze rattled the bamboo leaves. He felt peace and contentment. Kim came and sat opposite him. Neither spoke.

Eventually, Nate broke the silence by saying in Vietnamese, "Thank you for letting me come here. I wish my mother could see her family home again and be with you."

"She is always welcome. I hope next time she will come with you."

"I hope so, too."

Another period of comfortable silence went by. Then Kim said, "You look like your father."

"You knew my father?"

"Yes, he came here to this house."

Nate stared at her, unable to form words around the questions that filled his head.

CHAPTER 15

Lindsey

When Vivian calls me at work two weeks after we met in Washington, it couldn't have been at a worse time. My family and close friends know not to call me during work hours, so when my cell phone rings just as I am explaining to the recalcitrant client the reason why I can't put all the functions on one screen, I think there's an emergency.

"Hello," I say, sure that the nursing home is calling to say my mother had a stroke.

"Lindsey! It's Vivian! I have a proposition."

"Oh, hi." I'm relieved and annoyed at the same time.

The client starts tapping his pen on the conference room table. I turn my back on him and take two steps toward the door. "Listen, Vivian. This is a bad time. I'm going to have to call you back."

"If you can catch me," she says and hangs up.

When I call Vivian back later that evening, the call goes to her message after three rings. "You've missed me. Try again later. Ciao."

How presumptuous! After an initial feeling of annoyance, I realize how programmed I am to being interrupted by my phone. It doesn't surprise me that Vivian, the ruler of her world, would choose when she wants to speak to someone or even get a recorded message. She lives life on her terms. I have to admire that, in spite of feeling frustrated at her lack of modern day communications etiquette. Of course, I can play her game, too. I don't have to call her back.

After a makeshift dinner of cheese, crackers, and a glass of wine, I forget about Vivian's call and stretch out on the sofa to read a book I found in the library about the last days of the Vietnam War. In spite of the dead end I had reached after scouring my grandmother's notebooks, I retain a glimmer of hope that my father still lives. Foolish hope, but after being introduced to the notion of a father I hadn't met, I don't want to, in spite of unrealistic odds, abandon him to death at the hands of hundreds of thousands of North Vietnamese soldiers.

My cell phone rings. I answer it with my mind still unraveling the dense prose about the complicated political and very real personal dramas unfolding at the end of the Vietnam War.

"Hello."

"Vivian again. I must have called you at a bad time before. I tend to forget that real people work 9-to-5 jobs. Now about the proposition I have for you. I am offering an all-expenses paid weekend in New York that includes a Broadway show and dinners at some of New York's finest restaurants."

"When?" I manage to ask.

"You pick the weekend, I'll make it happen."

I mentally review my schedule and say, "Weekend after next would be great."

"Good. I'll mail you the particulars."

Click. She hangs up.

Just when Vivian's arrogance becomes unbearable, she apologizes and defuses my annoyance, like she did in Washington. Sometimes I feel she is playing me like a game fish.

*

Ten days later, I turn my three-year-old silver SUV down a ramp to a private Fifth Avenue underground parking garage into a space Vivian reserved for me. "When you get off the parking elevator, Dion will take care of you," she had written.

I wheel my suitcase into an elevator that takes me up four sub Manhattan levels into a green and gold deco foyer with a massive arrangement of dried and fresh exotic flowers on a round table in its center. A dark-skinned, middle-aged man sits at an ornately carved wooden desk with a nameplate that reads, "Dion."

He looks up at me. "Good evening. You must be Vivian's guest. She's expecting you. May I take your bag?"

"How did you know who I was?" I ask.

He smiles. "You are the only blonde, statuesque, brown-eyed beauty I've seen all day. It was easy."

Yes. Dion is taking care of me. I follow him to a more elaborate elevator with an interior of beveled mirrors and dark polished wood that smells of lemon oil. He selects floor number 16, hands me my bag, and bows slightly. "You have yourself a wonderful evening."

When I ring the doorbell to apartment 1605, the door opens and a man about my height stands before me. He has closely cropped brown hair and a four-day growth of beard.

"Oh, I'm sorry. I must have the wrong apartment," I say, backing away.

"No, you don't. I'm Geoff, Vivian's favorite nephew." He smiles and his shadow of a beard can't hide a dimple in his left cheek. "Come on in. She's expecting you."

Nephew? What is Vivian up to? Is she trying to set me up with a lonely family member?

But my suspicion soon disappears when Geoff kisses his aunt goodbye because he is about to leave for a trip to climb Mt. Kilimanjaro. On his way out the door, he says, "A pleasure to meet you, Lindsey."

"Well," Vivian stands to greet me. She is wearing a flowing caftan of purple with gold threads that looks like it was made in Guatemala or some third world country. Her earrings are wooden elephant heads complete with tiny tusks, probably of real ivory, and when she puts her hand out to me, her signature bangles of gold jangle up her arm. "You look lovely, as usual, my darling."

"And you look magnificent!" I say, letting my gaze go past her to the wall of glass that looks out on the Manhattan skyline. Far below, the blur of moving car taillights almost forms a red line. "Nice view," I say, an obvious understatement.

"Yes, it keeps me amused. Twenty years ago I had a far broader view, but that new building to the east has blocked it. Cocktail before dinner? We have reservations for eight."

"Not unless you're having one.'

"I've already had mine. It's a tradition. I toast the sunset every evening with my drink du jour. Lately, it's been a cosmos."

When I decline a cocktail, Vivian shows me to my room decorated in shades of yellow from mustard to pale lemon with an abstract painting mostly in cobalt blue that dominates one wall. "We're going to one of my favorite places," she says. "No need to dress formally. I'll change into another outfit, but it's fairly casual."

After Vivian closes the door behind her, I look closely at the painting and see a stylized "V" in the bottom right corner. It must be one of Vivian's works. It's dramatic and bold, and I'm not sure if I like it.

*

The restaurant is a high-class Vietnamese place. When I enter, I smell something sweet, pungent, and fishy, but it isn't offensive, and also something fried—perhaps onions. Every table in the place is occupied, and there is the low buzz of voices.

Vivian is greeted with familiarity and taken to "her" table, a booth in a far corner with tan leather padded seats.

"Have you experienced *real* Vietnamese food before?" she asks me.

"I can't say that I have. I'm looking forward to it," I say.

"It's like Thai, and related to Chinese, but there's a freshness that distinguishes it. Lots of raw vegetables and herbs."

I ask Vivian to order for me, something I'm sure she would do anyway.

As we sip a refreshing green tea drink with infused fruit while waiting for our food, Vivian looks closely at me. "Tell me what's happened since I saw you last."

It's impossible to keep anything from Vivian, so I start telling about my meeting Cousin Sarah and Uncle Mark and continue with what I found out from reading my grandmother's notebooks.

"So you've given up?"

"I suppose I should, but hope is a tease that won't go away."

The food arrives in courses, first small spring rolls on a platter of fresh herbs with a pale amber dipping sauce that explains the fishy smell I noticed when we entered the restaurant. Next come rice and an assortment of delicately stir-fried dishes of beautiful vegetables and thinly sliced meats in unusually flavored sauces. My favorite is a clear soup with beautiful ingredients—a single perfect shrimp, a piece of carrot carved like a flower, some thinly sliced white disks that are sweet and crunchy, mushrooms of a variety I'd never seen or tasted.

"This was superb!" I say, leaning back in my seat.

"I hoped you …" Vivian starts to say and then looks behind me with surprise. "Geoff!"

Standing at our table with his dimple-inducing grin was Geoff. "Just in time for dessert, I see." He sits next to his aunt, making her slide over toward the wall.

"And what are you doing here? I thought you had to catch a flight to Africa."

"Changed my mind. I can always catch a flight to Africa." He smiles at me.

I notice his eyes have unusually long lashes.

"Actually, the flight was canceled because of a suspected bomb threat. Just as well. This is not the optimal time to climb Mt. Kilimanjaro. But it looks like it's the optimal time to have dessert with you ladies. Have you ordered yet?"

Smooth talker. I've seen his type before.

After some deliberation, they order mango mochi—mango ice cream wrapped in rice dough called mochi, which they agree is actually a Japanese dessert, but close enough.

"Did you know," Geoff says to me, "that mangos, Mangifera

Indica, are considered the king of fruit and are in the same plant family as pistachios and cashews?"

I look at him with interest. "How did you know that?"

"Facts stick to me like burrs. That's why I'm burly." He grins.

I have to laugh. Nobody has made me laugh in a long time.

CHAPTER 16

Nate

Nate arrived back in San Jose midday on a Thursday after spending two weeks in Vietnam. Sophie had decorated the apartment with pink and green crepe paper streamers and a large homemade sign that said, "Welcome home, Mr. Nate."

"Why Mr.?" Nate asked her after he picked her up and twirled her around in a circle. "I thought I was Uncle Nate."

Sophie, still laughing, said, "'Cause Mommy said to."

Nate noticed that Sophie had lost another front tooth while he was away. He turned to Rosy and wrapped his long arms around her. "What's this Mr. business?"

"You'll figure it out," she said into his chest.

Feeling like he was receiving mixed messages, Nate looked at the welcoming elaborate decorations and the distancing "Mr." Rosy usually wasn't subtle.

"Well, Mr. Nate here has something in his suitcase for you ladies."

Nate unzipped his bag and removed two wrapped packages, the larger of which he gave to Sophie.

"What is it? Can I open it now?" Sophie hopped on one leg and then the other.

"Go ahead."

She ripped off the paper to reveal a doll with straight black hair under a wide cone-shaped straw hat, and a dress of blue silk with a fitted top and two flowing panels over white satin pants.

"Cool!" Rosy said. "Great outfit. Is that what all the women wear over there?"

"Only for special occasions," Nate said. "They wear black pajamas every day. In the cities they dress like we do."

"It's sexy without being obvious. Nice." Rosy took the doll over Sophie's protests, and examined its outfit. "Yeah, I remember studying this in school. It's called an ow dee or something like that."

"Mine!" Sophie took the doll back from her mother.

"Ao dai," Nate said. "I should have brought you one instead of this." He handed her a small box.

Rosy looked at him with narrowed eyes as she shook the box. Something inside clunked. "Hmmm." She slowly unwrapped the paper, dragging out the moment.

When she saw what was inside, Nate was gratified to see that her eyes widened with pleasure. "It's beautiful!" she said, holding up an intricately carved jade chrysanthemum blossom on a delicate gold chain. "Help me put it on."

As Nate fastened the necklace around her neck, Rosy wrinkled her nose and said, "What stinks in your suitcase?"

"Oh, probably the Vietnamese fish sauce I brought for my mom."

Rosy gagged and ran to the bathroom.

"Mommy's sick again," Sophie said. "She's sick a lot lately."

So, Nate thought with a mix of fear and elation, *that explains it.*

*

After giving Mai her gifts of several varieties of rice and Vietnamese food delicacies, Nate waited for her reaction. He expected her to be bubbling with questions about his trip and meeting her family, but she was silent. She sat with her hands in her lap and her head bowed. Finally, she looked up at him and said in Vietnamese, "They well?"

"Better than well," he said. "They have a good life and are happy. They all send their love."

Nate had rarely seen his mother cry, so it surprised him when she began sniffling and had to wipe her eyes with her apron.

He began to tell her, from the beginning, of meeting Uncle Tran, the ride to the farmhouse, and seeing the family. He gave details about each one, dwelling on his Aunt Kim and Cousin Binh, his favorites.

By the end of his narrative, she was smiling and asking questions, wanting more specific information about how each one looked, their personalities, and their interests.

It was late and Nate was exhausted from travel, but he had one question he had to ask—the question his Aunt Kim would not answer except to say, "Ask your mother."

"When did my father visit your family farm and why?"

All the joy that had softened his mother's face vanished. "Oh, Nate. That day the worst day of my life. I no can talk about it. I never tell anyone. Maybe someday, but not today."

"I need to know."

"Not tonight, Nate. You tired, I see it in your eyes, and Rosy needs you. Yes, I know. She no tell me, but I see things. You have happy time now you need to think about, not about bad past."

Nate rose from his seat at the table. "You're right. I'm tired. But soon you need to tell me about my father."

CHAPTER 17

Lindsey

Geoff calls me the day after I return home from New York. "Lindsey," he says, "I'm going to be in the Boston area this week and wonder if you would help me decide between a Celtics game or the Boston Symphony on Saturday evening."

Having played the French horn for most of high school and been part of my local orchestra for years, it was an obvious choice. "If it were me, I'd pick the Boston Symphony," I say.

"Great! I'll get us tickets."

It was a strange way to ask me out, but I was pleased. Geoff had joined Vivian and me the second day I was in New York, and his upbeat intelligence and charm made me understand why he was Vivian's favorite nephew, although I didn't hear how many other nephews she had. All she told me about Geoff was that his ex-wife expected a different lifestyle than Geoff provided her. From what I could analyze after an evening and a day with him, he was self-assured, not at all mainstream, and pursued many interests. I wasn't clear what he did for a living, if anything.

The topic of my father had come up at Vivian's, and Geoff was very interested in my dilemma. "I think most of us wonder if we're a foundling, especially when we have issues with our parents. We ask, 'How can I be a product of such idiotic/ stubborn/misguided people!' I know I've said that. Many times. Think of the possibilities when you find out your birth father isn't the father who raised you! You finally understand why you have personality traits your parents don't have. It all makes sense!"

He turned to Vivian. "Are you sure I don't have a different father or mother than the ones I grew up with?"

She rolled her eyes before saying, "Anything is possible in your family, Geoff."

Geoff grinned. "When I was little and my mother was exasperated with me, she'd say, 'I think we found you under a cabbage leaf in somebody else's patch.'"

Again, he made me laugh, and because he was interested in my situation, I was drawn even more to him. He went on to say that he thought I should pursue learning more about my father and perhaps go to Vietnam to see where he spent the last year of his life.

I entertained that possibility for about a second. How would I get time off without using my entire vacation? And Vietnam? A third world country? Do I really want to go there?

*

Saturday morning, I awake feeling that something important is going to happen, but I'm not sure if it will be good or bad. I decide to go to the gym before breakfast to work out some of my nervousness about the upcoming evening with Geoff. After running two miles on the treadmill and spending half an hour on the elliptical, I'm sweaty and calmer.

Back home, I go online to discover that the Boston Symphony

will be playing, in addition to other works, two of my favorite pieces, both by Bohemian composers—Smetana's Moldau, a work that transports me every time I hear or play it, and Dvorak's 6th Symphony, where the horns' impressive presence gives me chills. Even if the evening with Geoff is not the best, the music will be.

Geoff said he would pick me up around 5:00 p.m. so we can get dinner before the concert. I insist on meeting him at the restaurant at 6:00 p.m. to save him the trip to my Boston suburb, but my real reason is because I don't want him to see my apartment, which is very ordinary compared to Vivian's. I'll take the train in so I don't have the hassle of parking in the city, and the address he gave me for the restaurant is a block from a T stop.

As I'm deciding what to wear, I can't remember if Geoff's eyes are blue or hazel. They aren't brown. One evening he had worn a dark green shirt that I remember thinking looked good on him, but I wasn't sure if it matched his eyes or his general coloring. Am I getting first date jitters?

I pick out a black and red outfit that has gotten me compliments before and match it with the red purse I found in my mother's trunk. I'll bring the Polaroid photo of my dad as well, and if conversation lags, I can jumpstart it with my show and tell.

I needn't have worried about conversation lagging. From the moment Geoff meets me outside the restaurant, we talk nonstop, only taking time to read the menus when the waiter asks us for the third time if we are ready to order. Geoff orders a steak, and I opt for striped bass, a fish I tell Geoff my grandfather routinely caught on his fishing boat. Geoff tells me his grandfather had oil wells in Texas and probably wrangled steer at one time or another. We smile at each other.

Eventually, I pull out the photo of my mom and dad as well as the letter, which I had kept in the red purse.

Geoff studies the photo carefully. "You look like your father." He pauses. "They look insanely happy."

After reading my father's letter, he says, "I think your father had every intention of coming back to your mother. What I don't understand is why he couldn't have at least written her. Was his assignment *that* classified?"

I had wondered about that myself and had forgotten to ask Uncle Mark if the family received letters from Steve once he went to Vietnam. I know Mark talked about his last conversation with his brother when Steve said he had met the girl of his dreams.

Geoff now looks intently at me with his eyes that I note are a clear blue. "Something happened to him at the end of the war but it's being covered up. Your grandmother's records hit a dead end. What about men on his team, people he worked with? Is there a way we can find out who they were and contact them?"

I like Geoff's idea and I *really* like his use of the word "we" when it comes to carrying out the idea.

Soon afterwards, we leave for Symphony Hall, and as happens every time I enter the immense gilded room, I am breathless with awe for a brief moment. Geoff takes my elbow. "Nice space," he says. He leads me to our seats in the mid orchestra section, seats I haven't been able to afford before. While the orchestra is tuning up, I explain to Geoff about the importance of the horns in the Dvorak piece and tell him the story of the trip down the Moldau River in Smetana's work. He listens intently to me and later to the music, absorbing it as he appears to wholeheartedly absorb everything he encounters.

After the concert, as we sit in a bar, he says to me, "Thank you for making symphonic music a personal experience for me. I've been to a symphony before when I was very young, but I didn't relate to it. Now you have opened up a new world to me. Will you play your French horn for me sometime?"

"Sure," I say, "But it sounds best in an orchestra. It's not the most beautiful—or common—solo instrument."

"That doesn't matter. You can serenade me tomorrow as I help you research your father's comrades."

I look at him with raised eyebrows as I take a sip of my martini.

He says, "I'll drive you home tonight."

I don't protest.

*

We take our time getting up the next morning. It has been a while since I have found someone I liked enough to have over for the night. Geoff, as I expected, is a sensitive, experienced lover. We share passion, with intermissions of humor, and develop an almost uncanny communication as if we can read each other's minds.

It feels comfortable having him sit at my kitchen counter, sipping coffee, in spite of my brief moment of embarrassment earlier over my ordinary digs. "Eggs or pancakes?" I ask.

"Whatever you feel like making."

I usually hate it when people are indecisive like that, but with Geoff, I feel he truly wants what I want, which is eggs over easy with a dense grainy toast and two slices of bacon on the side.

Geoff eats heartily, and when he finishes, he says, "So far, I've discovered nothing but positives about you. And the icing on the cake, so to speak, is that you can cook!"

"You may need to take that back," I say. "You've only had one breakfast."

"I'd like to stay and sample more of your cooking." He smiles at me.

"I smile back at him. "You're quick on your feet, Geoff. And how are *you* in the cooking department?"

"Terrible," he says, "but I know good cooking when I taste it, and I'm a whiz at cleaning up." He proceeds to gather the dishes, rinse them, and load them into my dishwasher.

I give him a thank you hug, and we hold each other a long time. It's a perfect moment, yet I'm realistic enough not to expect all future moments to be perfect. We part slowly, and Geoff says, "I know you have to work tomorrow, but I'd very much like to help you research your father. Because of my business, I have access to search engines most people don't have."

When I look at him quizzically, he says, "I inherited the job of running my family's charitable organization. We send relief to disaster areas. We also interact closely with government agencies, and I have some security clearances that might get us access to information that can help you."

I lead him to my laptop. He asks, "Do you know what branch of service your father was in?"

"No. Just that it was military intelligence with some connection to the Purple Dragon, which dealt with cryptography."

Geoff types an Internet address and then a user name and password that brings up an interface I'm not familiar with. He asks, "Your father's full name was Stephen...?"

"C. Nathan."

"Do you know what the C stood for?"

I had discovered that from my grandmother's notebooks. "Campbell," I say.

As Geoff looks intently at the computer screen, I notice that his hair is slightly wavy in the back and that he flares his nostrils when he concentrates. I feel a wave of tenderness toward him that ignites sadness because I'm sure I'm not the only woman in his life. Someone like him, handsome, assured, and wealthy, most certainly can have any woman he wants.

"Look," Geoff points to the screen. "It appears he was in a loosely organized, very special unit of just a few men, but it doesn't name the unit or the men. Did your grandmother mention names of his friends?"

"No." Something in the back of my mind nudges me. I saw a name of someone recently who possibly served with him. Where did I see that? Why didn't I contact that person?

Then I remember. Comments from the Wall of Faces. One of the comments for Steve Nathan was from a friend who didn't leave an email.

"Let me look something up quickly," I say, and Geoff stands so I can take the chair he has warmed. I quickly find the web page and locate Steve Nathan's photograph, information, and comments left by friends and family. "Here it is!"

POSTED ON 7/2//03 - BY WILLI HENDERSON
My name should be on the wall. Not yours.

Steve resumes his seat and types Willi's name into his program, along with all the information we know or suspect about him, such as Vietnam War veteran and military intelligence. A screen appears with information about a William Jacob Henderson from Richmond, Virginia, and several addresses that appear to become more recent as we scan down the list. The last address and phone number is in Hampstead, New Hampshire, one-half hour away.

Geoff looks at me. "You game?"

"Sure."

I tap the New Hampshire number into my phone and put it on speaker. A querulous voice answers, "If you're selling something, I don't want it!"

Geoff and I share a smile.

"I'm not selling anything, Mr. Henderson. That is your name, right?"

"Yes, but I'm not answering 'we'll take just a moment of your time' questions, either." Willi's voice jumped into a falsetto briefly.

I'm afraid he will hang up if I don't catch his interest immediately, so I say, "I'm Steve Nathan's daughter, and I'd like to talk to you."

Silence.

I continue slowly, "You were together in Vietnam, weren't you?"

"He wasn't married."

"I know. He met my mother right before he left for Vietnam in 1974."

A long silence. I continue, "They met on my grandfather's fishing boat."

"I heard about her. Dark-haired beauty. He carried a photograph of the two of them."

Of course. If one Polaroid was taken, why not two? "I have a photograph of them, too."

"So, what do you want?"

I gather the words carefully in my mind before speaking

them to this crusty old person who obviously has all his mental faculties. "I've just recently found out that Steve Nathan was my father, and I'd like to learn more about him."

"That's legit, I guess. But I'm gonna tell you right up front, I hate talking about the war."

"I'm truly sorry to remind you of it."

I wait. Eventually, he responds in a softer voice, "Your dad was my best friend. I guess I owe it to him to speak to his daughter."

"Thank you. Do you mind if I come see you? I don't live far from you."

"Give me an hour."

"Thank you, Mr. Henderson."

*

An hour later, Geoff and I pull into the ice-crusted dirt driveway of a log cabin on a lake that is well off the beaten path. The house has a broad deck overlooking the water and a large fenced-in garden covered with snow. Geoff walks over to admire a neatly stacked woodpile while I take note of an anemometer mounted on a shed that I guess is a chicken coop based on the sounds inside it. Willi Henderson is not only mentally active and involved in the world around him, but he appears to be physically active as well.

The driveway is rutted and crunchy with frost, which makes me place my feet carefully all the way to the front door. Geoff joins me and says, "I like this guy already."

There is no doorbell, so I knock on the solid pine door.

"It's not locked!" a voice says from inside.

We open the door and see a cluttered room with comfortable

slip-covered chairs in a multi-colored floral print and large windows facing the lake. Every horizontal surface is covered with stacks of books, notebooks, and newspapers with random empty mugs precariously placed at the edges. A woodstove crackles and spews warmth along with the smell of a room that has been entombed for months and heated with wood.

A wiry man with intense eyes stands as we enter. He looks at me and slowly nods his head. "You're his daughter, all right." And then, as if remembering his manners, he extends his hand. "Will Henderson."

I shake it. "Lindsey Casselton," I say and motion to Geoff, "my friend Geoff Davis."

"Judith," Willi calls in the direction of the kitchen, from which a gray-haired woman wearing jeans and a navy blue Patriots sweatshirt soon emerges. "My wife and gardener," he says with unmistakable pride.

Geoff smiles his single-dimpled smile at her and says, "I was impressed with the ambitious size of your garden as we came in. What all do you grow?"

The two of them begin discussing garden lore while Willi and I sit in two chairs facing the windows that open to a wide view of the lake and a sky layering up with scalloped gray clouds. I hand him my Polaroid photograph, and Willi studies it in silence.

Finally, he clears his throat and says, "We were so damn young and idealistic. And what did it get us? Death for him and a stain on my soul that won't wash out. Time has faded it some, but it's still here." He thumps his chest with a clenched fist.

I have a million questions, such as was he able to write letters home, but a deep instinct keeps me silent. Willi hands the photo back to me.

"Your father," his voice breaks and he closes his eyes. "Let me start with the happy things. You know, like camaraderie. Going out to the bars together. Talking about home—what we were going to do when we got back. I was a couple years older and had more experience. It was my second 'Nam deployment, his first. He was a natural leader but young and inexperienced. He wasn't jaded like the rest of us.

"The war was over. Paris Peace Treaty was signed, but he was raring to go, had incredible instincts, saw things the rest of us missed. As a result, he became a target."

Target? What does that mean?

Willi puts his face in his hands and his voice is muffled. "That last day, he insisted on going to Phan Thiet to get the equipment even though I was the obvious choice. I could have gone in disguise, and I spoke the language. He was big and obviously American, even though he dyed his hair and darkened his skin."

I venture a question. "Equipment?"

"We had an office four hours away in the coastal town of Phan Thiet, manned by South Vietnamese. He had wanted to go earlier, but our boss couldn't accept that it would come down to the indignity of fleeing for our lives and waited until the last day. We had sensitive cryptographic equipment there and documents that needed to be destroyed so as not to get into the hands of the North Vietnamese and especially the Chinese and Soviets. There was no way to communicate to our people there. One of us had to go, or so our boss thought. Damn idiot!"

"So my father drove out of Saigon into the North Vietnamese army that had surrounded the city on the last day Americans were in the country?" I say, astounded.

"That's pretty much it. He took a civilian car and one of our trusted drivers. He lay low in the back seat. It was a doomed cause."

"Wait a minute," alarm bells are going off in my head, "You said earlier that my father was a target. Do you think this was a setup by your boss?"

Willi gives me a long look. "I've had decades to wonder about that."

Geoff by now has been listening in to the conversation. "Do you think any of your Vietnamese office workers in the town, what was its name—Phan Teet? are still alive?"

"Possibly. And they probably turned over the equipment and papers to the North Vietnamese, assuming Steve never made it there. Hate to say it, but it would have been a good way for our Vietnamese team there to show they were no longer on the American side. Not that I ever heard anything about our information falling into enemy hands."

"Just how sensitive was that information?" Geoff asks.

Willi takes a breath then says, "What the hell. It's all water over the dam by now anyway. I might as well tell you. At the time it was pretty sensitive, especially because it named the Soviet Union as the major reason the NVA broke the Paris Peace Treaty and began the final wave of attacks on South Vietnam. And none of our superiors believed the analysis about the Soviets that Steve and his team came up with. But in the end, they ordered him to risk his life to go get the equipment that gave him that information." He covers his face with his hands and sobs.

Geoff and I look at each other. Then we look at Judith, who shakes her head sadly. It is time to go. I touch Willi's shoulder tentatively and say, "Thank you. I'm sorry to put you through this." He doesn't look up.

Judith walks us to the door. Nobody says anything until we're outside, and I thank Judith and ask if there's anything I can do to undo the damage I've done.

"He'll be grouchy for a week or so. Then he'll get over it," she says. "There's nothing you can do." She has obviously been through this before with him.

We're silent in the car, going back to my place. Mental images of my tall, blond father in Vietnamese disguise occupy me. I see him being driven through one NVA checkpoint after another, possibly being shot at, interrogated, and tortured, just because his boss was an idiot or worse.

I have almost forgotten that Geoff is with me until he says, "We need to go to Phan Thiet."

CHAPTER 18

Nate

Stephen Felipe Huong was born at 3:16 a.m. after an unusually short labor. Nate had barely enough time to call his mother to come stay with Sophie before Rosy's labor pains intensified and were coming two minutes apart. In the cab on the way to the hospital, Rosy panted, as she was taught in the prenatal classes she and Nate had attended, and Nate urged the driver to go faster.

Because Nate appeared calm in spite of the urgency of the situation, the doctors allowed him into the delivery room and even let him assist with the delivery of his squalling 7 lb. 8 oz. son.

Later that morning, when Mai brought Sophie to meet her new brother, Sophie was uncharacteristically shy. But Mai eagerly held the tiny bundle swaddled in a blue blanket and let her tears flow unchecked. The baby had a full head of straight black hair and skin the color of a café latte. Nate hugged his mother and his son together and shed tears of his own—tears of relief that all went well, mixed with awe at the miracle of life that he had just witnessed, and an overwhelming sense of responsibility and commitment to protect this little bundle that carried his DNA.

Six months earlier, he and Rosy had married in an elaborate

ceremony orchestrated by her parents, Maria and Felipe, and attended by all 195 of her cousins. Although Rosy said only 100 guests were invited and less than twenty were cousins, Nate could swear he encountered close to 200 people who all looked like they were related to Rosy, but he might have been seeing double. Rosy and he had formed a comfortable relationship that revolved around Sophie, the restaurant, and now the child they had created together.

Rosy was a matter-of-fact mother, who took only one week off from her job as manager at Rice. Little Stevie came with her to work and slept in a tiny crib in an alcove next to the kitchen. He was an easygoing infant who only complained when his stomach was empty, and Rosy took care of that by stepping momentarily into Mai's living room to breastfeed him. When he outgrew the crib, one of Rosy's cousins was hired to watch him at Grammy Mai's conveniently accessible apartment behind the restaurant.

Sophie accepted her brother with only a tinge of jealousy. He was placid enough to let her hold him and dress him as if he were a limp doll. When he began to smile, Sophie could make him smile more than anyone else in the family.

At two months old, Stevie lost all his straight black hair. Eventually it grew back as thick dark curls. By the time he was three, he looked like any other little Hispanic boy until he turned to gaze solemnly at you with his light green, slanty eyes.

"We have our United Nations' child," Nate said to Mai, remembering when it had been a joke.

"You be careful, no make fun, Nate," Mai countered. "Maybe he be president someday."

By the time Stevie started going to day care, Rice Two was in the planning stages. Nate had found a good location across town, and a young black Asian American sous chef, whom Mai had trained, showed extraordinary promise and responsibility so that Nate and Mai were comfortable letting him be head chef of the new Rice Two, with Nate as manager.

Since his trip to Vietnam, Nate had been ordering rice and other specialty food from his relatives, and now with the coming expansion of Rice, he thought it was time to make another trip to Vietnam.

"Ma," he said one Sunday morning, the time he and his mother set aside each week to drink Vietnamese iced coffee and discuss the business, "I think it's time for me to visit the relatives again and see what food trends I can bring back to us, especially now that we will have two restaurants. Rather than offer two identical menus, we might want to experiment with something different in one of the restaurants."

"One menu, two restaurants," Mai said firmly.

Nate expected pushback, so he was not surprised. In fact, he agreed that Rice Two should not be named that if the menu was different from Rice One. What Nate really wanted were new food ideas to offer the loyal regulars who had made Rice a success— ideas that could be offered in both restaurants.

"Okay, so does that mean you don't want new dishes for the menu?"

"I change menu all the time." Mai was becoming defensive.

It was true. Mai changed all but the most popular dishes seasonally. But the seasonally appropriate dishes were becoming predictable. Festive dishes for Tet (Vietnamese New Year), lighter fare for the summer months, heavier fare for the colder months.

"You are right," Nate said, backing down, knowing that by doing so and giving his mother space, she might come back to him with the idea as if it were her own.

The next Sunday as they sat sipping Vietnamese iced coffee and eating cinnamon toast, Mai said, "I think we need new food ideas. We have always the same menu."

Nate smiled inwardly, but with a serious face said, "Everybody loves our menu."

"Yes, but time for new things. You go to Vietnam, find new ideas. I call my brother, tell him you come."

Nate was prepared for her to change her mind, and now he took the opportunity to open a topic that had been closed since he had returned from Vietnam years ago. "I won't go unless you tell me more about my father. I am a father now, and it is important that I know more about mine."

Mai looked at her son for a long time. Nate met her gaze. Other times when he had asked about his father, she had said it was too painful to talk about or that it wasn't a good time because of the moon position or because the wind was coming from the southwest. But now he saw resignation in her dark eyes and noticed her body slump as if he had punctured her spirit somehow.

"Yes. You need to know," she finally said. Her head was lowered, and in a whisper that Nate could barely hear, she said, "I kill your father."

"What!"

"No. Not me shoot, but because of me, your father die."

Nate waited.

"Your father my boss. I work hard. I good worker. Your father like me. I like him."

Mai began speaking in Vietnamese, obviously more comfortable with its minimal grammar and the familiar echoes of the story she had more than likely told and retold in her head for decades.

When she was finished, Nate stood and folded his depleted mother in his arms. "I love you, mom," he said as she wept into his chest. "You are the best mother anyone's ever had."

PART 2 – VIETNAM

CHAPTER 19

Nate

Fourteen years later when Nate decided to take his sixth trip to Vietnam, he wanted to go during Tet, and he wanted to bring his mother. Mai had begun allowing people she trained to take on more responsibility at the restaurants. She could no longer be on her feet for hours, and Nate convinced her it was time to let others do the drudge work while she saved herself for the more important tasks of planning menus and ensuring the quality of each dish served.

But persuading her to leave the restaurants for several weeks to go visit her family during Tet in Vietnam was a daunting task. It took Nate months to get her used to the idea. Knowing his mother, he started with a mere suggestion. He gradually inserted descriptions into daily conversation of the family compound and funny incidents about what happened on his previous trips. When he asked her to describe her memories of Tet as a child on the family farm, he was able to get her to recount stories he had never heard before, some of them bittersweet because of the constraints of war.

Finally one day in late fall, an incident at Rice One influenced Mai's decision. It was a Friday evening, and every table was taken. Nate had hired a new manager, one with years of experience, but new to Rice. A special that evening was crab and asparagus soup, something the head chef had developed on her own. Mai was in the kitchen, sitting in her special chair where she could see all the stations, when a loud, angry voice from the dining area brought her through the swinging doors. A bowl of crab and asparagus soup flew through the air and crashed onto the tile floor in front of her, spewing hot soup and bits of broken china.

The new manager walked calmly to the disgruntled customer and said, "Is there a problem, sir?"

"Damn soup has asparagus in it!"

"Yes." The manager did not raise his voice. "That was in the soup description. Crab and *asparagus* soup."

"But I *hate* asparagus."

"I'm sorry you hate asparagus, sir, but we have a policy in this restaurant that does not allow customers to throw soup bowls. That bowl could have injured someone. Please come with me, or I will have to call the police."

"What kind of fuckin' restaurant is this! You give me asparagus when I hate it, and now you threaten me..."

The manager pulled out his phone and dialed 911. The woman with the disgruntled customer looked like she was ready to cry, and several other diners stood up, ready to leave. The manager turned to them and said, "Sorry for this disturbance. You may wait outside until the police arrive. Your meals are on the house tonight."

Meanwhile, the soup thrower was pounding the table, his face contorted with rage, as the woman next to him quietly pleaded with him to stop.

Most of the customers left their tables and went outside, while a few stood in the corners or by the door to see what would happen. Mai was frozen in place.

In a matter of minutes, the sound of sirens announced the arrival of two policemen, who entered the restaurant and escorted the angry man and the mortified woman outside. Most of the remaining customers returned to finish their dinners, and Mai was amazed that most of them declined the offer of a free meal.

Later, after she recounted the incident to Nate, who had been at Rice Two, she said, "My restaurants are good. I have good people. I can go see my family now in Vietnam."

Nate agreed, and after making ticket reservations for two to Vietnam, he gave the new manager a raise.

*

One of the reasons Nate wanted to go to Vietnam again was to investigate the possibility of importing coffee. Since his taste of real Vietnamese coffee on his first visit there, he had tried to buy coffee beans from Vietnam in the US without success. He and Mai served a coffee drink at both Rice One and Two, but its base was not from Vietnam. It was a blend of coffee from other countries that most likely contained a percentage of authentic Vietnamese beans. He learned that although it is the second largest coffee producing country next to Brazil, Vietnam gets no name recognition, unlike Sumatra, Java, Hawaii, or Ethiopia.

Part of the problem, Nate realized once he started looking

into the situation, was that most Vietnamese coffee is a Robusta variety that has more caffeine and less acid than the more popular Arabica variety common in other coffee-producing countries. The American palette was used to Arabica coffee, so large companies acquired cheap Vietnamese coffee and carefully incorporated it into their blends, balancing it with enough acidic Arabica coffee to still appeal to American taste buds.

When Nate ordered Vietnamese coffee from established import companies, he was sent a pre-ground variety that disappointed him every time with the flat-tasting brew it produced. Yet the coffee that Nate drank in Vietnam was remarkably good with a mocha aftertaste and an appealing aroma. This trip, he would go to the highlands where it was grown and learn why the coffee in Vietnam tasted so much better before it was imported to the United States.

But first, he and his mother would go to Aunt Kim and the family in their farmhouse compound just outside Phan Thiet, something he did each time he went to Vietnam.

CHAPTER 20

Lindsey

A month and a half after my first date with Geoff, we are at the San Francisco International Airport, awaiting our flight across the Pacific Ocean to Hanoi, Vietnam. Vivian gave us a grand sendoff from JFK earlier that included champagne and smoked salmon.

Geoff has been to Vietnam before, several times apparently, and he has connections, so he made arrangements with a person named Minh who will be our guide, and from what he says, Minh talks like a guidebook, so I don't need to buy one. I can just enjoy the trip. I am learning that Geoff has many connections and unusual privileges that most people don't have, yet he doesn't flaunt them. For example, he told me that a senator on the Veterans' Affairs Committee of the US Senate is a friend of the family, and he asked me if it was okay to talk to the senator about my father's situation. Of course I said yes.

Even though our main reason for going to Vietnam is to visit where my father spent his last days and see if we can uncover a reason for his disappearance, Geoff has persuaded me to take a tour of Vietnam first. "Vietnam is beautiful. There are subtleties you'll come to appreciate as you learn about the culture. If you understand the country, it might help your search for answers about your father, and hopefully, you'll enjoy it no matter what."

Geoff and I have seen each other every weekend since that first date in Boston. There were times when I felt this trip together was the most natural thing for us to be doing and other times when I questioned what I was getting myself into, both in regard to the trip and the relationship. It frightened me that I had allowed myself to feel happy and content around him because something this good can't last. At least that's what experience has taught me.

To try to resolve my issues before the trip, I took a day off work last week and drove to Sue Ellen's little cottage that she, her live-in Joe, and their three children share on the coast of Maine.

Her children were in school, and Joe was in his woodworking shop, making the beautiful handmade furniture he is known for. Sue Ellen and I sat at her round kitchen table, one of Joe's amazing creations, and sipped herbal tea.

"Does Geoff make you happy?" she asked.

"I've never been happier."

"So is your question, Do I go on a life adventure to Vietnam with a guy who makes me happier than I've ever been in my life?"

I had to laugh. Put that way, it was a no-brainer.

"Joe and I," Sue Ellen said, "take it one day at a time. When I got pregnant with our first child, I must admit I was afraid. Joe didn't have his business at the time, and I had to pay the bills. Things were tough financially for a while. But I believed that he would find his niche, and he did. We have grown strong together. He supports me and my yoga classes as much as I support him and his business."

I think of her parting words to me as Geoff and I wait at the airport gate. "Open yourself to new experiences, Lindsey. Embrace life wherever it leads!"

The waiting area for our international flight at the airport is huge and filled with more Vietnamese than I have seen before in one place, most of them well-dressed families, some elderly American men with Vietnamese wives, and gangs of unattended children running, laughing, and screaming along the edges of the room. Geoff nudges me and says, "I hope they wear themselves out now so they sleep on the plane."

"Is it really seventeen hours in the air?" I ask.

"Yes, seventeen." Geoff grimaces. "I brought some pills to help us sleep. I don't know about you, but I can never get comfortable enough on a plane to fall asleep naturally."

The chatter around us is a prelude to the language I'll be hearing for the next three weeks—tonal, monosyllabic, with "ng" sounds from the back of the throat, and hard "k" endings.

"Maybe I should have taken a crash course in Vietnamese," I say to Geoff.

"It wouldn't hurt, but it really isn't necessary. You'll be surprised at how many Vietnamese speak English. We should learn the basics, however—hello, goodbye, and thank you, but Minh will teach us that when we meet him."

Geoff starts a conversation with a young Vietnamese man next to him who wears a large carved jade Buddha on a thick gold chain on the outside of his jacket. Geoff asks the man why he is returning to Vietnam. The man says in broken English, "to see his famery." Geoff asks more questions and learns that he works in a spa doing pedicures and manicures. He came to the

US five years ago on a visa and is going home for Tet.

Tet! I nudge Geoff with my elbow. "Are we going to be in Vietnam during Tet?" The first thing that pops into my mind when I hear the word "Tet" is "Tet Offensive" from my reading about the Vietnam War, and although I know it means more than that, the word has an ominous feel.

Geoff asks the Vietnamese man when Tet is. The man says, "Next week."

We look at each other. "I think it's a good thing," Geoff says. "Minh didn't mention it, so it must not be a problem."

"What exactly is Tet?" I ask because Geoff is kind of like an encyclopedia. His memory amazes me.

"It's the Vietnamese Lunar New Year, but it's also celebrated by the Chinese. It's their most important holiday. You've seen news coverage of Chinese New Year celebrations with dragon dances and firecrackers. They'll probably have similar celebrations in Vietnam, and I think it's serendipitous that we're here for it."

Serendipitous! I shake my head at Geoff. Not only does he know everything there is to know about everything, but he knows words most people don't!

"You are incredible!" I say and kiss him on the nose.

He looks me in the eye, "So are you!"

*

After a claustrophobic eternity on the Boeing 737 with only three hours of medicinally induced sleep, we arrive in Hanoi near midnight. Minh is there to meet us. He is heavier than most Vietnamese I've seen, though not at all overweight, and has a perpetual grin on his round face.

I'm beyond tired as we drive in Minh's Toyota through dark streets, slick with drizzle, and pass a park where a cluster of red flags decorated with yellow hammers and sickles stand in a circle around a huge monument. A picture of a man's face, a thin face with a straggly beard, is centered on the monument and next to it, a poster of a giant pig. I think I'm hallucinating.

"Did I just see a pig?" I ask.

Minh laughs and says, "This is the year of the pig. You will see many, many pigs of every kind on this trip."

When we get to the hotel, I barely acknowledge the spacious room and comfortable bed, which I fall into.

*

I awake disoriented yet sensing the now familiar warmth of Geoff next to me. Then my mind is flooded with fragments of flitting images and sensations from the past 24 hours—red flags with golden hammers and sickles next to a giant pig, feeling damp and bone tired, peeling warm aluminum foil off steaming squares of food I would not normally eat, and the sound of the fretting child two seats behind us.

Taking a deep breath, I sit up and look at the room, which I hardly noticed last night. It's surprisingly spare and modern and offers no clues that it happens to be in Vietnam. A digital clock on my side of the bed says 8:34. I'm assuming that's 8:34 a.m. because I understand we are exactly twelve hours earlier than Eastern Standard Time, having dropped a day and a half somewhere in travel over the Pacific, which we will recoup on our return.

After showering, I gently nudge Geoff awake.

"Who am I?" he mumbles. "Where am I? Who are you?" He buries his face in the pillow then turns to say, "How did I get so lucky?"

The man is a comedian even when half asleep.

An hour later, we make our way to the breakfast room filled with the aroma of coffee. A breakfast buffet caters to every taste, offering Western style cereal, eggs, bacon, sausage, toast, and pastries, as well as what must be Vietnamese breakfast foods warming in large pots. An entire table is filled with exotic fruit of every imaginable color, many of which I've never seen much less tasted before. I recognize pineapple and mango, but draw a blank on a hot pink oval fruit that's white inside and embedded with what looks like poppy seeds.

The coffee is amazing, smooth and strong without a hint of acidity. Across from me, Geoff, who had to sample the Vietnamese breakfast, gamely swallows some kind of rice gruel and makes a face. He gets up and brings back a plate of eggs, sausage, pastry, and fruit.

"Minh wants us to call him when we're ready to go," he says. "Does 10:30 sound about right to you?"

I nod, having just sampled the hot pink fruit and finding it crunchy and bland—not as its bold exterior advertised. "What's on the agenda for today?"

"Anything we want. Minh booked rooms for us in several cities and towns he thinks we'll find interesting, but what we do there is entirely up to us. If something piques our interest, we can stay all day. But if a museum or ancient ruin bores us, we can move on."

"Sounds good to me!"

At 10:30, Minh meets us in the lobby and suggests we sit for a minute and talk about what we'd like to see and do today. He suggests we go to the Water Puppet Theatre, something unique to Hanoi, but we need to pre-purchase tickets and might not get in until tomorrow evening. Other options for the day are the Hanoi Hilton where Senator McCain and other American POWs were detained, the Hanoi Art Museum, Ho Chi Minh's tomb, or a drive to a village that makes rice paper. He describes each option briefly, then waits for our response.

Geoff looks at me. I say, "The Water Puppet Theater sounds fun. Let's go ahead and get tickets for whenever. As for the other options, as tough as it may be for me, I'd like to learn about the Americans who were here during the war, and I guess I'd like to try to understand the whole thing—the reasons for the war, why the North won and we lost."

"She's a flighty one, no depth whatsoever," Geoff says and shakes his head in mock bewilderment.

Minh, who hasn't stopped smiling since the moment we saw him, nods approvingly. "I will order tickets for the Water Puppets now, if you do not mind, and then we will begin."

A moment later, wearing raincoats and carrying umbrellas, we go out to the car through cold, gray drizzle, which is the same as what we experienced last night. But the road activity has changed. Motorbikes clog the roadways, darting every which way like unpredictable windup toys. One has an impossibly large five-foot potted tree with oval orange fruit strapped to the back seat.

"That is a kumquat tree," Minh says. "You see, it brings prosperity for the New Year because the fruit is orange and represents gold. Most families will buy a kumquat tree at Tet for luck. See, there is another one!" He points to yet another motorbike with an oversized potted tree tied to the back. The tree changes the weight distribution of the ride, but the driver is unfazed as the motorbike wobbles and weaves through traffic and spitting rain.

"Yellow and orange symbolize prosperity," Minh continues, "so you will see many yellow flowers like chrysanthemums for sale at Tet time. And sometimes people wear yellow-colored clothing for luck."

My mind drifts with the color symbolisms. If wearing yellow or orange brings prosperity, perhaps red brings love, and green brings life? Does white bring chastity? What about black? Or brown? Or blue?

"Geoff," I ask, "What's your lucky color?"

"Khaki," he says. "It symbolizes decisive action, as in the military. But my other lucky color is light blue for something softer, say tenderness. Contradictory qualities, but they show two extremes of a complex character. What's yours?"

"Teal. It's neither green nor blue, but combines the virtues of both. Green for growth and abundance of life; blue for the sky and unlimited possibilities."

We smile at each other.

Minh parks across the street from a gray, square-cut stone building with a raised center that is surrounded by manicured lawn and guarded by three uniformed men. They are dressed entirely in white and march crisply in front of the entryway. They stop and change direction every few minutes—back and forth like impeccable, stiff-legged robots.

"This is Ho Chi Minh's tomb, which is modeled after Lenin's tomb in Moscow," Minh says. "Ho died in 1969, six years before the end of the war. He did not want a fancy tomb. He lived a simple life and requested a simple burial. But his body is on display here at the mausoleum for the people of Vietnam. We will not go in, but we will go past it to the area where he lived in a very small house. He could have lived in the palace built by the French for their governor, but he chose not to."

As we walk to Ho's very humble house behind the tomb, Minh says in a low voice that only we can hear, "I must tell you that my family was on the American side during the war, but I honor Ho Chi Minh. He unified my country and freed it from foreign control. This would not have happened without Ho Chi Minh. You see, he loved his country, my country, more than his life and more than the lives of his people. He sacrificed himself and the people of North Vietnam in order to win, first the war against the French, and later the war against the Americans. Millions of Vietnamese died in these wars, but their belief was so strong, they would have fought to the last man to free their country."

Unlike the South Vietnamese, I think, remembering from my reading about corrupt and well-fed officers who avoided conflict. They lacked the passion of their Northern countrymen.

Minh continues, "Ho was born in 1890, the youngest of three children. His father was a teacher who rebelled against French rule. Ho became a rebel like his father and decided he would go to France to learn about the enemy. He became a cook and worked on a ship going to France. In France, he worked at many jobs and even went to United States for a couple years. Ho liked the United States' Declaration of Independence and tried to present his views to President Wilson in 1919 and asked for help to remove the French from Vietnam. When President Wilson ignored him, Ho joined the Communist Party. You see, he didn't believe in communism, but he needed help from somewhere to free his country."

We get back to the car and stand a moment, watching the white-uniformed guards marching back and forth in front of the entrance to the imposing building. Getting back into the car, Minh suggests that because it is our first day and our bodies are still on US time, we make it a short one. He will drive us around the city to give us a feel for its layout, and then we'll have lunch and call it a day. That sounds perfect to me.

In the center of Hanoi is a long lake, which we drive around, noticing colorful stands selling pig memorabilia and gaudy flowers. Not all the flowers are yellow, and many are made of red paper with gold streamers. It's as though the entire city is in circus mode, trying to compensate for the gray sky and severe buildings.

Minh takes us to a local Vietnamese restaurant, which he says serves some of the best spring rolls, a favorite Tet appetizer. The spring rolls are smaller than any I've experienced, about the size of a man's pinkie, and deep-fried to a delectable crunch. He suggests dipping them into a popular sauce called nuoc mam pha made of fish sauce, lime juice, sugar, and thin slices of hot red pepper. Geoff eats a half dozen without pausing for breath.

"Let me go out on a limb here," I say. "I'm guessing you like these."

He nods and devours his seventh spring roll.

*

Back in our hotel room after we kick off our shoes and shed our wet raincoats, Geoff sits in a chair and presses his fingers along his eyebrows—a sign that he is deep in thought. Eventually he says, "I admire Ho Chi Minh for attaining his goal to unify the country, but I don't admire the great cost for his success! Millions of Vietnamese were killed. When you think of Mahatma Gandhi, Martin Luther King Jr., and Nelson Mandela, who achieved their goals through peaceful means, Ho is less admirable."

I am quiet a moment before I ask, "How does Ho compare to, say, George Washington, who fought for our freedom from the British and shed American blood? And General Eisenhower, who led thousands of Americans to their deaths to save us from Nazi Germany? Wasn't Ho doing the same thing for his country?'

"You're right," Geoff says. "Some wars are justified. I wouldn't want Hitler's swastika on our flag and the SS watching our every move. And perhaps Ho can be justified because he felt as strongly against outside control over his country."

"But what about our part in the Vietnam War? We lost 58,000 people for what? Why were we here anyway? We weren't defending our freedom."

Geoff nods. "It was a senseless war. I'll never forget a question posed to the Senate Foreign Relations Committee in 1971. It was, 'How do you ask a man to be the last man to die in Vietnam? How do you ask a man to die for a mistake?'" Then realizing what he said and how my father might well have been the last man to die in Vietnam, Geoff reaches for me and holds me tight. "I'm so sorry I brought that up," he says into my hair.

I sniffle into his shoulder for a minute, then look up at him, feeling a surge of resolve. "If I'm not able to look at the facts—all the facts—then I shouldn't be here. You don't have to coddle me."

But he does. For the rest of the afternoon.

CHAPTER 21

Nate

The morning before Nate and Mai were to leave for Ho Chi Minh City, as Nate and Rosy shared their daily ritual of eggs and salsa on toast, Rosy asked, "Has Mai seen her family since the war? You know—did she visit them when you were growing up?"

"No." Nate took another spoon of the fresh, homemade salsa Rosy prepared each morning for their breakfast. This was their only uninterrupted time of the day, and it had become the hinge on which the rest of the day swung. "For some reason, she avoided going back, even though many of her friends did. Maybe it was for financial reasons."

Rosy snorted as she set down her coffee mug. "If Mai wanted to go back, nothing would have stopped her!"

"You're right." Nate paused, thinking about his complicated mother. Then his thoughts turned to the two wonderful children he and Rosy shared. In addition to Stevie Felipe, who was now 14, they had Maria Mai, a spitfire 10-year-old. "Someday I'd like to take you and the kids."

Rosy shrugged. "The kids, maybe. I don't need to go." Rosy was no longer working at Rice and had started an online design assistance hotline. She called herself the "Dear Abby of Interior

Design Disasters."

Nate continued, "Sorry I'll miss Stevie's art show at school. He's been so excited about it. And Maria's soccer tournament. Will she forgive me?"

"Don't worry. I'll bring my family, and they'll make a big deal about it. You need to go get your cultural fix, I know. Commune with the ancestors." She gave him a half smile. "I get you."

Nate reached over and gently touched her cheek with the back of his fingers. "And I'll never get you!"

*

Mai was restless on the long plane ride. It wasn't any longer than the ones Nate had taken on his other five trips, but it felt longer because he was responsible for his mother, who was having difficulty sleeping and otherwise occupying herself in the small, confined space. She didn't want to watch the movie. The food was inedible, she said. When she closed her eyes as though to sleep, she rocked her head from side to side and sighed.

She's worse than a small child! Nate thought. *What possessed me to bring her along?*

But that all changed when they landed at Tan Son Nhut Airport. Mai emerged from the plane, focused with all senses alert. All around them, families cheered and greeted passengers as they exited customs. Nate had emailed Binh that he knew the way to the family compound and there was no need to meet them at the plane. Yet when they walked through the exit, someone yelled, "Nate! Mai!" and they saw Danh, Kim, and Binh waving excitedly at them to the right of the exit.

Kim and Mai, about the same stature and weight, came

together like magnets. Nate shook Danh's hand and then hugged Binh, who was now a grown man working at a software development company in Ho Chi Minh City. Eventually, they made their way to Danh's car, a locally assembled Ford, and loaded the luggage, which was much more than double what Nate usually brought.

Getting out of the airport took almost an hour because of the crush of cars picking up relatives. Mai and Kim didn't seem to notice. They were deep in conversation, attempting to catch up on over 40 years. Mai looked up once and said in Vietnamese, "Much more traffic now." And again when they passed the towering skyscrapers of downtown, "Is this San Francisco?"

From the back seat, Binh filled Nate in on his life after graduating from a university in Australia. His English was excellent, and Nate was proud of his little cousin, who confided that in the coming year, he was marrying a young woman he worked with named Hoa. She would be coming to visit on the third day of Tet so Nate would meet her. Binh said in English, "She's a looker, and smart, too!"

After getting through Ho Chi Minh City, they started the drive to the family compound. Kim brought out banh mi sandwiches, which Mai accepted with enthusiasm.

Nate was relieved when, about a half hour into their drive, he looked back to see Mai sound asleep, her head on Kim's shoulder. He smiled at his aunt, who smiled back.

CHAPTER 22

Lindsey - Hanoi

The next morning, Minh takes us to a stone and yellow cement block building with a sign above its arched doorway that reads, "Maison Centrale."

"French?" I ask as we enter through the arch into a dark cement interior.

Minh tells us, "It was built by the French in late 1800s for political prisoners. You see, before that, the land was a potter's compound, named Hoa Lo, which means 'potter's kiln' in Vietnamese. That name makes people think 'fiery furnace' and 'Hell's hole.' The American name 'Hanoi Hilton' is because a pilot Bob Shumaker, who was a prisoner here, carved 'Welcome to the Hanoi Hilton' on the handle of a bucket he gave to a new American prisoner, Lt. Robert Peel."

Inside, a man at a desk collects 10,000 Vietnamese dollars from each of us, worth about 50 cents US, then lets us through to a room full of glass cases of pottery. Even though I was just told the compound used to be a potter's community, it feels odd to see jugs and bowls displayed in a world-renowned place of torture.

Minh explains, "Most Americans want to see where the

American prisoners stayed, but that part of the prison was torn down to build the Hanoi Towers buildings behind us. There is very little about the Americans here. What you will see here is where the French kept Vietnamese political prisoners."

Geoff and I look at each other. He shrugs and I whisper, "At least we're out of the rain." The next room we enter is filled with rows of life-size models of Vietnamese prisoners with a strange shiny blue cast to them, almost as though they were dead bodies. Their feet are shackled.

I shudder. Was my father put in such a place? The next room is a dungeon for solitary confinement with only a small, shoebox-size, barred opening.

I can't help but imagine how it was when it was occupied—the smells of human waste, rats, moans from the ill, screams from people being tortured…"I need some fresh air," I interrupt Minh, who has been talking about the French abuse of political prisoners.

He leads us to an enclosed garden with little potted palm trees lining a courtyard. Moss grows between paving stones. It looks peaceful except for an imposing gray wall engraved with figures in various poses of torture.

"Are those figures Americans?" I ask naively.

"No," says Minh. "This is a memorial honoring the North Vietnamese dead—the men and women who died in the 'American War.'"

"Let me understand this," I say, getting personally involved. "The French built this prison and tortured Vietnamese in it. Then the French were defeated. During the American War, the Vietnamese used the same building to torture American POWs. Now the Vietnamese vilify the French for their inhumane treatment and memorialize that at this museum when, a few years earlier, they used the same facility to torture our POWs. Do people ever learn from the past?"

I had momentarily forgotten about Minh and turn to see him looking down at his feet. "I'm sorry, Minh. I'm speaking like an ignorant American, and I'm sure we also did unspeakable things during the war." I take a breath. "I detest the way war twists human beings into monsters."

Minh looks up at me. "You are right. My family was pro American during the war, and they were punished when the Americans left. There was much suffering on both sides, and no one is without blame. But I think there is more to see. The few things from the American POWs are around this corner."

We follow an arrow that leads up a staircase to a modest room with glass-enclosed cases and framed black-and-white photographs. The room smells musty. The photographs show destruction and burned bodies.

"What are these photographs supposed to mean?" I ask.

Minh says, "I believe this room shows the harm that American planes did to the Vietnamese. Perhaps it is to explain why American pilots were imprisoned here."

The next room, similar in ambiance and smell, has photos of American prisoners— impossibly thin—gardening, praying, preparing Christmas dinner, being attended by Vietnamese doctors. Prominent in the room is a glass case with Senator McCain's flight suit and personal effects. We walk around silently absorbing it, and I am imagining Steve Nathan in an even worse situation because there was no accountability by the time he was possibly captured.

"Lindsey, look at this!" Geoff says next to me. He points to a sheet of framed paper with red writing, the top in Vietnamese, followed by English.

SOME PICTURES AND OBJECTS

OF UNITED STATES PILOTS IN HOA LO PRISON

UNITED STATES GOVERNMENT CARRIED OUT A SABOTAGE WARFARE BY AIR FORCE, AND NAVAL FORCE AGAINST THE NORTH OF VIETNAM FROM 05 AUGUST 1964 TO 15 JANUARY 1973.

THOUSANDS OF PLANES WERE SHOT DOWN, HUNDREDS OF UNITED STATES PILOTS WERE ARRESTED BY THE NORTH ARMY AND PEOPLE. SOME OF THEM WERE IMPRISONED HERE.

DURING THE WAR, THE NATIONAL ECONOMY WAS DIFFICULT, BUT VIETNAMESE GOVERNMENT HAD CREATED THE BEST LIVING CONDITIONS TO US PILOTS FOR THEY HAD A STABLE LIFE DURING THE TEMPORARY DETENTION PERIOD.

UPON THE AGREEMENT ON WAR TERMINATION WAS CONCLUDED IN MARCH 1973 IN PARIS, ALL THE ARRESTED US PILOTS WERE RELEASED TO US GOVERNMENT BY VIETNAM GOVERNMENT.

SOME OF THE PICTURES AND OBJECTS ON THESE TWO EXHIBITION HALL SHOW SOME DETAILS OF US PILOTS' LIFE WHEN THEY WERE TEMPORARY IMPRISONED AT HOA LO PRISON.

"Let's go back outside." I say, shaken and angry, confused and sad. Back in the courtyard, Geoff sits down on a wooden bench. I slowly sit next to him. Minh, as if realizing his presence is awkward, tells us he has to make a phone call and will be back later.

"How long were Americans 'temporarily' held here?" I ask.

Geoff, who knows everything, says, "Everett Alverez was the first prisoner captured in 1964. He was a Navy pilot and they held him nine years. Senator McCain was held five-and-a-half years."

"And I doubt they were treated as well as the Vietnamese claim."

"True." Geoff pauses and reaches inside his jacket to bring out a notebook. "I did some homework," he says and gives me a small smile. "In the beginning, American prisoners weren't allowed to communicate. Many were in solitary confinement. Can you imagine years of solitary confinement? Years of not being allowed to communicate with another American?"

We are silent. In this place, Geoff's words are incredibly powerful. I am about to ask to leave when Geoff says, "The Americans early on were not allowed to speak to each other, but they did communicate here at Hoa Lo. Look at this."

He opens his notebook to a page with numbers and the alphabet that formed a matrix.

	1	2	3	4	5
1	A	B	C	D	E
2	F	G	H	I	J
3	I	L	M	N	O
4	P	Q	R	S	T
5	U	V	W	X	Y

"A code?" I ask.

"Right! Each letter of the alphabet could be conveyed by a code that was tapped on the wall. Using the matrix, you tap the number horizontally then vertically to identify the letter. For example, the letter 'I' is 4 taps then 2 taps." He taps his pen on the side of the bench.

He continues tapping—2 taps/3 taps (L); 5 taps/3 taps (O); 2 taps/5 taps(V); 5 taps/1 tap(E); 1 tap/5 taps(U); I am drawn into decoding his taps, unsure at first whether they were random, until the meaning becomes obvious.

He taps in an off-handed manner, clicking his ballpoint pen in or out after each letter. When he finishes, I wrap my arms around him and whisper into his ear, "I love you, too."

*

That evening after yet another Vietnamese meal, which was good and quite similar to all the others, we walk to the Water Puppet Theater, a short four blocks from our hotel. The drizzle has stopped, the sun has retreated for the day, and because it is a few days away from the new moon, there is no visible moon in the sky. Our only light comes from the myriad colored lights and flashing displays in honor of the Lunar New Year.

Vietnamese air smells different from any air I have ever breathed before. I mention it to Geoff, who laughs and asks me to describe it for him.

"Like wet earth and fish and charcoal smoke all mixed together," I say.

He laughs again and hugs me.

"This way!" Minh, who is ahead of us, calls because we are dawdling. We enter a building that is solid with human bodies. Minh pushes through them, and we follow him up a flight of stairs. The show has already started when we open a door leading to a warm, dark room. It takes my eyes a moment to adjust.

"There in the middle," Minh whispers, pointing to two seats in the middle of the theater.

We cause a ripple of rising theatergoers as Geoff and I make our way to the last two seats available in the theater. On the stage, wooden farmer puppets appear to be planting rice. There is a nasal singsong voice and drums and wooden instruments I've never heard before. I can't understand the story, and the music is unusual. But the lighting and the uniquely carved puppets are interesting, especially when I realize their stage is a pool of water.

Geoff leans over and says, "The puppeteers manipulate the puppets while standing waist-deep in water."

"How did you know that?"

"Burrs, remember?"

I laugh as I remember his first joke about facts sticking to him like burrs and settle into my seat. The room is very warm. Too warm. My eyes close involuntarily, and I begin to relax for the first time that day. The music fades. I sleep.

A sudden drumroll, long and loud, wakes me. Where am I? My head is resting on something soft and a little bit scratchy. It's someone's shoulder. I smell aftershave, faint but distinct, a mix of grass and citrus. Then I realize the shoulder is Geoff's inside his nubby oatmeal-colored sweater, and I smell the new aftershave I bought him right before we left the US.

Apparently I slept through most of the performance and woke for the finale. People applaud and then stand up around us to begin the slow caterpillar crawl out the only exit.

"How was it?" I ask.

"You missed the best part," Geoff says. "The water rose up into two walls, and the farmers crossed safely to the other side."

"Different ancient story," I say, shaking my head and laughing.

Minh meets us outside the theater with his perpetual smile. "How did you like it?" he asks.

Geoff says, "Very unique. Let's go someplace where we can sit and talk about it."

Around the corner from the theater is a café that serves coffee, tea, and little French pastries. We find a table in the back, and after ordering, Minh proceeds to tell us, "The Water Puppets began long ago around the 11th century in North Vietnam, and they started as entertainment when farmers' fields flooded. In Vietnamese, the name means 'making puppets dance on water.' The people who make the puppets dance are behind a bamboo screen in the back and use long bamboo sticks and strings under the water to move the puppets. Knowing how to do this is passed from father to son for generations, and sons must train for three years.

"Teu is one of the main characters; you must remember him, the one with the big smile who wears a loincloth. He is a jester who makes jokes during the ancient stories of living and growing rice, harvesting, fishing, and celebrations. Life was difficult, but Teu and my people learned to laugh no matter what happens. You see, they made theater when floods ruined their rice crops!"

And they are welcoming us Americans back into their country after we were their enemy, I think, remembering the openness and acceptance I've felt since I've been here in Hanoi. Everyone from maids at the hotel to airport officials appear to not hold it against us. When I mention this to Minh, he says, "We are a people used to war, but we have no war for a generation now, and the young people don't remember it. To them, American tourists mean money, and that is good. Also, it is Tet time and everybody is happy. You come at a good time when people are in a good mood. The only trouble is that it will be crowded—hotels, roads, and sites, because everybody is on holiday and visiting their families."

Geoff says, "And we appreciate you working during this holiday, showing us around. Don't you have family you want to spend time with?"

"Yes." Minh hesitates. "I want to ask you, but it is no problem."

"Really," Geoff persists. "We can change our schedule. Just leave us in a good place for a few days while you celebrate the holiday with your family."

Minh appears to consider the offer and finally says, "If it is okay with you, next week is the beginning of Tet, and the first three days are most important to be with family. Perhaps I can leave you in Saigon for those days and then you fly to Dalat, where I meet you. Then we drive from Dalat to Phan Thiet.

"By all means! I wish I had thought of it earlier!" Geoff says.

"Good!" Minh beams.

CHAPTER 23

Nate – Tet Nien

Each time Nate visited the family compound, he felt like he was coming home, and this time being with Mai, he expected to feel the familial connection even stronger. He wasn't sure how she would react, because Mai rarely showed emotion. Of course, seeing her little sister Kim at the airport after decades of separation brought a flood of tears, but that was to be expected. What Nate didn't expect was what Mai did when they reached the house.

It was near midnight when Danh turned the family Ford into the dirt driveway, sheltered by night-darkened bamboo. Nate was asleep; his time-conflicted body had succumbed to exhaustion. The car came to a stop, and he became aware of the commotion of doors swinging open and excited voices. He opened his eyes to hubbub and saw from the dim overhead light in the car that Mai was still in a deep sleep in the back seat. Kim was shaking her gently.

Mai opened her eyes slowly and appeared confused about where she was.

"Mai." Kim jostled her. "We are here. Home!"

"Home?" Mai whispered, barely awake.

She climbed out of the back seat like an old woman and fell to the ground. Alarmed, Nate went to assist her until he realized she was bowing, her forehead in the dirt, and mumbling something he couldn't understand, which alarmed him even more.

The rest of the family seemed unfazed and proceeded to unload the car with an army of small children who appeared out of nowhere. Kim waved Nate on into the house as she waited by her sister.

Eventually the two of them came indoors, where Kim led Mai to the bedroom/toolshed that used to be Binh's and was now upgraded to a legitimate bedroom. Most of the men, including Nate, were relegated to cots arranged outdoors and covered with mosquito nets.

"Goodnight, Ma," Nate said, looking at her closely as she settled herself on the shelf of a bed that was usually his.

"Goodnight, Nate." She closed her eyes with an undecipherable expression on her face.

*

The next morning, roosters woke Nate and sounded as if they were crowing next to his head. The beams of morning sun that penetrated the bamboo thicket looked filmy through the netting. He smelled a charcoal fire even though, from the conversation he'd overheard last night between his mother and Aunt Kim, they had upgraded to a modern stove that used bottled gas.

Small children began wandering around, laughing, infected with the anticipation of the biggest holiday of the year. It was impossible for Nate to fall back asleep. He stretched and found his way out of the netting to stand and survey the yard. A new cement patio extended from the kitchen, and in its center was a long wooden table that could seat perhaps half the family. At two corners of the patio were huge pots of small trees, one a kumquat with a multitude of small oval orange fruit and the other a blooming peach tree with delicate pink flowers.

As Nate approached the kitchen, he saw that there was already a great deal of activity there, more than was usual before breakfast. Aunt Kim was at the center of it, directing the other women and young girls. Mai was not among them.

Nate wandered over to Binh and another cousin with morning-tousled hair, standing at the edge of the property.

"Chao," he said informally. They returned the greeting in English.

Nate continued the conversation in Vietnamese, "Busy time of year."

The younger of the two cousins, one of Tran's grandsons, said, "This is Tet Nien, the week before Tet, and it is crazy until Monday when Tet officially starts. We have to clean the entire compound and prepare all the food in advance because you cannot work during Tet, plus our ancestor's graves need to be cleaned before Tet officially starts. Stay away from the women. They are in charge of it all, and if they see you, they will give you a job." He grinned.

Nate grinned back. "Why do you have to work so hard?" Although he and Mai had celebrated Tet every year, he had no extended family growing up to share in the festivities, so they had kept it simple.

Binh said, "You know, you have family and visitors coming and everything has to be perfect and the food has to be better than what other people serve. It's a contest. At least the women seem to think so. Plus, you want the new year to be lucky, so everyone is on their best behavior—no fights or arguments to spoil the coming year."

Nate had heard much of this before, although he and Mai did not practice it beyond attending the parade and then going to the Buddhist temple for their annual visit. Obviously theirs was a watered-down version of Tet. He was curious about the traditions he had missed.

"Why do you clean the ancestor's graves?"

Binh proceeded to answer in English. "My parents believe the ancestors are with us all the time and control our luck. The dead live in another dimension, but the living must tend to their needs, and in return, the ancestors give the living advice and bring good fortune. So before Tet, the family must remove weeds and clean the graves and make them pretty. Also, we need to give offerings to the ancestors at the family altar."

Nate had noticed the family altar in the corner of the central room of the house when he walked through last night. What usually occupied a small area on a top shelf, was now a dominant display in the room, complete with burning incense, which permeated the entire house, floral bouquets, plates of food, and handwritten inscriptions in ancient Chinese characters. He would have to go back and check it out.

Binh continued, "And the most famous of our ancestors are the Kitchen Gods. You know the story?"

"I might have heard it as a boy. Refresh my memory."

"Seven days before Tet, the Kitchen God, who lives in every family's kitchen, goes to Heaven to tell the Jade Emperor how the family behaved all year. His report decides the luck of that family for the coming year. So families bribe the Kitchen God with cookies and sweets, so he will give a good report." Binh shook his head as though he couldn't understand how people could be so stupid. "Maybe I don't believe all of it, but I like that it is a new beginning. So even if you had a crappy year before, you can start over at Tet and hope to have a better year."

Nate had to smile at his cousin's mastery of slang, and his words jogged a memory of something he'd read recently that said Tet is a shortened version of Tet Nguyen Dan, which means "Feast of the first morning of the first day."

Right about then, Mai appeared, and after nodding to Nate and her grandnephews, to whom she had not been formally introduced, she headed straight to the kitchen. Nate heard the exclamations of welcome when she entered the crowded lean-to.

Well, Nate thought, *I won't see her much from now on. She has found the element that for her is as essential as oxygen.*

But he was wrong. A few minutes later, she reappeared with a bowl of congee for him, and as he spooned the hot gruel into his mouth, she said, "You finish, come with me."

He handed her the empty bowl, which she gave to Binh to take back to the kitchen, and motioned Nate to follow her. They walked to a far corner of the property where a path led through the giant bamboo. Although he had explored most of the area around the house, Nate didn't remember this path. It was narrow and wound through the dense undergrowth to end at a clearing with a rock-enclosed area of earth. Incense stuck out of the dirt, and pots of flowers lined the edges.

"Your grandparents," Mai said and went down on her knees in front of the grave. She touched her head to one of the rocks that formed the edge. After a moment's hesitation, Nate followed her example.

Nate didn't recall hearing much about his grandparents as he grew up except they were killed by an American bomb while working in the rice fields. Obviously the bomb didn't destroy their home or their children, who must have been teenagers at the time. How could his mother go to work for the Americans after they killed her parents?

Nate stood and waited for his mother to lift her head before he asked, "Didn't you hate the Americans for killing your parents?"

"Yes, but the NVA worse. We have war. My parents unlucky and in wrong place. Americans good to us and help us. Give Tran good job. Then I get good job." She paused and stood, looking around. Breathing deeply, she walked to an area outside the rocks where a mound of earth was barely visible through vines and tangled ground cover. She appeared to be looking for something. Suddenly, like a woman possessed, she knelt and began tearing at the weeds, yanking them out by the handful and sobbing hysterically.

"Ma!" Nate grabbed her by the shoulders and pulled her upright. "What are you doing?"

Mai pushed him away with her muddy hands and fell back to her knees.

I shouldn't have brought her here, Nate thought. *She's having a nervous breakdown.*

He knelt next to her and put his arm carefully around her weeping form and waited until her sobbing subsided.

"You all right?"

"No. Your father is here, under the ground."

CHAPTER 24

Lindsey - Ha Long Bay

Leaving Hanoi the next morning, while waiting for a traffic light, Minh turns to us in the back seat. "Ha Long Bay is," he looks at each of us, "a very romantic place."

"Will it be sunny?" Geoff asks.

"Maybe, maybe not." Minh shrugs. "This is the winter in North Vietnam and it rains most of the time."

"What is Ha Long Bay?" I ask.

Minh says, "It is where there are nearly 2000 limestone islands of incredible beauty. Ha Long means 'where the dragon goes into the sea.' It is a place of many legends, for example, the legend of how it was created. A great dragon came to this coast from the mountains. He destroyed everything with his tail along the way, making valleys before he ran into the sea. The dragon sank, and his spine is now many islands."

On to more practical things, Minh continues, "We will take a small boat out to the junk in the bay and will go on a cruise around the beautiful islands. We will eat on the junk and then spend the night in modern cabins."

After a couple hours of driving between impossibly green rice fields divided by straight paths of mounded dirt, we arrive at a parking lot edged by the sea and filled with cars and buses. I look toward the fog-shrouded dark shapes in the bay, which must be the "islands of incredible beauty." At least the drizzle has stopped for the moment.

There are two launches rapidly filling up with a large group of tourists who speak a language I'm not familiar with. "Portuguese," Geoff says.

The dock is at the bottom of steep, rain-slick stone steps, and as we carefully make our way down, placing our feet sideways on the narrow treads, I hear one launch noisily revving its engines. Clouds of diesel smoke arise as it turns and begins to move toward what looks like a yellow and red ferryboat topped with orange sails.

Behind me, Minh says, "There is our floating hotel for the night. It is a new one. Good!"

So this is to be our "very romantic" digs here in Ha Long Bay, along with a boatload of Portuguese tourists.

Minh must have seen my look of disappointment because he says, "During Tet, it is not possible to find a private boat, but you have a very good room."

We board the launch and sit alongside well-dressed middle-aged couples who enthusiastically gesture as they speak nonstop to each other between moments of explosive laughter.

I take a deep breath as the launch slows to a wobbly stop and inches over to a lowered set of stairs that lead to the main deck. Geoff squeezes my hand as I step off the bobbing launch onto the equally bobbing stairs and says, "Did I ever tell you about the time I sailed in a leaky wooden dugout down a piranha-infested river?"

"Right!" I have to laugh and shake my head at my amazing

companion, who knows how to read me and when to interject humor.

We walk single file up the makeshift stairs to the landing and into a common dining area beyond which are two corridors of staterooms. Minh motions us through the room, back outside, and then up a metal stairway to the top deck. We go inside again to another shorter corridor of staterooms, and Minh opens the last door into a compact but very comfortable suite with a private deck looking out the stern.

"This is wonderful," I say, noting our private dining area and the expansive view out a sliding glass door where limestone islands loom like giant stalactites.

"I am next door, if you need me," Minh says. "Your dinner is at 6:00, and they bring it to you here."

After Minh leaves, the boat's engines rev and we begin to move. Geoff and I stand at the glass, looking at the widening wake. I say, "Better than a leaky wooden dugout."

*

This is my third day in Vietnam, and my equilibrium is off. It isn't just that time has turned upside down—midnight is noon and my internal alarm clock for rising in the morning goes off when it's time to wind down for the day. What really upsets my equilibrium is being around Geoff 24 hours a day, which is like overdosing on stimulants. His coded message to me at the Hanoi Hilton doesn't help.

During the infrequent quiet moments I've had since, when I try to understand that message—not the words, but what they imply—I become confused. Surely Geoff didn't mean he wants a long-term, exclusive relationship with me. It wasn't a proposal for marriage or an invitation to cohabitate. And how would I feel if it were?

These disquieting thoughts aren't allowed to fester, however, because exotic scenes and smells invade my space, and I have to interrupt my internal analysis to deal with them, the most recent of which are the oddly shaped limestone islands that pass us as the boat glides by.

Geoff and I are out on our private deck in polar fleece and rain gear, getting coated with mist from the cool, damp air.

"Look! There's the dragon's spine!" Geoff points to a lumpy string of islands that look connected. "And those two rocks are roosters facing each other."

I usually have an active imagination and see human faces in wood grain and animals in cloud formations, but those two rocks are not roosters.

"I don't see them," I say.

"Actually, they aren't roosters. They are a pair of nuns with billowing robes. And they are pissed at each other. You can see it in the angle of their bodies—bent forward at the waist, one is shaking her finger at the other..."

"You are too much, Geoff Davis," I say, burying my laughing face in his wet sleeve. He moves to hug me, and we stand entwined, swaying to keep our balance on the rolling deck as dragons and roosters and nuns pass by.

*

That evening we invite Minh to eat with us in our cabin. He appears grateful to avoid sharing a dining room with people who speak no Vietnamese or English. The boat has anchored and is gently rocking, a soothing and rhythmic movement. Outside, it is still light enough to see that the wind has picked up and is swirling the slowly darkening fog.

"Is it always overcast here?" I ask.

"Often it is foggy, which is beautiful. And in the summer it is sunny, and beautiful in a different way."

Someone from the kitchen comes and lays a white cloth on our table and sets it with an elaborate array of plates, glasses, and silverware, including chopsticks. When the food comes, I find that I'm starving. Apparently the damp cold has increased my appetite so the now common spring rolls have a fresh appeal, as do the ubiquitous rice and stir fry vegetable dishes with the usual variety of meats. One new and striking dish is a whole fish with crispy skin coated in a sweet and sour sauce. Other than the intact eye that stares up at me, it is a welcome addition. Geoff notices my aversion to the eye and covers it with a piece of cucumber garnish.

Minh says, "It is good fortune when things have a head and a tail. My son especially likes to eat the fish eye."

Geoff quickly says, "Tell us about your son. How old is he, and do you have other children?"

"We in Vietnam are encouraged to have only two children. No more. So my wife and I have a son, 12 years old, and a daughter, 10 years old."

"What are their names?" I ask, "And do you have pictures?"

Minh brings out his cell phone and proudly shows us pictures of An and Duong, smiling little dark-haired children, through various stages of growth.

Geoff asks, "Do you mind if I ask about your experiences

during the Vietnam War?"

"Yes, you may ask," Minh says, "but first I must say that we call it the American War."

"Makes sense," Geoff says. "And you must have had the French War before that and Chinese Wars even before that."

"Right!" Minh beams.

We wait a moment as Minh swallows a sip of tea.

"My family was originally from Nha Trang. My father was a businessman who traded with the French and then with the Americans. My older brothers fought on the American side."

"What did your family do after the Americans left?" I ask.

Minh shrugs. "It was not easy. My father was a political figure, a prominent pro American. My second older brother was high in the ARVN, and he was taken away after the war. We never saw him again."

I remember from my research that ARVN is an acronym for Army of the Republic of Vietnam, the South Vietnamese army. Minh fumbles with a handkerchief. I want to put a reassuring hand on his shoulder but am unsure if, in this culture, that would be an acceptable gesture from a female who is not a family member.

He composes himself and continues. "My family moved to the Mekong Delta, where we became rice farmers. We had to destroy all papers that identified us, and we got new identities. Three of my brothers and sisters escaped during the time of the boat people. One lives in Arizona, one is in Chicago, and my sister lives in Canada."

"Your family is far apart," I say.

"Yes, I have many nieces and nephews I have never seen. But some day perhaps they will come to visit. They may want to see where their family came from."

I try to process how I would feel if I were talking to someone who indirectly was responsible for the disappearance and assumed death of an older brother, someone whose country let his family down so they had to destroy their identities and take on a life of hard labor, someone whose government disrupted his family life to the point where siblings fled to other countries and left family ties behind.

"I'm sorry," I say, and this time I touch Minh's shoulder, not caring if I'm violating a Vietnamese custom. As the daughter of a Vietnam vet, I feel a personal connection to this man's difficulty.

Geoff says, "Your English is very good, and I know you are one of the most popular tour guides for English speakers in Vietnam. Where did you learn it?"

Minh takes another sip of tea. "You have heard of the boat people, right?"

"Yes."

"My two older brothers and one sister who escaped Vietnam were boat people who left soon after the war. It was very dangerous, and they were lucky to make it alive. Pirates raided the boats. Storms sank them. Between 200,000 and 400,000 Vietnamese died in these boats. I was very young at that time, too young to leave my mother and father, but several years later at age 16, I wanted to leave Vietnam and go to America. It was my dream.

"So in 1982, I left with 17 other people. I didn't say goodbye to my mother because she would make me stay. We took a bus in the middle of the night to Cambodia. There we took a boat, again at night, to go 300 miles across the Gulf of Thailand to Malaysia. The boat was only 23 feet long. We had two outboard motors, but we ran out of gas. So we drifted and soon ran out of food and water. Thai pirates boarded our boat and raped the women and stole all our possessions. One woman they killed, a beautiful young Chinese woman."

Minh's story rivets me. My Internet research told of hundreds, no, thousands of boat people who died in their attempt to flee Vietnam. The large numbers dehumanized them. But Minh's story is a very personal one about someone I am sitting next to. I feel a huge lump in my throat and try unsuccessfully to swallow it.

Minh begins to tear up and reaches into his pocket for a handkerchief. "It was a nightmare. Then a storm came and filled our boat with water. The boat was sinking. We were rescued by Thai fishermen who took us to a refugee camp on the coast of Malaysia. The refugee camp was very crowded. It was built for 4,500 refugees, but more than 40,000 were there. There was not enough food and water from relief organizations. Sanitation was a very big problem. Many of us were sick.

"Once a year, people from United States and other countries gave us a test to help them select people for resettlement. Every year I studied very hard for the test. I was there for four years and I was not selected. Married couples and young families were selected. Young women were selected. But most of the young men like me were not selected."

I say. "How could they do that? That's so unfair!"

Minh nods. "Yes. But there was one good thing about the refugee camp. They provided education. Every day I listened to the BBC English language program and learned English. For four years, that was all I did every day, while I waited to be selected to go to America."

Geoff asks, "Why did you come back to Vietnam?"

"Every year, we had the opportunity to return to Vietnam. If we returned, the government did not punish us for leaving. So finally, after four years, I decided to return to Vietnam. It was better than the stinking refugee camp. And now that you see it, Vietnam is beautiful, is it not?"

Geoff and I nod in agreement.

Poor Minh. I can't imagine how humiliating it would be to suffer the indignity of not meeting the standards of governments that were screening refugees. To return home, a failed boat person, was added humiliation. How could he smile so much? And his poor mother. He disappeared one day as a 16-year-old, and she probably thought he was dead. Yet he showed up four years later. It must have been shocking yet wonderful.

When I come out of my reverie, I hear Geoff and Minh talking about plans for one of the upcoming cities. Geoff is saying, "I'd like to visit the orphanage there because it was one that we set up several years ago after the typhoon in 2008."

"Not a problem," Minh says.

That night, in spite of thoughts of marauding Thai pirates, I manage to sleep, lulled by the rocking movement of our red-sailed ferryboat.

CHAPTER 25

Lindsey - Hue

I awaken to the sound of boat engines starting and the sight of a tentative ray of sunlight through the brightening fog. We make our way back to the dock and Minh's Toyota. We'll be in the car for most of the day.

Our next stop is the ancient capital city of Hue. When I first saw the name in writing, I pronounced it "Hugh" until I was told to say "whey."

As Minh explains on the drive, Vietnam is a thin country about 1000 miles long. Geoff puts it into more relatable terms. "It's like a thin sliver of the East Coast from New York City to Miami. We're driving about a third of that today on roads that are paved, but not the superhighways we're used to."

Minh apologizes that we have to drive when, if we had come any other time of year, we could have flown from Hanoi to Da Nang and driven north a short distance. But because it is the week before Tet, all airlines are booked solid. He was able, however, to get us a flight to Dalat on the fourth day of Tet when most families have already arrived at their destinations.

"And good news is that the weather gets better as we go south," Minh says. "Maybe not sunny in Hue, but soon we will see the sun."

I am surprised at how cold it has been so far in Vietnam. Fortunately, Geoff advised me to bring warm clothing; otherwise, I would have assumed that, because it is a tropical country, Vietnam would be hot and muggy. Not so in the north during the winter, apparently.

"Ho Chi Minh City will be very warm," Minh promises. "And we are to be there in four more days."

Normally the long drive would have been a perfect time for Geoff and me to talk, but Minh's presence is a deterrent. So, I put my head on Geoff's shoulder and doze for much of the journey, or pretend to as I fantasize about our future together at every stage of our relationship from friendship to marriage. And to prepare myself for the worst, I imagine a horrible incident that comes to light from his past or a revelation about a lurking, unknown personality trait that will turn me against him. But I have to admit that my greatest fear is he will disappear from my life after this trip, as if I meant nothing to him other than a temporary diversion.

*

The next morning, I awake with anticipation. We are finally in Hue, the ancient capital of Vietnam and home of the former Vietnamese emperors. Supposedly a beautiful city, it doesn't appear so as we drive through nondescript streets on yet another gray, drizzly day. We are going to the Citadel.

Minh has filled us in about the multi-walled old city of the emperors surrounded by a moat with water from the Perfume River. I can't imagine any river here smelling like perfume!

The city was built in concentric walled squares. The outermost wall enclosed the city called the Citadel. Inside that was a wall around the Imperial City, where the emperor's high officials did business. In the heart of the Imperial City was yet another wall around the Purple Forbidden City, reserved for the emperor's family.

In spite of Geoff telling me I didn't need one, I bought a tourist guidebook for this trip, and now I open it to Hue and find the section on the Citadel. There's a list of facts that I skim over:

Started in 1803 and finished in 1832

Walls protected an area of 2 square kilometers

Emperor Gia Long wanted to replicate the Forbidden City in Beijing

Tu Duc, longest reigning Nguyem emperor (1848-83) had 104 wives and countless concubines, but he had no offspring—the theory was he was sterile from smallpox

Poor guy. In spite of having access to all the women he wanted, probably the most beautiful women in the empire, he couldn't produce an heir. Probably sex for him became a driving obsession to produce an heir and wasn't much fun after the first year or two. Smallpox. Hmmm. He likely was pockmarked and ugly.

Geoff and Minh are discussing what happened in Hue during the American War, as I now think of it. Apparently the Citadel was a significant battleground during the Tet Offensive of 1968.

We arrive and park on the outside of the old city, crossing a wide stone bridge over the moat to a gatehouse. If it had been a sunny day, the Citadel might have impressed me more. The drizzle gives a sheen to the yellow roof and gray stone walkways, but the colorful ornamentation on the gate is blotched with black mold. I do notice the dragons—dank, dirty cement dragons festooned along curved rooftops, dragons painted in red and gold in sacred pavilions, and open-mouthed fearsome ones in multi-colored enamel over ornate gates. I also notice the bullet holes desecrating the few ancient buildings left standing.

Minh points out the massive walls 30 feet high and 20 feet thick that surround the city and says, "A very sad thing happened here during the Tet Offensive. Both Vietnamese armies entered the Citadel and, while fighting inside it, destroyed their common cultural treasure. However, it is now a UNESCO World Heritage site. You see, the world recognizes that it is an important historical place that should be restored."

Minh leaves us to wander on our own through grassy plots around crumbling buildings and courtyards in the midst of being restored. When we get to the center, the Purple Forbidden City, I try to imagine 104 wives cohabitating with countless concubines in this very spot. Talk about intrigue and jealousy, and sadly, women who were trapped in a life where they had little control.

Geoff takes me by the arm and motions me to sit down on a sheltered cement bench. "I brought a recording with me that I want to play here in this spot. It was made by my Uncle Herb, who was at the Citadel during the Tet Offensive. It's graphic and disturbing, so you don't have to listen to it."

Graphic and disturbing. Do I need to hear something like that?

I respect Geoff for wanting to honor his uncle by listening to his words in the spot where he fought. He's not *my* uncle, but his words are part of the history of this place. And Geoff has gone out of his way to take me on this trip so I can learn more about my father. The least I can do is listen to his uncle.

"Go ahead," I say.

Geoff sets up his phone and holds it in his hand between us. Soon an old voice speaks.

This is Herbert Davis recounting an incident that happened to me in Vietnam during the Tet Offensive when I was stationed there as a medic. The day started like any other day until my commanding officer stood in front of me and said, "They need corpsmen in Hue. Get your gear."

I grabbed a travel pack of medical supplies and followed him to a waiting CH-46 helicopter, which was larger and slower than the Army Hueys. I found a seat among the boxes of supplies.

"Get a move on!" the pilot said. "Weather's marginal and getting worse by the minute. 200-500 foot ceiling and less than a mile vis. All hell's broke loose up there."

The pilot was chatty. Must have been nervous. "Just brought out a load of wounded. Heard there were 35 dead in a matter of minutes. No time for them now."

The Marine on my left made the sign of the cross and bowed his head.

The pilot increased the speed of the rotors and talked louder over the noise. "A four-man NVA sapper team dressed in ARVN uniforms killed the guard at the Citadel gate and opened it for their men. They've taken over half the damn walled city and are flying the NVA flag from the tower. Pushed the ARVN into the northeast corner and set up snipers along the wall. Heard they have anti-aircraft missiles, too. We'll be lucky to drop you off and get more wounded out of there tonight."

The man on my right said, "I thought Charlie asked for a

ceasefire during Tet. What happened?"

"It was a damn trap," the pilot said. "They pulled this Tet Offensive on all major cities just when we let our guard down."

Everyone was quiet. Finally, someone in the group said, "Heard Charlie's been massacring the civilians in Hue. Wild dogs are roaming the streets, eating dead bodies."

A man across from me asked, "Isn't the Citadel a sacred city or something? Protected from our bombs?"

"The whole damn city was protected," the pilot shouted. "We weren't supposed to go near it. But you should see it now! It's destroyed."

"Who destroyed it?"

"The damn Vietnamese! ARVN headquarters was inside the Forbidden City and now the NVA have penetrated, and both sides are pounding it from the inside. It took two weeks for the ARVN to ask us to help them out. So now we're dropping you in and flying out the wounded. It's door-to-door street fights—something we weren't trained to do in Quantico."

We started to descend and the pilot stopped talking. Nobody talked.

The first anti-aircraft missile whizzed past my side of the helicopter. Then they came at us from all sides. It was a miracle we landed intact.

"Go, go, go!" Hands reached up to take boxes of supplies. Just beyond, rows of stretchers held the wounded.

The men raced to get the boxes out and the stretchers in. The rotors spun faster, the big, slow CH-46 tilted and rose to leave.

No time to watch it. Had to find cover. The whoop, whoop, whoop of the rotors grew fainter. I headed for a bunker to my right. As I got close, I heard an explosion. The foggy sky lit up. All

I saw was a ball of fire that had been the helicopter.

That's about all I remember. The rest is a blur. Somehow I survived, but I'm not sure how.

*

Back at the hotel, Geoff holds me for a long time. My mind can't absorb the fact that I was at the very spot where a helicopter exploded in midair, and on the ground, dead men were lined up until it was convenient to fly them out—the same spot where wives and concubines battled a different kind of battle a century earlier, and who knows what kinds of life interactions happened there before and in-between. The air should have felt different. Surely particles of horror must still be swirling around, jarred loose from their normal molecular orbits.

And my father. What kind of trauma did he experience? Was there one final trauma that ended his life? Will I be able to feel it in the air if I go to where he last stood on this earth?

Trying to comfort me, Geoff says, "This afternoon we're going to a much more uplifting place, an affirmation of life after disaster."

"Where are we going?"

"A Buddhist orphanage."

"That's life affirming?"

"Yes. When caring people pick up the pieces—the pieces in this case are little children who lost their parents—that's a positive thing and shows strength in spite of adversity. The caring people are Buddhist nuns who run an orphanage sponsored by my organization. You probably didn't hear about the typhoon of 2008, but it devastated Vietnam. Many people died and so many families were destroyed. We try to use elements of a culture to help repair damage within that culture, and although Vietnam is Communist, Buddhism is still strong. The people trust the Buddhist priests and nuns, so we funded them to build an orphanage here in Hue where the damage was greatest."

This is a side of Geoff I'm not familiar with, yet I would have expected him to be a savvier businessman. "You weren't afraid the Buddhists would misuse your money?"

Geoff laughs. "I trust them as much as I do any religious organization. Their purpose is to minister to their constituents, and they're far more accepted here than a Christian organization. Today will be the first time I've had a chance to visit them, so we'll see how they're doing."

From battlefield to orphanage. Somehow I didn't expect to experience both in one day.

*

Minh pulls the Toyota into a paved courtyard lined with pruned bushes. As we get out of the car, a swarm of small boys runs out to greet us. They gravitate to Geoff and throw their arms around his legs, competing with each other to attach like little frogs with suction cup toes. A woman with a shaved head comes out bobbing and half bowing. She says something to Minh who translates.

"The children rarely see men," he says. "You see, the nuns are women, their teachers are women. Men are special to them."

Geoff reaches down and tousles the boys' hair and then attempts to walk with three on each leg, exaggerating each step until finally he staggers and pretends to fall. The boys shriek with laughter.

Minh and the nun are talking, and from the expression on her face, she had not known who Geoff was and had not expected his visit. She quickly claps her hands and orders the boys off Geoff. Then she bows almost to the ground in front of him.

Minh translates her verbal stream of words. "Welcome, Mr. President. You find us in the middle of preparing for Tet, but please come in, and I hope you will join us for our simple meal."

Geoff responds. "We don't want to interrupt your preparations for Tet, and it is not necessary to feed us. But we do want to see you and the children and hear about their progress."

She leads us into a cement building that smells of incense and disinfectant, and in what looks like the main foyer, she sets out three green plastic chairs for us. "Wait here, please." She scurries off down a long hallway. Children peek at us from around doorways.

When she returns, she brings an older woman, also with a shaved head, who bows respectfully to Geoff and nods at Minh and me.

After an interchange of words, Minh says, "This is the head mistress. She wants you to know that she is honored by your visit. Tea and refreshments are coming. While we wait, she wants to tell you about this orphanage."

Geoff nods and smiles.

Minh continues to translate. "We have a total of 152 children from babies to teenagers. In addition to academic subjects, the children are taught common skills such as cooking, cleaning, and gardening to prepare them for life when they leave the orphanage. We are like a very large family where the older ones help care for the young ones."

A tray arrives with a pot of tea and several cups, along with a plate of candied dried fruit, nuts, and something wrapped in green leaves. Another nun pours each of us a cup and passes the plate around. I try something that turns out to be coconut. It's sweet and crunchy.

Geoff asks, "The typhoon when so many children lost their parents was many years ago. Do you get many babies now?"

"Yes. There are always babies whose mothers can't raise them. It doesn't take a typhoon to make that happen." She smiles and we all smile back. "We take any child who needs a home and education. When they leave us, we make sure they have a job and can care for themselves. Some come back and work for us. Two of our oldest ones are going to marry each other, and we are very happy for them."

She stands. "Do you want a tour?"

The baby room is wall-to-wall cribs with small aisles between and around each, and it smells like dirty diapers and disinfectant. Many of the babies stand up in their cribs and look at us solemnly. A few women hold babies and croon into their soft, wispy hair.

In the kitchen, older children are wrapping what we learn is sticky rice in banana leaves for Tet. The kitchen smells of steamed rice, coconut, and charcoal.

We tour the classrooms, which smell of chalk dust.

Everywhere we go, dark eyes and the sound of giggles follow us. They're happy kids, and I imagine their anticipation of Tet is much like American children's the week before Christmas with its magic and traditions.

We are quiet in the car on the way back. In our room, Geoff sits motionless, deep in thought.

I touch him gently on the shoulder. "Are you happy with the way the Buddhists are running your orphanage?"

"They're doing a damn good job, better than I ever could," he says.

I wait.

He continues, "I have to be reminded sometimes that happiness isn't dependent on stuff, or power, or accomplishment.

"When I think back to my happiest moments, there's always a human connection. My mother rocking me to sleep or comforting me after a skinned knee. The frenzy and camaraderie of winning a soccer game. Going with Aunt Vivian to an art gallery where she is the queen and I'm her favorite court jester. And just tonight, when little Vietnamese boys clung to my legs and infected me with their exhilaration."

He takes my hand. "I hope you understand that, too. Because being here with you and sharing so much," he looks at me significantly, "makes me very happy. I love making you laugh, feeling your curiosity, and even sharing pain. You are allowing me to have a genuine connection with you, and that's what it's all about."

CHAPTER 26

Lindsey - Hoi An

By morning, after muddled dreams, I'm still not sure what Geoff meant by his heartfelt talk last night. Unless, and this is hard for a person like me who always wants to know what comes next, he was simply stating how he felt that very minute and wasn't thinking about the future. Of course, I could ask him, but I don't want to do that prematurely and jinx the rest of the trip. I decide to take an early morning walk and quietly slip out of bed so as not to wake Geoff.

It's not raining, although there is heavy cloud cover, and already people are bustling about. Along the sidewalks, vendors are setting out the most beautiful fruits and vegetables spread out on the ground in circular baskets—oranges, limes, mangoes, that hot pink fruit I now know is cactus fruit, and purple passion fruit. I had my first passion fruit at breakfast on the boat in Ha Long Bay and discovered its unusual musky, creamy yellow center full of seeds.

Looking at my surroundings and noting them clears my head. It reminds me of the class on mindfulness I took after I had to put my mom in the Alzheimer's unit. It helped me accept her situation, but I haven't kept up the practice. Sue Ellen had recommended the class to me. I laugh now as I remember her words, "Lindsey, we both know you are the world's biggest control freak, and although it's good to have a control freak as a friend because I know I'll always be taken care of, whether I want to be or not—it's not good for you to have the responsibility of the world on your shoulders. Lighten up a bit!" After the class, she wanted me to join a local meditation group, but I became busy with other things, and I guess the logical part of me has trouble letting go.

When I told Sue Ellen about my newly discovered father, she said, "Whatever has happened to your father has already happened, and if he is dead, you're not going to bring him back. I'm happy that you've found a new purpose in life—to learn about your real father, but be prepared to be disappointed. And accept whatever happened. Nothing you do can change that."

If Sue Ellen were here now, she would probably advise me to enjoy these moments with Geoff and expect nothing in the future. I imagine her walking next to me, avoiding puddles and baskets of fruit and hear her say, "Lindsey! Wake up, girl! You're on a crazy adventure with the man of your dreams. Savor each and every moment and don't spend a second worrying about the future! The future will be whatever it turns out to be!"

Thank you, Sue Ellen, I say and smile at a little girl holding a huge bunch of yellow flowers. Her eyes open wide in alarm and she drops the flowers as she runs to hide in her mother's wide black pant leg. The mother turns to see me, and when I smile at her, she gives me a half smile and reaches to touch her frightened child reassuringly on the back.

Most people are wearing the typical peaked, cone-shaped straw hats. Good rain deflectors, I think, noting how they look like miniature umbrellas that channel rain away from the head.

By the time I get back to the hotel, I'm damp but invigorated and glowing with renewed purpose to simply enjoy each day as it comes. Until I see Geoff's face as he stands rigid by the front desk.

"Where were you?" he asks, his voice strained.

"I just went for an early morning walk."

"I was worried sick, and thought you'd been kidnapped and held for ransom. Seriously! People around here could know who I am."

Minh stands next to him, inexplicably smiling.

"Don't do that again!" Geoff is dead serious.

"I had no idea…"

"Now you do. Please. Don't just go off on your own." He softens his stance and puts his arms around me. "You're too important to me."

My bruised pride at Geoff talking to me as if I were a three-year-old is salved by his last statement, but I pull away from him with my emotions doing jumping jacks. It isn't until we are in the car with palm trees whizzing past us that I acknowledge to myself that I was in the wrong. Going off on my own in a strange country, even without being associated with Geoff, was daring and possibly dangerous. Geoff, who is clearly a very wealthy man, made my action stupid, and his anger is finally justified in my mind. Logically I was satisfied. Emotionally I still felt bruised.

*

As we near our next destination. Minh says, "Hoi An is an ancient town that was not bombed during the war and is a favorite place for tourists. Some of the wooden houses there are very old and show Chinese and Japanese design. That is because Hoi An was the largest port in Southeast Asia for many hundreds of years and the people traded with many countries."

We park outside the town center because the streets are shut off to traffic due to the coming holiday. The main street is festooned with colorful lanterns, and if we had forgotten it was the Year of the Pig, we are soon reminded by replicas of every kind of pig imaginable from cartoon characters to realistic photographs, one a life-size sow suckling a litter of piglets.

It is lunchtime and we pass a little tea shop that advertises what look like submarine sandwiches. Several tables are outside under an overhanging roof covered with a lush green vine. "Let's stop and get a sandwich," I say, eager to avoid yet another five-course Vietnamese meal.

"Yes, yes. Whatever you wish," Minh says.

We find a table, and Minh, after reading the menu, tells us they serve sandwiches on French bread and our choices are spicy pork, processed meat, or vegetarian. Geoff orders the spicy pork, and I go for the processed meat, expecting ham, maybe chicken or salami. When the sandwiches arrive, I'm surprised at how good the bread is with a nice crisp crust, but the cold cuts taste like nothing I've eaten before. Geoff thoroughly enjoys his spicy pork and shares a bite with me. It burns my mouth, but is clearly better than my sandwich.

After lunch, we wander by the river that goes out to the ocean harbor. An elderly Vietnamese woman sits motionless in a canoe-like boat as though posing.

Minh says, "The elderly in Vietnam have little income, especially if their sons were killed in the American War. This woman is what you call a 'photo op.' Take her picture and give her some money. This is her job."

Apparently she *is* posing. I take out my cell phone and nod to the woman, who gives me a large smile that shows black teeth. Minh tells us the older generations of women blackened their teeth with lacquer to cover teeth stains that resulted from chewing betel nut. Geoff reaches down to the woman and hands her a wad of Vietnamese currency. The woman tucks it inside her jacket before turning her black smile to the next group of tourists.

"How about a boat ride?" Geoff asks me. He's looking at a boat anchored nearby with a canvas roof and bench seats. A wobbly plank connects it to the shore.

"Sure," I say hesitantly.

Geoff asks Minh about hiring a boat for us and soon we are walking on a heaving plank to a vessel that smells of hot, minimally processed fuel. We have the boat to ourselves, so I pick a seat in the middle with a 360-degree view.

Black smoke billows as the boat turns out into the river, and I grab a rusty metal pole for stability that feels damp.

Geoff smiles at me. "Are we having fun yet?"

I shake my head at him, unsure how to respond. I don't want to be a poor sport, but this greasy tub of rust doesn't even make it to the bottom of my bucket list.

"Look what they have for us." Geoff hands me a large, smooth green fruit with a straw sticking out of a hole at the top. "Fresh coconut juice!"

I take a tentative sip. It's not chilled and doesn't taste at all like the coconut juices I've had out of cans or plastic bottles. "Great presentation," I say and hand it back to him.

He makes a big show of sipping it and puts his head back with an exaggerated "Ah-h-h!"

I shake my head again at him and reach for another sip. I could use some of his joie de vivre.

The boat goes down the ever-widening river out to where its brown banks gradually become white sandy beaches that open into a natural harbor. Fishing boats of every size and shape pass us, coming home from a day on the sea. Geoff and I sit quietly, letting the life on the river glide past us.

I find myself relaxing for the first time since this morning. The rough rumble of the engine is strangely soothing, the salt air reminiscent of languid days at the beach, and Geoff next to me is warm and solid, his high positive energy temporarily in idle mode. Life at this very moment is calm and good.

The sky is still overcast, but the cloud density thins as the afternoon goes on. By the time we return and the sandy banks are back to brown, a low rosy sun peeks from an opening in the clouds. We watch it lower and redden until it becomes a fiery red ball that slides into the water and turns the palm trees on the shore to black silhouettes. The boat show is over.

I put my arms around Geoff and look him in the eye. "Thank you!" I say.

CHAPTER 27

Lindsey - Nha Trang

The promise of the sun from the previous evening is delivered the next morning as we drive south past Da Nang. By the time we near the seaside resort town of Nha Trang, the sun is out in full with a background of blue sky and puffy white clouds. We ask Minh to pull over to a sandy beach where we take off our shoes and jackets and walk with the feel of the sun on our faces and warm sand between our toes.

It's heaven after so many gray days in a row. I wonder if my father ever came here for vacation. Or did his superiors, possibly jealous, conniving men plotting to snuff him out, prevent him from enjoying time off? It probably wasn't as prosperous a place as it appears to be now. I notice the tall buildings in the distance; many, according to Minh, are hotels for world travelers.

"Look!" I point to a thick cable that appears to cross the bay to an island. It isn't obvious from where we are what it is, but it looks like some kind of cable transport.

Geoff looks at it and says, "I think that was completed after my first visit here." He turns to Minh, "Isn't that the cable line for gondolas that go to the amusement park that opened a few years ago?"

"Yes," Minh says. "Many people complain that it is very expensive. Tries to be like Disneyland, but not the same."

"I think we can skip it," I say, now noticing rectangular black objects moving along the cable.

Back in the car, we continue toward the city, where Minh says he has a treat for us. He wasn't able to get us a bungalow at the resort on Vinpearl Island in Nha Trang bay, but we will take a motorboat to the back side of an island, which has the most beautiful beach in the world.

Sun, blue sky, most beautiful beach in the world—I think I can handle it.

After settling in at yet another comfortable but not ostentatious hotel, Goeff and I look out our window over the harbor, where enormous passenger ships are anchored. The name on the closest one looks Scandinavian. Minh told us that the Japanese are building a deep water cargo port in the vicinity, and the old Cam Rahn Bay Military Airbase is now a bustling international airport frequented by people from many countries, especially Russians.

"What a contrast to Hoi An," Geoff says, looking down at the streets clogged with motorbikes. "Vietnam is obviously thriving, but I like the pace in Hoi An better."

"Me, too."

It's late morning, and Minh calls to suggest we walk the short distance to the harbor for our transport to the world's most beautiful beach. We quickly pack bathing suits, towels, sunscreen, and a couple of water bottles that are ever present in every hotel's bathroom, and join him at the front desk.

Workmen are hanging lights connected like an airy blanket over the main intersection and wrapping strings of them around pillars erected at even intervals on both sides of the street. Again, there are pigs everywhere, outlined in lights, on posters, even pig topiaries in a park we pass. The cacophony of horns, revving engines, hammers, excited voices in Vietnamese, German, French, and what might be Russian fill the air like an almost visible solid.

The roads are so heavy with traffic that in order to cross the street to get to the harbor, Minh suggests that we link arms and go en masse, walking into the fray with faith and foolhardiness. After holding my breath and gripping Geoff tightly, we make it alive to the other side.

The crowd is dense, and Geoff reminds me to hang onto my pocketbook, which I hug in front of me as we zigzag our way to the water. There, we see low-slung tourist ferries encrusted with rubber tire bumpers. Minh negotiates with the captain of one of them, and we board along with a dozen other people. This is not going to be the peaceful ride that we had in Hoi An.

The boat roars to life and maneuvers its way out into the harbor. I notice an unusual amount of floating garbage in the water, multi-colored islands of it, bobbing and emitting a disgusting odor. We soon leave them behind as the motorized boat goes full throttle, bumping over the waves, sending spray through the open sides.

Geoff says something to me, but the wind snatches the words from his mouth and tosses them behind us. Then I see him pointing at something. Perfectly round baskets in several sizes that hold from one to three adults are bobbing out in the harbor, close to land. It appears that people use a pole to maneuver them.

Our engine slows to make a wide turn, and Minh takes the opportunity of relative quiet to explain that the baskets are made waterproof with the sap of a particular tree. People use the basket boats, much like Americans use dinghies or zodiacs, to go to and from larger fishing boats.

All around us are islands, some more inhabited than others. The boat heads out to the open ocean, keeping a small island on our left, until we come to a dock next to a curved beach. As we get closer, I notice thatch umbrellas dotted here and there around what looks like a row of concession stands and bath houses on a slight ridge that looks down at pure white sand and a rippling ocean of an intense shade of blue. Without garbage. Perfect!

Only half the passengers get off, and the beach doesn't look at all crowded. I breathe in the salt air mixed with the smoky smell of meat grilling, not with barbecue sauce, but with the pungent smell of fish sauce, which I am learning to like.

Geoff and I select a thatch umbrella more removed from the others, and I'm grateful that the lounge chairs under it are comfortable. Minh says he will watch our things while we change and take a swim.

The water is not too cold or too warm, and the smooth sand bottom slopes out gradually. Geoff is an accomplished swimmer and acts like a playful dolphin jumping waves and diving beneath the big ones to grab my legs and pull them out from under me. We laugh and cavort like two teenagers until my rumbling stomach tells me it's time to eat.

Dripping salt water, we go to the concession stands and order grilled kabobs, which we take back to our umbrella. The kabobs are delicious, especially when eaten in the balmy outdoors with the backdrop sound of sea gulls and crashing waves. Peace.

Below me to the right, I see two families spread out on blankets in the sun. I can hear that they are not Americans. Their language is guttural. Probably Russian. The women are young and large in every way, yet they proudly flaunt their bodies. I envy their self-confidence. They are wearing the smallest of bikinis. One lolls suggestively on the blanket and laughs as her husband pats her substantial behind.

I am fascinated.

"Zoftic," Geoff says. He sits upright in his lounge chair, watching the Russian women. Then he turns to me and smiles. "But they're not my type."

"What *is* your type?" I ask boldly.

The butt-patting husband is now astride his laughing wife as they playfully wrestle.

He ponders a minute, then points down the beach to a young topless woman with an almost invisible bikini bottom walking toward us. She has a perfectly proportioned body with long flowing dark hair that blows around her face.

"She'll do," he says, not taking his eyes off her.

A surge of hot emotion explodes in me. Men! They're all the same. You can't trust them because their hormones or testosterone or whatever takes over their brains. And when you have someone like Geoff, who obviously has deep pockets, he can buy any woman he wants—including me, it appears.

I stand up, wrap a towel around my waist, and start walking briskly back toward the concession stands.

I'm a fool! An intelligent, handsome guy suggests I go to Vietnam with him, and although I pay for my airfare, I let him arrange everything else. Isn't that just like being paid to be with someone? And when he tires of me, and some nubile, young thing comes along, he can conveniently dump me for her because, after all, he's in control, and I made an unconscious agreement with him to be just a temporary diversion.

I stub my toe on a small rock in the sand, which brings tears to my eyes. I hop on one foot and hold the sore toe for a second, then ignore it and continue my charge down the beach, my toe bleeding little dots into the sand with every step.

The concession stands blur past me on the right. Eventually there is nothing but beach, sea, sky, and the horizon where I see the skyline of Nha Trang in the distance. I plop down on the sand and hug my knees, resting my face on them, breathing heavily.

My husband duped me before. You'd think I'd be smart enough to shield myself from caring about a man again. If only I could numb the caring part of myself and simply have a good time with a guy and expect nothing other than the moment I'm in. Emotions complicate everything.

My breathing slows, and I remember my imaginary talk with Sue Ellen yesterday morning. I didn't take her advice to "Savor each and every moment, and don't spend a second worrying about the future! The future will be whatever it turns out to be!" Apparently my future isn't with Geoff, and I've blown the rest of this trip by angrily stomping off. Now what do I do? Geoff hasn't committed to me. He doesn't owe me anything. I'm the one who acted poorly.

I could pretend I was restless and needed a walk. Or that I wanted to get some more food from the concession stands, except I don't have money and can't return with another kabob or a drink. Or I can simply walk back and sit down as if nothing happened.

On the walk back to Geoff under the thatch umbrella, I let the steam out of my brain and simply allow the slight breeze to swirl around me and gently cool the warmth of the sun on my bare skin. By the time I reach the umbrella, I decide I won't pretend anything. If I've learned one thing in life, it's that cover-ups make things worse.

Geoff watches me approach, and by the time I sit back down on the lounge chair, I see his eyes are questioning. I look directly at him and say, "Sorry about that. I can explain later." Minh is on the other side of Geoff, apparently savvy enough to be looking away from us down the beach.

We are quiet. I pretend to doze, and Geoff takes out a book he brought to read.

*

"There is an interesting story about the Kitchen Gods," Minh says suddenly into our uncomfortable silence. "A very long time ago, when Earth and Sky met in the Valley of Whispers, a poor woodcutter and his wife lived in the forest. They had little money and were often hungry. The man began to drink to escape his lot in life, and took to beating his wife. One night she had enough and ran away. She wandered for weeks in the forest until her feet were torn and bleeding. Finally, she came upon a hunter's cabin. The hunter was a good man who fed her and tended her wounds. She stayed with him as his housekeeper and eventually they were married. They were happy together and lived very comfortably."

Geoff and I look at each other, eyebrows raised.

"One day," Minh continues, "while the husband was out hunting, a beggar came to the door. The woman recognized him as her first husband. She took pity on him and gave him money and rice. But she was afraid her new husband would be jealous, so she hid her first husband in a pile of straw. The hunter returned soon afterwards with a bounty of meat. To cook the meat, he set the straw on fire and burned the first husband to death. The wife, upon seeing her mistake in hiding him in the straw, jumped into the fire herself. The hunter, distressed by his wife's action, also jumped into the fire. This story so moved the Jade Emperor that he gave all three of them the title of Kitchen God. And we remember the three kitchen gods because of the three supporting posts on our charcoal clay stoves."

Minh finishes and gets up from his lounge chair. "Now I will take a walk."

When Minh is out of earshot, his back to us, Geoff and I look at each other and burst out laughing. It feels good to release some of the tension.

"What is the moral of that story?" Geoff asks.

"Don't hide former husbands in piles of straw?"

We laugh again.

"Never take pity on someone who did you wrong?" I suggest again.

Our cultural bias is making the story difficult to understand.

Geoff thinks for a minute, serious again. "I think it illustrates the Vietnamese inability to chart their course in history. They were thwarted over the centuries by stronger powers, such as China. So their folk heroes are not swashbuckling 'save the maiden from the fire' types, but self-sacrificing 'throw yourself into the fire' types, who are rewarded by the gods for their martyrdom."

"That doesn't feel right in our culture," I say.

We are quiet again. Finally, I get up the courage to say, "My husband left me for another woman, and I'm very sensitive to rejection."

Geoff looks at me. "My wife and I divorced because of irreconcilable differences. We each wanted the other to be somebody else. She wanted me to be the country club type who bought her expensive jewelry. I wanted her to be like you."

I hold myself very still, afraid to believe his words.

He continues, "I'm a man. I know you've heard that excuse before. We're swayed by our animal instincts, but that doesn't mean they control us. Yes, I was attracted to the young woman walking down the beach, but I can't help that. I *can* control what I do about it. You can't help feeling jealous when you see me attracted to somebody else. Yet you can and did acknowledge it and apologized for getting angry about it. Now I need to apologize to you for my male reaction, which hurt you."

I can't believe a man is saying those words. A man I now realize I'm over-the-moon in love with.

Geoff isn't finished. "The good thing about this is I now know you care enough about me to be jealous." He smiles his one-dimpled grin as I go to his chair and lean over him.

Nose to nose, I say, "I have a very good feeling about this relationship."

CHAPTER 28

Nate – Eve of Tet

Mai's breakdown at the gravesite of Steve Nathan seemed to release the flood of pent-up emotion that had caused her previous trepidation and discomfort. It was as if a dam had finally given way and released decades of angst.

After she composed herself, Mai and Nate walked back to the house to get tools and returned to finish clearing the weeds from the mound of earth in silence, each with unspoken thoughts.

Nate's thoughts centered on what to do about this knowledge of his father's remains. The US military should be notified. Up until now, Nate had not considered the fact that his father's body had not been accounted for and that there were American relatives who most certainly mourned him. Was his father married? Did he have children?

Perhaps his mother knew, but Nate didn't think it was appropriate to ask her at this time. If Steve was married, it probably had been a sore point in her relationship with him. Nate would have to research the matter when he returned to the States. Best not to let his mother know of his plans to report his father's grave.

It was peaceful, loosening the dark soil to release the roots of vines and plants, some of them with thorns. As he dug with his three-pronged bamboo garden tool, Nate couldn't help but imagine what was beneath him. Were there only bones and teeth left? Could they be positively identified? Somehow he didn't feel grossed out. The man whose grave he crouched next to was unknown to him except for a single snapshot and a few stories reluctantly told by his mother.

When the grave was cleared of the encroaching jungle, Mai stood and said, "Now we make it pretty."

Together they went to the house, where Mai took several sticks of incense, a plate of candied peanuts, and a branch from the blooming peach tree. "Steve like these peanuts," she said as they walked back to the grave.

Nate wondered how his father would have felt about the Vietnamese ritual they were about to perform with incense, flowers, and peanuts. Even though he might have liked peanuts when he was alive, there was something weird about offering them to an American ghost. Then reality kicked in, and Nate understood that the ritual was for the living, not the dead. It didn't matter what his father, long dead, might feel if he were still alive.

Back in the noisy kitchen, Mai joined the women making the traditional Tet rice cakes. She was a different person. Nate stood to one side and marveled at the transformation as she laughed and joked with the women, telling them how terrible purchased rice cakes were in America.

"Kim," she said. "Tell my son the story of how rice cakes came to be."

Kim motioned Nate to come inside and take a seat on an empty stool. Without stopping what she was doing, she began to speak in a singsong voice. "Many lives ago, Emperor Hung-Vuong gave a challenge to his many sons to help him decide which one would rule after him. He said whoever brought him the most delicious and unusual food would become the new emperor.

"Now his sons were talented, some in martial arts, others were scholarly, but the youngest son, Tiet-Lieu loved nature and went to the countryside, where he became a farmer. The older sons immediately started looking for unusual foods in the forests, on the seas, and even in other countries. But Tiet-Lieu went to his rice field and picked a few grains of glutinous rice that was ready to be harvested. He smelled their delicious aroma. The rice was at the peak of perfection. So he and his family harvested it and ground it into flour. His wife mixed it with water to form a soft paste and his children helped wrap it in leaves and cook it over a charcoal fire. Some of his children made round cakes and others made square cakes with green beans inside. The round cakes they called banh day and the square ones they called banh chung.

"On the first day of spring, the sons came to present their food to the emperor, and Tiet-Lieu brought his two kinds of rice cakes. His brothers brought exotic dishes, such as roasted peacock, lobsters, and rare mushrooms, and they laughed at Tiet-Lieu's simple offering. But after the emperor tasted all the dishes, he liked the rice cakes the best. He said that it was the purest and most meaningful of all the food because it was made only of rice, the food of the people. So the emperor named his youngest son the new emperor."

Nate applauded. "But, Aunt Kim, I see you putting other things in the banh chung you are making. Isn't that pork and bean paste?"

"Yes." She smiled at Nate. "People always want to make a good thing better, so we add things to make the cakes richer. What you add to your cakes shows your creativity as well as your wealth. The poor cannot afford to add much besides rice. Of course, some people are purists and don't change the original recipe. But Mai and I, when we were young and poor, wanted to make them the best that we could. So we added what we had and believed we were food artists."

Nate watched the women wrap the cakes in banana leaves and tie them with long flexible bamboo slivers. He noted their camaraderie tinged with competitiveness, and he knew there would be gossip when he left. It was family—the very thing he had wanted Mai to experience with him in Vietnam.

*

The next evening, the family celebrated the eve of Tet, similar to New Year's Eve. The following three days would be like Christmas and everyone's birthday all at once with celebrations starting at home with close family and gradually extending to friends and business acquaintances.

Nate was glad he had gone to the bank before he left California and picked up 100 crisp two-dollar bills in US currency to put into the red envelopes that people gave to each other. American dollars were welcome in Vietnam and a two-dollar bill was unique and considered lucky.

That afternoon, five cases of Vietnamese beer were delivered, several vats of local rice wine, two specially roasted pigs that were a regional delicacy—all this food was in addition to the rice cakes and special Tet dishes that the kitchen full of women had been working on for days. These people were ready for serious partying. In addition to Mai, her brother Tran, sister Kim, and their children, the children's spouses and offspring, Danh's family and Tran's spouse's family were all included in the first day of close family celebration. If Nate had been overwhelmed by Rosy's family at his wedding, he was about to be even more overwhelmed by the size of his Vietnamese family.

The celebration on the evening before Tet, however, was limited to a smaller circle of immediate family. Mai chose to be included in Kim's immediate family group. Tran's larger group would meet separately in a spacious common room he had added recently to his wing of the compound, where he had another altar set up.

Nate had not seen much of his Uncle Tran since his first visit to Vietnam when he pretended to be an importer of rice. Tran was an enigma. Yet Nate had just heard his mother say that he worked for the Americans during the war. How could he have a high-level position in the Communist government if that were the case? That and other questions about his mother's family in relation to the war and his father were swirling in his head, but it didn't seem appropriate to ask them on the eve of Tet. Everyone was determined to be happy and positive, as if by doing so, they could control the mood of the coming year.

The last meal of the year was a very important one. Traditional dishes would be placed on the family altar for the ancestors first, and then taken outside to the large new table and consumed by the living family.

In addition to the family altar inside, Nate had noticed a small altar, like a little cement house, at the edge of the property.

Binh explained that this was for wandering spirits called hungry ghosts, who had no living relatives to care for them. People set out rice and salt, the basics of life, and lit a few incense sticks to satisfy them and keep them from bringing bad luck to the family.

While waiting for the festivities to begin, Nate stood in front of the family altar. Each deceased family member was represented by a photograph or personal item. Nate studied the black and white photograph of his grandfather, a serious man in a stilted pose. Uncle Tran had inherited the old man's eyes, but there was little resemblance to his mother and Aunt Kim. His grandmother had no photograph and instead was represented by a small wooden bowl worn perfectly smooth and filled with yellow apricot blossoms. Wispy tendrils of incense smoke wove among the carefully placed items, among them an envelope-sized palm leaf basket at one side of the altar that Nate hadn't noticed before.

No one else was in the room when Nate picked up the basket. The top half slid off and a military dog tag on a stainless steel chain fell out, followed by a pocketknife that hit the table with a clunk and bounced to the floor. A set of keys with a lacquer heart-shaped key ornament tumbled down with a jangle of metal. Stuck inside the basket, a corner caught in the weave, was a square of stiff paper. He reached in and pulled out a faded Polaroid photograph. It showed Steve Nathan smiling broadly with his arm around a dark-haired, white American woman.

CHAPTER 29

Lindsey – Ho Chi Minh City

At breakfast the morning after the relaxing yet emotionally charged day at the beach, Minh approaches us with a handful of papers. Almost bowing, he says, "Thank you for allowing me to see my family on Tet. I am very grateful."

"Glad to do it!" Geoff says. "What do you have there?"

"This is what you will need in the next few days. Here are plane tickets from Da Nang to Ho Chi Minh City. And after three days there, you have tickets to Dalat. I will meet your plane in Dalat. Is that all right with you?"

"Of course!" I say.

"Now here," Minh brings out another sheet of paper, "is the reservation for your hotel in Ho Chi Minh City where you stay for three nights. It is a good hotel, not 5 stars, but still very good. You can walk to many sites and restaurants. And on this paper here are many places you can visit. There are more than you can see in three days, some historic, some pleasant and beautiful, so you choose the ones you like. You can get a taxi to all of them. And here," Minh brings out a final sheet of paper, "are the good restaurants in Saigon. We have many good ones from many countries. Italian, French, even Moroccan. You choose. The one

I suggest you try is a small noodle shop for pho. Perhaps for lunch. Very authentic and something you don't get every day in America."

We shake Minh's hand and wish him a very happy new year with his family. I am overjoyed to be on our own and in one place for three days after almost a week of city hopping down the coast of Vietnam. Sightseeing can be exhausting.

Geoff, however, is scanning down the list of places to visit and placing checkmarks next to many of them. "Oh, look, the Cu Chi Tunnels. I was there several years ago. It's an amazing and horrifying place. And here, you must see the War Remnants Museum. Positively mind altering. Um, oh, the Rex Hotel's rooftop bar where correspondents hung out during the war. We have to go there for a drink. And the Reunification Palace."

"Excuse me," I say. "Do I get a choice?"

"Of course!" Geoff looks at me quizzically. I guess my tone was sharper than I realized.

"Look," I say in what I hope is a more pleasant voice, "we've just had a week of wonderful but tiring visits to strange cities and slept each night in a different bed. I'd really like a day off. My brain is overstimulated right now and I need to veg for a day. You can do whatever you want and I won't mind, but just count me out for a day or so."

"Not a problem." Geoff studies the list again before looking up at me. "I'm glad you told me." But I think I see disappointment in his face.

*

.

It's afternoon when we arrive at our hotel in Ho Chi Minh City. It's the most sophisticated of all the places we've stayed and clearly reflects that the Saigon of a war-ravaged country is now an up-and-coming contender among world cities. Skyscrapers tower at its center and proclaim it is not a provincial center.

Our room is on the 17th floor and looks out over a wide expanse of city. I'm thankful that the room is well air-conditioned because it is obvious that South Vietnam, unlike the north, is in the tropics.

Geoff has been quiet most of the day. Soon after we settle into our room, he says, "I think I'll take a walk."

I look at him, trying to determine his mood. I'm guessing that he didn't invite me because he's giving me a chance to veg or perhaps he's annoyed with me. I decide to be positive and say, "Enjoy. I'll be here when you get back."

After he leaves, I feel oddly happy. We had been together 24 hours a day for the past week, and my perspective is changing from "me" to "us." It doesn't feel like a bad thing and I don't feel I'm losing my identity completely, but my assertion this morning at breakfast was the first time I pulled away from the new "us" back to "me." And now it appears that Geoff is doing the same by choosing to walk without me.

When Geoff returns a couple hours later, he brings me a Vietnamese coffee.

"Thank you! I missed you," I say, giving him a big hug. Then I say the line I'd been preparing for his return. "Didn't the poet Kahlil Gibran say something about having spaces between lovers?"

Geoff quotes, "But let there be spaces in your togetherness and let the winds of the heavens dance between you. Love one another but make not a bond of love: let it rather be a moving sea between the shores of your souls."

We look at each other a long time before Geoff says, "Before we let the winds of the heavens dance between us, would you come with me to a hamburger place I discovered a block away from here?"

*

The next day, Geoff decides to go to an experimental rice plantation in the Mekong Delta where they grow a new variety of rice that is drought resistant. We'd agreed that I would have the day off to sleep all day or whatever I felt like doing as long as I texted Geoff if I left the hotel. We had checked into the hotel under an assumed name, so he wasn't as fearful about me being kidnapped.

After sleeping in and ordering room service for breakfast, I sit by the window that looks out over the city as I review my options for the day. I could read the book I brought with me or walk two blocks to a little park that I can see from the window. It looks like there's a fair of some sort because it's very colorful.

I quickly dress in a lightweight skirt and a sleeveless blouse and text Geoff that I'm walking to a park two blocks from the hotel. He texts back, "Love you. Have fun."

Outside the hotel, I breathe in the humid air and marvel again at the difference between Hanoi and Ho Chi Minh City. Where Hanoi was cold and bleak, Ho Chi Minh City is hot and pulsing with energy. I walk to the end of the block and look for the traffic light that will stop the endless flow of motorbikes so I can cross the street. There is no light.

A man next to me steps nonchalantly into the traffic. A car slams on its brakes and several motorbikes slow, making wide circles around the man as he walks into the fray. I hold my breath until he steps onto the sidewalk on the other side. It reminds me of slipping between the ropes in Double Dutch, something I was never good at.

Other pedestrians walk through the traffic, as if each were Moses parting the Red Sea. I am about to give up and go back to the hotel when a gentle voice says in English, "I help you, okay?"

Next to me is a young woman in her twenties, her hair pulled back into a single long braid that reaches her waist.

"Thank you," I say.

Like a traffic cop, she steps into the street and stands with her arms upraised. Amazingly the flow comes to a stop. People stand astride their motorbikes and rev their high-pitched motors. Self-consciously, I cross one lane, as my diminutive personal traffic cop stops the other lane's flow for me.

Safely across, I take a deep breath and look for the young woman. She is halfway down the block. I call out the phrase Minh taught us as a new year's greeting, "Chuc Mung Nam Moi!"

She stops, gives a brief nod, and goes on her way.

The park is situated between two major thoroughfares and is about the size of two city blocks. It's full of flowers. Not just flowers on bushes or trees, but large, ornate displays of dragons, and pigs, and unknown mythical creatures composed of flowers, fruits, and nuts. It appears to be an art and flower show with one section of the park full of pots of bonsai and another with orchids. There's a full row of almost identical flowering pink bushes forced to remain about two feet high with fleshy, exposed roots like twisted gray sweet potatoes.

I wander among the displays, marveling at their intricacy and the time it must have taken to make them. One goofy dragon has googly eyes beneath bushy eyebrows and wears a red pepper necklace. It makes me laugh, so I snap of photo of it with my phone to show Geoff later.

In the center of the park, an enormous dragon about fifty feet long is covered with flowers. Musicians play strange-looking instruments around it and people dance and clap. Only one little child is crying.

The happiness around me is palpable. People smile at me and nod. It's as if what we Americans did here over 40 years ago is forgotten by this next generation who are busy making lives for themselves. And my father, did he experience a Tet here? Did the people dare laugh and feel optimistic about a new year as they looked at the devastation around them?

I sit on a bench next to a graceful bamboo arbor that provides shade for delicate orchids. My father. I haven't thought about him in days, and he was the reason for my coming here. Getting to know this beautiful, exotic country and falling in love with Geoff Davis have sidetracked me from my original mission. But after our visit to Dalat, Minh said he would take us to Phan Thiet and help us question the people there. Who knows what, if anything, we'll find?

*

"The War Remnants Museum," Geoff says the next morning in the cab, "is someplace you should see, but it's not pleasant."

He had already told me that it opened in 1975 as the Exhibition House for US and Puppet Crimes. Its name changed in 1990 to

Exhibition House for Crimes of War and finally changed to its current name in 1995. Ironically, the building that housed the museum had once been the United States Information Services (USIS) building. Now, as I look at the gray rectangular structure with its name in bright gold Vietnamese and English letters, I can't help but think of its drastic metamorphosis.

As we walk through the front courtyard past a Huey helicopter alongside an M48 Patton tank, two attack bombers, an A-1 Skyraider and an A-37 Dragonfly, Geoff warns me that I will see anti-American propaganda. We climb some steps to the first floor.

I think I'm prepared for an ugly American slant as I stop at the first display. Next to a quote from our Declaration of Independence, the one about all people being created equal, is a photo of a smiling US soldier holding an enemy head. The caption reads, "After decapitating some guerillas, a GI enjoyed being photographed with their heads in his hands."

My stomach turns. True, the US involvement in this war was a huge mistake, but we suffered as well, and our young men died fighting for the South Vietnamese cause. I move on. I can barely focus on the blatant photos and poorly worded Vietnamese/ English statements about our atrocities. A larger-than-life letter from President Eisenhower says that we needed Vietnam for its tin and other resources, therefore justifying us to protect it from communism. It makes me gag. It's too much. I tell Geoff I have to leave.

Geoff says the second floor is less biased. I hurry to the stairs, taking deep breaths. I have never before been ashamed of being an American.

The upstairs exhibit may have been less biased, but it is no less disturbing. Stories and photographs of Agent Orange victims, Vietnamese and Americans alike, line the walls. The photographs are gruesome, the stories heartbreaking. After reading two stories, I can read no more. I take Geoff's arm and leave the exhibit.

Across the way is another exhibit called Requiem that Geoff strongly urges me to visit. I see in fine print that it was donated by the State of Kentucky. Odd. I read further and learn the photo exhibit is the work of photojournalists from both sides of the conflict, who died during the war. Interesting and equitable.

"Requiem," Geoff reminds me, "is a mass or hymn of mourning. In this case, it is a grouping of photographs displayed as a memorial for the dead photographers and their tragic subjects, who suffered or died in the war."

The first picture is a visual contrast to the ugly Americans portrayed on the first floor. It is of American crew chief James Farley weeping in a supply shack after a tragic mission. It shows that we Americans were feeling human beings after all.

In a grouping of photos by North Vietnamese photographers, I am struck by how young the soldiers are and that there are young women as well as men.

Wall after wall shows the horror, the travesties of war—people being tortured, weary men with filthy uniforms, slogging through mud, carrying heavy equipment. There are shots of explosions and dead bodies, of men comforting the dying. But the most touching photos are of the Vietnamese women and children, their lives disrupted by the despicable horror around them.

I stand for a long time in front of the Pulitzer Prize-winning photograph by Kyoichi Sawada. In it, a Vietnamese woman and her four children are swimming across a river to escape American bombs. Their faces show desperate fear and something else—a grim determination to get to the other side and survive. It is gut-wrenching, yet I can't turn away.

The next photograph that transfixes me is one taken by Henri Huet. A Vietnamese woman and two children are triangularly framed by a standing American soldier's spread legs. Each of the Vietnamese is fearfully looking in a different direction toward at least three different menaces approaching them. They look distrustful, cowed, overpowered, pleading, and helpless. I stand there with tears running down my face, wondering what we did to inspire their fear; reminded anew of what war does to rip apart the fabric of normalcy and human decency.

Geoff puts his arms around me, and we share something deep and sorrowful, something beyond words.

A little later as we cross the courtyard again, I say, "Geoff, you were right. I needed to see this."

PART 3 – THE MEETING

CHAPTER 30

Nate

After celebrating Tet as he never had before, surrounded by myriad uncles, aunts, and layers of cousins, Nate drove back to Ho Chi Minh City with Binh and his fiancée. Nate was to catch a flight to the highland city of Dalat, where he would be staying several days to learn about Vietnamese coffee. One of his first cousins, Uncle Tran's youngest son Chien, was manager of a large coffee plantation just outside the city and would be showing him around. Mai chose to remain at the family compound as Nate expected.

Binh's fiancée had come to celebrate the third day of Tet with her new family-to-be, and Binh was justifiably proud of the beautiful young lady. As the two young lovers spoke of wedding plans in the front seat, Nate in the back relived the moment of finding his father's personal belongings on the family altar.

Normally he would have approached his mother about them and asked why they had not been turned in to the US government. The dog tag was government property, and it was wrong to keep it. But because it was the day before Tet, Nate knew enough not to poke a hornet's nest on the eve of the day when all should be positive and happy. One accusatory sentence, and he would be blamed for jinxing the new year. That night as he closed the palm leaf basket, however, he removed the Polaroid photo and slipped it into his pocket. He might need it for locating his father's American family.

Nate's flight to Dalat left at 4:00 p.m., and he had several hours to kill before then. He asked Binh to drop him off near the Central Market where he'd grab a bowl of pho before catching a cab to the airport.

Rice served pho, a rice noodle soup dish with a meat of choice, usually beef or chicken, and garnished with an assortment of fresh herbs and sauces. Nate was pleased with his mother's version, but this particular restaurant in Ho Chi Minh City did something to the broth that made it unique. Nate took every opportunity to sample it and try to determine the ingredient that gave it the flavor he craved. He had spoken with the restaurant owners, but they wouldn't divulge their secret. He knew that for the beef broth, sometimes beef tripe and cinnamon were boiled along with the usual beef bones and oxtail, but Mai had tried them, and neither turned out to be the mysterious ingredient. The same flavor was in the chicken version, which required boiling an entire chicken for its broth. Before they returned home to San Jose, he'd have to bring Mai to the restaurant to see if she could discern what the magic ingredient was.

Entering the small eatery off a busy street that was one of many that dead-ended at the Central Market, Nate inhaled the aroma of those wonderful broths. The restaurant was small with six large communal tables that held at most eight people each. In the center of each table were three sauces—nuoc mam pha, the most common Vietnamese dipping sauce; a dark, soy-based sauce much like Chinese hoisin; and a spicy red sauce like sriracha.

The restaurant was full, and several tables held foreigners who spoke English. Nate was disappointed that tourists appeared to have discovered his little haven of perfection, but he figured it was inevitable. There was one empty seat next to a woman with long blond hair pulled back into a ponytail, which she tossed as she laughed at something her companion said.

The owner of the restaurant recognized Nate and came over to him and greeted him in Vietnamese. Nate asked about the man's family and commented on the restaurant's popularity. After the requisite polite conversation, Nate ordered beef pho.

As he waited for his food, Nate couldn't help but overhear the conversation of the couple next to him who had just been served steaming bowls of pho.

"What do we do now?" the woman asked. She was looking at a huge plate of basil, mint, bean sprouts, cilantro, and green onion in front of her.

"Anything you want," her companion said, and she laughed again, tossing the ponytail so it almost brushed Nate's shoulder.

Nate sighed, then said, "Excuse me. Is this your first time eating pho?"

"Yes." She flashed an embarrassed smile. "I could use a little help." She was pretty in a wholesome, no fuss way.

"The key is the broth," Nate said. "First take a sip of it and savor it."

They both did as Nate suggested, and the woman closed her eyes. "Wonderful!" she said. "I've never tasted broth quite like this before."

"Now, decide what you want to augment that flavor. Do you want it to be a little more pungent, or spicy, or fresh with the taste of herbs?"

"I like it just the way it is," the man said.

"I like basil," she said and reached for some, "and maybe just a hint of something citrusy."

"How do you feel about fish sauce?" Nate asked. "There's lime juice in it, but it can overwhelm people who are not used to it."

"I like fish. My grandfather was a fisherman. And I'm getting used to this fish-sauce-with-every-meal business."

"Then try the light yellow sauce—just a little to start. You can always add more."

She put a small spoonful into her pho and after sampling it, added another. "Delicious!" She turned to Nate and said, "Thank you! And by the way, your English is perfect!"

Nate sat perfectly still for a moment. Then he said, "So is yours," and looked directly into her dark brown eyes.

She was startled and frowned at him a moment before recovering her equilibrium. "Where are you from?"

"San Jose. And you?"

"The Boston area."

CHAPTER 31

Lindsey

We see the unusual Vietnamese/American man with the green eyes again at the airport. I'm not sure I like him after his sarcastic response to my compliment. He gives us a quick nod of recognition before looking down at his cell phone.

The airport is busier than when we flew in three days ago on the first day of Tet. As Minh had explained, by the first day of Tet, most people are already at their ancestral homes. Now, on the fourth day, I look around the waiting area at the small children decked out in new clothes and shoes, still infected with the magic of the holiday.

It's a two-hour flight to Dalat on a Boeing 727 with every seat taken. Geoff and I are unable to sit together, and I see that he is seated next to our "friend" from the noodle shop. They appear to be deep in discussion. I wonder what they are talking about.

The airline attendants are all slim, young women who wear the traditional flowing dress over silk pants. I ask one for a bottle of water and then settle down with the book I've barely started.

In no time, we're circling the Dalat airport, and I look below at dark green forests contrasted with bright orange soil and rolling cultivated fields with perfectly parallel rows next to white gauzy greenhouses in the shape of Quonset huts.

After landing, the pilot welcomes us to Dalat in French and Vietnamese. When the door of the plane opens, we're met with refreshingly cool air that smells of pine. Nice. I gather my backpack and connect with Geoff inside the terminal.

"Lindsey, this is Nate Huong," he says, introducing me to the noodle shop guy. "His cousin runs a coffee plantation, and he offered to take me there tomorrow. You're welcome to join us."

"Coffee?" I say, unaware that Vietnam grew it. "Sounds interesting." Wasn't Vietnam known for its rice? Geoff had come back from the Mekong Delta full of enthusiasm for rice. Now it's coffee.

Just then, Minh locates us, and after happy inquiries and answers about his family and their Tet celebration, he is told of the plan. "Vietnam produces much coffee, second largest country next to Brazil," he says. "You should take time to see the coffee plantation tomorrow. I can show you other things today."

Geoff and Nate trade phone numbers, and Nate says, "See you tomorrow at 8:00. No, it's vacation for everyone around here. Let's make it 10:00. I'll text you the particulars."

Our hotel is a renovated French villa on the side of a mountain with gorgeous formal gardens on three sides.

"Dalat was a French resort," Minh tells us. "It has an altitude of over 1500 meters. I think you would say 5000 feet. The French came here to escape the heat of Saigon. Now it is a popular vacation spot and the biggest flower producer in Southeast Asia. The greenhouses grow gerbera daisies, roses, and other flowers to export to Australia, Japan, and many countries."

"What do we have on the agenda for the afternoon?" Geoff asks.

"We can visit a silk factory and see how they make thread from the silk worms and weave it into cloth, and we can visit a cricket factory—a new treat in Vietnam."

"Sounds very buggy to me," I say, and Geoff and I laugh, but Minh is dead serious.

"We can also visit some flower greenhouses to see the beautiful flowers."

Geoff looks at me. "Your choice."

I realize that Minh would prefer to be with his family than with flippant Americans like us. However, we are paying him and he's trying to do his job. So I say with 60% sincerity, "They all sound very interesting. Can we fit them all in?"

Minh smiles. "Yes. Let me make some phone calls."

*

After eating a ham and cheese sandwich on the flakiest croissant I've ever had, I continue to sit at our table in the garden of the hotel surrounded by flowers that look pumped up with steroids. The sun at this high altitude is warm without any of the cloying humidity we've experienced elsewhere in Vietnam. I close my eyes, half wishing I could stay in this spot for at least the rest of the day, but it is not to be. I hear crunching gravel on the driveway as Minh's Toyota approaches. The day of rest in Ho Chi Minh City has enabled me to continue this crazy tourist pace, but not with enthusiasm.

Geoff and I stand up from the table, and on the way to the car, I inspect a perfect, cobalt blue delphinium, one of my mother's favorite flowers that she never had much success with in her garden. Perhaps all she needed was air and soil from Dalat.

The greenhouse we stop at shows further proof that the unique qualities Dalat has to offer are magical for flowers. Under the semi-sheer gauze of domed greenhouses, we see row upon row of catalog photo ops for roses of every color.

"You are allowed to pick one flower," Minh tells us like an indulgent schoolteacher as he hands us each a pair of clippers.

Geoff selects an unusual apricot colored rosebud just starting to open, and solemnly presents it to me. "This beautiful flower pales in comparison to your beauty."

"Thank you!" I kiss him on the cheek. I snip a fragile yellow rose and, after inhaling its scent, give it to Geoff. "Here's to sharing the beauty and fragrance of many more experiences this trip!"

"I'll toast to that!" We touch our roses together with an imaginary clink.

Our next stop is the cricket factory that produces the newest snack craze in Vietnam. I'm highly dubious, but Geoff seems intrigued. The sign outside a modest one-story building shows a pair of giant green crickets, one on top of the other, obviously mating as another giant cricket looks on. The only word in English is "Welcome."

"Cricket whorehouse," Geoff says to me under his breath. "Peeping Toms allowed." I try not to laugh.

We enter a salesroom/kitchen that smells of fried food. It has a table to the side with a plate of fried crickets beautifully displayed inside an edging of thinly sliced cucumbers. Chopsticks are conveniently set out. We learn that in addition to the crunchy fried crickets, the establishment makes cricket wine from fermented crushed cricket juice. My mind refuses to dwell on that thought.

Minh leads us past the cricket table to another room in the back, which is the breeding room. Shelves line the walls, filled with pastel tubs covered by perforated lids. Minh opens one of the tubs to reveal strips of newspaper covered with crawling black crickets of every size. A distinctive odor, one I have never smelled before, makes me gag.

"I need fresh air," I tell Geoff as I head for the only other door in the room. It leads to a dark closet-like space, and my eyes take a minute to register large brown crocks. The air smells even worse. I back out and take Geoff's arm for support.

"Um, I think I'll go back to the car," I say.

"Wait," he says. "I need you to take a picture of me eating a cricket."

We go back to the first room, which smells much better than where we've been, and Geoff dramatically uses chopsticks to pick up a cluster of tangled brown cricket bodies and hold them in front of his mouth as I snap the photograph. Then he pops them in and breathes an exaggerated "Mmmm!"

"How do they taste?"

He swallows and thinks a minute. "Somewhere between buttered popcorn and dried seaweed. Very tasty!" He reaches for another bite as Minh looks on with an approving smile. "I think I'll buy a box to send to Aunt Vivian. She'll love them!"

*

We are on our way to the silk factory when Geoff's cell phone rings. He listens intently to the person and says, "Thank you. Great job." After a period of deep thought, he taps Minh on the shoulder and says, "I need to get back to the hotel. You can just drop me off and continue the tour with Lindsey."

"No need to take me to the silk factory," I say quickly. "Let's just call it a day."

Regularly throughout the trip, Geoff has used his laptop to do what appears to be business. After all, he is the CEO of a worldwide charity and has other responsibilities he doesn't elaborate about. Once he had a conference call late at night, Vietnam time. Usually right after breakfast, he logs on, and for about an hour, he focuses intently on his emails. When Geoff focuses, he focuses. I've never seen anyone before who can shut out everything around him to the degree that Geoff does. I've learned to check my mail at the same time and write to friends about my adventures in Vietnam. I promised Vivian I'd stay in touch, so I often send her an email and attach whatever photos I've taken.

Now, back at the French villa, in our room that has an amazing balcony with an ornate metal railing that looks out over the hills of Dalat, Geoff opens his laptop. Before he becomes entrenched with that faraway look he usually has in front of his computer, he looks up at me and says, "There's something I need to talk to you about."

It sounds serious.

"You remember I asked if I could talk to my senator friend about your father."

I nod.

"Well, he has done his homework. Apparently he contacted Willi Henderson and others who worked with your father. Then he opened old, highly secure files and discovered some disturbing shit. He's sending me the report."

"Oh." I sit down on the bed. Disturbing shit? How disturbing?

If there was foul play and my father died to cover other people's mistakes, it would be disturbing and infuriating. Yet knowing the truth wouldn't bring my father back. Even if people were punished for wrongdoing, it wouldn't bring my father back.

"You all right?" Geoff sits beside me, his arm comfortingly around me, his eyes inquiring into mine.

"I think so. It's just…" I hardly know how to express myself. "I came on this trip mostly to find out what happened to my father. And now that I'm close to finding out, I'm scared. Maybe scared isn't the right word. I've tried to see things through his eyes on this trip, imagining him at the places we've been. I know the country was at war when he was here, but he *was* here, and he saw the same mountains and probably swam in the same ocean and ate some of the same types of food we've been eating. It's weird, like I've been sharing things with him and gotten to know him in my imagination."

I feel foolish. I'm making no sense. "Sorry. I'm being maudlin. I'll be fine, and I want to see what's in the report, no matter what kind of disturbing shit is in it."

Geoff hugs me hard and rocks me slowly as he says, "One of the things I love most about you is that you allow yourself to feel things, but you are not at all maudlin. You are strong, and curious, and real."

"And you," I say with my head on his shoulder, "are the most amazing person I've ever met."

Eventually, we sit down in front of Geoff's laptop and together read the report. Afterwards, Geoff holds me tightly for a very long time.

CHAPTER 32

Nate

Chien was the most relaxed of all Tran's children. This may have been because he was the youngest and born after the war ended, and also because he inherited his mother's personality. Chien's mother, An, was a jolly woman, larger than most Vietnamese, and the first family member after Kim to make Nate feel welcome. She stayed at the family compound more than at their home in Ho Chi Minh City because she said she liked the smell of the country and waking up to roosters crowing.

When Chien finally showed up at the Dalat airport to pick Nate up, he said, "We will have a good time together. You like to eat, right?"

Nate tried out a Vietnamese adaptation of "Does a bear shit in the woods?" He said, "Does a water buffalo piss in the rice paddy?"

Chien roared with laughter as he clapped his taller cousin on the back.

Because Geoff and his blonde girlfriend had already left by the time Chien arrived, Nate was unable to introduce them to his cousin. He was fairly confident that his cousin wouldn't mind the couple touring the coffee plantation with him, but just to be sure, he said, "I sat next to a man on the plane, an American, who is very interested in Vietnamese agriculture. He made a special trip to the Mekong Delta to learn about rice production and visited your father's experimental farm there. He and his friend would like to visit your coffee plantation tomorrow, if that's okay with you."

"Of course," Nate's affable cousin said. "And if you want, they can join us at my favorite restaurant afterwards."

Nate shrugged. "Maybe. If we still like them by the end of the tour."

Chien clapped Nate on the back again and guffawed.

When Chien led him outside to a brand new red Mercedes sedan, Nate thought, *Coffee must be a lucrative business.*

"My birthday present for Tet," Chien explained, stroking the glossy fender.

"Nice!" Nate breathed in the new car smell as he slid into the gray leather passenger seat and thought about the beat-up minivan that he had traded in last year for a new hunter green hybrid SUV with cloth seats. Not that the restaurants weren't doing well, but he had one kid in college and two more to go.

They wound their way through pine-forested hills that gave way to rolling fields around clusters of greenhouses. Chien's house was outside of town on the coffee plantation he managed. It was a two-story stucco square perched on top of a mountain, surrounded by coffee trees, and at a slightly lower elevation were small boxes of houses for the workers. Chien explained that most of the workers were tribespeople indigenous to the highland area.

"The government doesn't like them to marry Vietnamese," he said," because then the bloodlines become mixed. But when they marry their own kind, they can have as many children as they like to prevent them from becoming extinct as a culture. We pureblooded Vietnamese, however, can only have two children at the most."

Nate couldn't help but think of the mixed bloodlines of his own children and was grateful he lived where the government didn't tell him how many children he was allowed to have. He also was gratified that Chien apparently was unaware that speaking to Nate of mixed bloodlines was potentially awkward.

Two children, a boy of about eight and a girl a couple years older, came running out of the house as Chien pulled into the driveway and turned off the engine. Nate had seen them just a couple days earlier at the family compound among the dozens of children darting about.

"Papa, papa," the boy said. "Can I drive the tractor today?"

"Maybe tomorrow." Chien patted the boy's head.

"You said that yesterday!" the boy protested. "It's vacation and nobody is using the tractor today. You promised."

Children are the same whether of pure blood or mixed, Nate thought, having gone through similar scenarios with his son, *and so are their parents*.

*

That evening, sitting out in the cool mountain air on the patio that overlooked neat rows of glossy green coffee trees, Nate and Chien relaxed after multiple local beers served warm. Chien's wife was an accomplished cook from the north and had prepared a Vietnamese specialty from Hanoi called bun rieu. What Nate found unusual about the dish was the tomato-based broth, uncommon in Vietnamese cuisine. Fresh water brown crabs found in rice paddies were pounded into a paste, shell and all, to flavor the broth. The soup was rich, but the pulverized crab was nicely balanced by the acidity of the tomato broth.

Nate had bought some Cuban cigars in Ho Chi Minh City as a gift for Rosy, but now because the conditions were perfect, he brought two out to share with Chien.

Rosy. He missed her. She was the no-nonsense constant in his life. Often after a long day at the restaurant, he'd return home to find Rosy and the children asleep, but she was always willing to get up and sit on their little balcony to smoke a cigar with him. He could only imagine her take on his Vietnamese family and was relieved in a way that she didn't want to come with him to Vietnam. The exposure of his family to Rosy and her to them might be educational for all and hopefully beneficial, but the process would be painful.

It was Chien's first cigar. After choking and coughing from inhaling, he followed Nate's instructions and became more confident with each puff, until he said in English into the smoky silence, "Godfather."

It made Nate choke and laugh out loud.

"Good one?" Chien said again in English.

"Yes. Very good."

"I watch all movies," Chien said proudly.

"Me, too."

They sat in silence again, watching stars alternately twinkle and disappear behind low scudding clouds.

Finally, Nate said in Vietnamese, "Your father. He doesn't talk to me."

"Yes."

"Why is that?" Since Nate's first visit to Vietnam when he went to Tran's office, disguised as an importer, he had not held eye contact or had a word with his uncle. He noticed, too, visible tension between Tran and his mother.

Chien stood up and went into the house and returned with two more bottles of warm beer. "We talk," he said as Nate popped the cap and took his first sip of the fizzy room temperature brew.

"My father had a difficult life," Chien began in Vietnamese. "During the American War, he was a young man who believed in America. It was common knowledge that countries prospered when they received aid from the US. My father wanted his country to prosper. But the Americans left Vietnam after nine years of a war that destroyed our country. What was he to do? Communists imprisoned or killed people who liked Americans. My brother was a baby. My father had a family to care for."

Chien looked at Nate as if it was a no-brainer. To survive in Vietnam after the war, one had to become a Communist. And obviously, a Communist could hardly acknowledge, much less welcome, American relatives.

"How did your father convince the Communists that he no longer worked for the Americans?

Chien shrugged. "He's a smart man."

CHAPTER 33

Lindsey

I couldn't sleep last night, so Geoff gave me one of the little pills he keeps for plane travel. The pill leaves me groggy this morning until I have two cups of amazing coffee, a flaky French pastry, homemade yogurt, and fresh mango juice delivered to our room on a bamboo tray. Although awake, I feel hollowed out, as if the emotions that surged within me trampled all other feelings before they subsided.

While Geoff is on his laptop for his usual morning office time, I send an email to Vivian with a picture of the view from our balcony and one of a topiary pig from the park in Ho Chi Minh City. I sometimes wonder if Vivian had a hand in setting me up with Geoff. From what I know about Geoff, although he adores his aunt, he wouldn't do Vivian's bidding unless it was something he wanted to do. Whether it was pure chance or Vivian's manipulation, I'm happy to have Geoff in my life, especially now that I'm dealing with, as Geoff terms it, "disturbing shit."

Last night after we read the report, we decided we'd do the coffee tour today and then leave for Phan Thiet tomorrow. This morning, Geoff let Minh know of our plans, so hopefully, he can book us a hotel room. I'm not sure what we can find out in Phan Thiet. The likelihood of finding someone who knows anything is slim, yet we feel we have to make the attempt. The report included the address of the American headquarters, and that's a logical place to start. At the very least, I can stand in the spot where my father was last seen, according to the report of the driver who took him there. We have the driver's name, and Minh is going to see if the man can be located.

Geoff stops typing on the laptop to check his phone. "Lindsey," he says. "Nate sent a text with directions to his cousin's house. We should leave in about a half hour."

It looks like it will be another day of sun and crisp mountain air. I bring a light sweater to put over my sundress and a broad-brimmed straw hat to keep the glare out of my eyes. Oddly, being closer to the sun at this high altitude makes it feel brighter but not hotter.

Minh drives us out of town along a road that winds between sloping fields of red dirt that contrast with the lush green of what I come to realize must be coffee trees. They come in all sizes from small bushes to a few full-grown trees at the top of the ridges. When I point that out, Minh says, "I don't know everything about coffee trees, but one thing I know is that they grow big, but the farmer wants to keep them small to make it easy to pick the beans."

We turn into a narrow paved road that transitions to dirt, which billows in a red cloud behind us as we climb to the top of a hill. We stop in front of a large house with 360-degree views. Coming at us from the other direction is a green tractor that appears to be driven by a small boy until I notice two men walking on either side of the slowly moving vehicle—one short, one tall. The tall man waves at us, and I recognize Nate. As they get closer, the other man jumps in next to the boy and guides the tractor into a shed next to the house.

Eventually, they all walk toward us. The boy, holding onto Nate's hand, swings their clasped hands back and forth as his feet do a little dance. A smile covers his face. Geoff gives him a thumbs-up, and although it doesn't seem possible, the boy's smile gets broader.

"This is my cousin Chien and his son Tran," Nate introduces the two.

We shake hands all around, and I notice how Nate towers over his much shorter, stockier cousin. Nate's height and of course his eyes are a dead giveaway that he has a Caucasian parent. I assume his father is an American who fought in the Vietnam War.

After Minh takes his leave with instructions to call him when we're ready to go back to the hotel, Chien says and Nate interprets, "We'll drive to the coffee fields first and then walk through the village of workers."

We climb into the back seat of a red Mercedes of which Chien is noticeably and justifiably proud. As we pass row upon row of vibrant green bushes, Chien says through Nate, "The coffee trees have just finished blooming, but you can see white blossoms left on some of the trees." He pulls the car over to the side. "There are trees at every stage in this field."

As we walk up the sloping field over loose clods of red dirt, I am glad I wore sneakers instead of the strappy high-heeled sandals that match my dress. Chien stops in front of a bush with clusters of white flowers. "Smell," he says.

The fragrance reminds me of gardenias, but it is more subtle. "Beautiful!" I say. "It must smell heavenly when the entire field is in bloom."

Chien laughs. "It can be too much of a good thing," Nate interprets as Chien pantomimes sneezing and wiping his eyes. We all laugh.

Next to the bush in bloom, which Geoff notes is a "late bloomer like me," is a bush with dried brown clusters of former flowers on the spine between drooping ridged leaves. Another bush has brown flowers that have turned into green berries. At the top of the sloping field is a very large tree-like bush that Chien says is the oldest, planted by the French, and it has flowers and berries at every stage we've seen so far, plus some bright red berries.

"We like trees that produce at the same time so we can harvest and process all the trees together. If my workers pick berries on a tree with flowers, it can disturb the flowers."

"How do you grow trees that produce at the same time?" Geoff asks. "Do you graft or cultivate from seeds or cuttings?"

Chien explains, "We find a healthy plant, a good producer of coffee berries, and we take the dried seeds from that plant to start new ones. The new plants grow fast. Coffee is actually a bush tree that needs to be pruned regularly because only one-to-two year branches produce flowers."

The men continue discussing coffee agriculture and get into the pounds/kilos of beans per acre, up from ten years ago, as we walk slowly back to the Mercedes. I zone out and breathe in the miracle of clear mountain air warmed by the sun, tinged with the smell of earth and a few lone coffee flowers.

"Now we'll go to the village where the workers live," Chien says as we get back into the car.

The village is two rows of tiny white boxlike structures on either side of a main road. Some of the structures have corrugated tin roofs and others have thatch. Pigs and chickens wander between the houses, and a host of small, dark-skinned, tousle-haired children, some of them naked, surround our car when we stop. A few of the children, who look no older than six, have babies strapped to their backs, tied on with a cloth.

"These are the children of tribespeople who have lived in the mountains for many generations. They are hard workers and have a good life here now. Plenty of food and many children," Chien says.

As we get out of the car, Nate reaches into his backpack and brings out handfuls of miniature chocolate bars. Soon the children are gathered around him, jockeying for position as he puts candy into each small outstretched hand. When Nate's supply is depleted, they dart away and look at us shyly as they eat their chocolate.

We walk down the narrow main street of red packed earth, and I say to Geoff, "Look!" On many of the tiny houses are strategically placed white satellite dishes. We laugh at the mix of cultures and laugh again further down the street when we see a bamboo pole strung with baskets of toothbrushes and washcloths next to the town water pump.

Chien takes us to a large square area just outside the village, where brown coffee beans are spread on hard-packed dirt. "These were handpicked yesterday when they were bright red, and now they are drying in the sun." He reaches down and picks one up. Inside the hard shell are twin green berries, which Chien says are what will be bagged and sent to the roasters.

"So let me see if I got this," I say. "You pick the coffee berries when they are bright red and fully ripe. Then you dry them naturally in the sun. What happens if it rains?"

"These berries are for the villagers' use," Chien says. "We have a manufacturing area I will show you this afternoon where heated rooms dry the coffee during peak harvest time. Then we have machines that mill the coffee to remove the shells and bag the beans to send to the roasters. Harvest time is not for several more months, so I can't show it to you in operation."

Chien then points further down the road to several houses under construction. They are two-storied and significantly larger than the one-to-two-room houses in the village. "See, my workers make good money and can build bigger houses." He seems proud of their success, and Nate nods approvingly as he translates his cousin's words.

Geoff comments, "Capitalism is alive and well in Vietnam." Nate and I laugh.

There is a gentleness about Nate that was not evident the first time I met him. Thinking about his response "And so is yours," to my compliment "Your English is perfect!" still makes me cringe. I suppose he was right to say it, but it made me feel stupid, and unobservant, and racist.

Now that I've observed his interaction with his nephew and the little tribes children and seen his easy rapport with Chien and Geoff, I'm changing my mind. Perhaps he's just defensive about his mixed race.

My opinion of Nate continues to improve after Chien invites all of us to go to lunch at a restaurant nearby. We are seated next to each other at a round wooden table. I have difficulty finding a good place for my large hat, and Nate kindly takes it and hangs it from a hook on the wall behind us. "I wish my wife would wear a hat like that," he says. "It's very flattering and makes me think of an Impressionist painting of women in flowing white dresses."

"Thank you," I say. "It's rather old fashioned, but it keeps the sun off. So, tell me about your family."

Smiling, Nate reaches for his phone and starts showing me photographs. "This is Sophie, who is now a junior in college in New York." The photo shows a smiling, dark-haired Hispanic woman with amazing brown eyes and a soft, yet unflinching look into the camera. "She is going to the same college her mother went to years ago. We're confident Sophie is going to be a very successful designer."

The next photo is of a young teenage boy, who looks young for his age because of a silly grin and impish green eyes that peer through a tousled mop of dark curls. "This is Stevie Felipe, at age 14, who is the easygoing one. He hasn't figured out what he wants to do yet, but I'm convinced he can do anything he chooses. And last but not least," Nate selects a photo of a little girl with tawny straight hair and dark hazel eyes that dare you to mess with her. "This is the baby, Maria Mai, who just turned ten. She was born in the Year of the Tiger, and my mother says that explains everything."

"What wonderful names you have for your children!" I say, picking up on the mix of Spanish, English, and Vietnamese in their names.

"Yes," Nate says. "We had to please everyone in the family, so Stevie is named for my father, Stephen Nathan, and Rosy's father, Felipe, and Maria Mai is named for ..."

I stop hearing the rest of the sentence.

CHAPTER 34

Nate

Nate was looking forward to sampling the spicy baby water buffalo dish that was the specialty of the little restaurant Chien took them to and was passing the time talking to Geoff's girlfriend when she began to act strangely. Initially, after their first meeting at the pho restaurant in Ho Chi Minh City, he was under the impression that she was like every other beautiful blonde, bubble-headed, privileged white woman he had ever encountered, starting with his girlfriend Janet during his sophomore year in college. But Geoff was an intelligent man, and he appeared to have a great deal of respect for Lindsey. Yes, that was her name. And during the tour, she made appropriate comments. The quality that Nate found most appealing was her positive attitude. While other women might have complained about getting red clay on their shoes and objected to walking a good two miles between rows of coffee trees, she was a good sport.

Yet as they were having a perfectly normal conversation and Nate was telling her about his children, she suddenly rose from the table and, with a face drained of color, walked to the restroom. Geoff looked after her anxiously, and after ten minutes, when she didn't return, he went to find her.

Eventually, they both came back to the table with strained faces just as the featured dish of the restaurant was set in the middle. Weird. They ate very little and were quiet during the meal that Nate thoroughly enjoyed. Although the buffalo meat was chewier than he expected, it still had an interesting texture and flavor that was almost obliterated by the spicy sauce. He would have cut the spiciness to allow the natural flavor to come through.

"Nate," Lindsey said when the meal was over. "I'd like to talk to you whenever it's convenient. I know you have the rest of the tour this afternoon, and I don't want to keep you from that, but perhaps later this evening, Geoff and I can meet you somewhere? We're going to cut the tour short and call Minh to pick us up here."

He looked into her serious brown eyes. She wasn't angry at him, but something huge was bothering her.

"Sure. In fact, if it's urgent, we can meet now. I can always have Chien show me the rest of the operation another day."

"That would work, if you don't mind." She paused and looked around the small restaurant that was now empty of other customers. "Is it okay to stay here, or should we go to the little park we passed on the way here?"

*

Chien now realized that something was up. Nate quickly explained what he knew of the situation, and Chien insisted that they all return to his house where Nate, Geoff, and Lindsey could sit out on his patio. He even offered to supply the beer.

It was a quiet ride back to Chien's house. In the back seat, Geoff held Lindsey's hand and patted it every once in a while.

Once they were situated on the patio in comfortable lounge chairs, Lindsey said, "Sorry for all this drama, but I have to ask you something to make sure I heard you correctly. Nate, did you say your father's name was Stephen Nathan?"

"Yes," Nate said, puzzled.

"Was he a Vietnam War veteran who most likely died near the end of the war?"

"Yes," Nate said again.

Lindsey momentarily looked down, then took a deep breath and said, "My father's name was also Stephen Nathan. We're here in Vietnam to try to find out what happened to him."

Nate remembered his rumination about whether his father had an American family who needed to be notified about his remains and dog tag, and now it appeared that a member of that family was here—his half-sister. That thought made Nate sit up abruptly from the recliner. *I have a half-sister?*

"Excuse me a minute," he said and got up from his chair to go to his room. Minutes later, he returned with the Polaroid he had taken from the envelope-sized woven palm leaf basket at the family altar.

Lindsey glanced at the photo and reached into her purse, producing an almost identical one. Side by side, Nate's photo was more faded, probably from being in the tropics, and it was creased as if it had been kept in a pocket or handled frequently. It had no handwritten inscription.

Nate sat down slowly. "Where do we begin?"

*

Several hours later, they were still in deep discussion. Chien knew enough not to hover, although he came twice during the afternoon to offer more refreshment.

Lindsey had started by telling her story about finding the Polaroid in her mother's dresser drawer and how that had sparked her search for information about her father. Nate heard about her trip to the Vietnam War Veteran's Wall and was not surprised to hear that there was a "+" next to their father's name.

Then Geoff told about their visit to Willi Henderson and the first indication that there might be foul play, and his follow-up with the senator and the report they'd just received that validated what Willi had said. "I'll bring the report to show you next time I see you," he said. "Bottom line, it was a complaint soon after the war ended by the men in Steve Nathan's unit, about their commanding officer. They submitted it at a time when nobody cared anymore about the war and everyone was simply relieved that it was over. Their allegations, however, were serious.

"Apparently, the higher-ups in intelligence at the end of the war were of the opinion that North Vietnam was complying with the Paris Peace Accord of 1973. That accord specified that US troops had 60 days to withdraw, all war prisoners were to be released, and North and South Vietnam were to be reunified through peaceful means.

"Steve Nathan, however, had information that indicated the North Vietnamese were in collusion with Russia and China, who were supplying them with arms and aid and urging them to take the South by force. His superior officers ignored him, even when it was obvious that the NVA was mobilizing and taking over areas in the western highlands and infiltrating the Mekong Delta. They insisted that the NVA gains would be minimal, and the US had plenty of time to bolster the weakening South Vietnamese government.

"When Steve proved them wrong and it became obvious that the NVA was marching against Saigon and would overtake it, his commanding officer, who had a personal grudge against Steve, sent him on a death mission to Phan Thiet to retrieve their intelligence equipment. It is a very old trick."

Geoff ended by saying, "That's all the information we have about Steve Nathan's disappearance. Do you have anything to add?" He looked at Nate.

Nate had listened intently to what gave him an entirely different slant to his mother's story about his father. When he realized that Lindsey wasn't the longtime grieving family member he first imagined, but an illegitimate child just as he was, he felt a budding kinship. His father had obviously loved two women—Lindsey's mother and his own—and the circumstance that precipitated that love was the Vietnam War, which, like any war, destroyed a young person's illusion of immortality and made him receptive to love wherever it was available.

Nate hadn't told anyone the story his mother had told him about his father's death. Not even Rosy. Mai had only told him with great reluctance because it put her in a bad light. But now, he felt he had to tell the story to Lindsey and Geoff.

"My mother worked for Steve Nathan as a translator and assistant. She came from Phan Thiet, where you say they had an office. She told me that she worked for him in Saigon, which is entirely possible. Apparently, they had a relationship. She has a photograph of them together where he is wearing a camouflage uniform and has his arm around her. It's similar to this Polaroid." Nate pointed to the two Polaroids side-by-side on the table and noticed that Lindsey winced.

"When she became pregnant, she didn't tell Steve. I don't know if she knew about your mother, Lindsey, and the fact that Steve carried her picture around with him. At any rate, the NVA was drawing close to Saigon, and things were looking desperate. She hinted that she wanted Steve to take her to America. He said he couldn't. They had a fight. She returned home to Phan Thiet and left him a note saying she was pregnant with his child.

"She didn't expect to see him again, but suddenly he showed up at the family compound in Phan Thiet in a nonmilitary car driven by a Vietnamese driver. His face was darkened and his hair was dyed black. 'Come,' he said. 'I'm taking you and my child to America.' Just at that moment, there was a burst of gunfire from the bushes, and he was killed. The driver grabbed my mother and put her in the back seat and drove her back to Saigon, where she was able to get on one of the last helicopters to leave the city."

Nate continued, "Just this past week during Tet, I helped my mother clear my father's grave. It was the first I knew about the grave, and I know I should notify the US government, and I will. In addition, I found the photograph," he indicated the Polaroid, "and a set of dog tags for Steve Nathan."

They sat in silence, ignoring their warm beers.

Eventually Geoff said, "Nate, how would your mother react if we questioned her?"

Nate pictured Mai across from these two well-spoken, highly educated, white Americans on a mission to dig down to the truth, one of them the love child of Steve Nathan. Then he remembered the time she was upset and used a cleaver to smash garlic cloves with great vigor and the hundreds of times she'd refused to use logical detachment to debate controversial issues with him. If he told her some people wanted to talk to her about what really happened to Steve Nathan, she'd probably say, "He dead. What I say no change that," and wave a machete at them.

"It won't work," he said. "She doesn't do well with the direct approach." As an afterthought, he added, "But she knows more than she told me. And I think her brother Tran does too. He sided with the Americans during the war and suddenly switched loyalties at the end."

Geoff said, "We're driving to Phan Thiet tomorrow. Is it possible for us to go to your family compound and at least see where Steve Nathan died?"

It took Nate a moment to reconcile Geoff's perfectly legitimate request with the complexity of how to deal with his mother. Then a potential solution popped into his head. "Let me see what I can arrange," he finally said. "I have your phone number. I'll be in touch."

CHAPTER 35

Lindsey

Chien tries to convince us to stay for supper, but neither Geoff nor I are hungry. I am mentally and physically depleted by the time Minh drops us off at our hotel. As we walk up the curved staircase to our room, Geoff puts his arm around my shoulders.

Inside the room, I collapse on the bed. Geoff suggests that he get us a couple of stiff drinks from the bar, and we sit on the balcony to watch the sun set. It sounds doable.

We are silent as the sun lowers behind a building bank of clouds, shooting beams out from chinks between the layers. The sky turns an impossible orange and fades to peach, then pink, and finally pale gray before turning off the show.

The drink and the sublime sunset help me turn my swirling emotions into tangible thoughts. When I discovered that my biological father was not the man who raised me, my world became disoriented, and now it has taken another dizzying spin. I have a half-brother who looks different from me, and I'm not sure I like him. It's not just because he's half Vietnamese and was snarky to me when we first met. It's more than that.

Geoff asks how I'm doing.

"Better," I say.

"You want to talk?"

"Yes, I think so." I wait a moment as I further organize my thoughts. "This might sound all jumbled up and strange, but just when I was getting comfortable with the idea of a mythical, perfect father who adored my mother and dreamed of coming back to her, I find out my father wasn't so perfect after all. Turns out he knocked up a Vietnamese woman and then risked his life to save her and his child."

"Your father, just like all of us, was human."

"But, what was he thinking? Where on his list of priorities were my mother and me? Or maybe he didn't know about me."

Geoff says slowly, "In the story that Nate's mother told him, Steve refused to take her with him to the States, and she became angry and left in a huff for Phan Thiet. It wasn't until Steve discovered that she was carrying his child that he came for her. Nate's mother may have known about Steve's girl back home and was in competition with your mother the whole time."

"What about Steve's orders to get the equipment from Phan Thiet?" I say. "Just how much of his going to get that Vietnamese woman coincided with orders from his superior to get the intelligence equipment?"

"We've heard two reasons why Steve left the security of Saigon to go on his wild ride to Phan Thiet. It's possible that he went for both reasons."

"Willi Henderson said he was willing to go but Steve insisted. Probably because he wanted to save his child."

I feel resentment, and yes, jealousy toward this other woman and her child, my half- brother Nate. If Steve hadn't gone to Phan Thiet that day, he probably would have returned to my mother, and I would have known my father and had a different life.

Geoff seems to sense my struggle and says, "I sometimes wonder what my life would have been like if I hadn't made the choices I did. When I start wondering about the choices my parents made or didn't make, it can really make me crazy!"

A thought pops into my head, something that Sue Ellen would say if she were here right now. *Lindsey Casselton, you selfish thing! You've had a perfectly good life, yet here you are wishing for something that would have condemned Nate to a much more difficult existence as a half-breed in postwar Vietnam. What are you thinking?*

"I need another drink," I say, and Geoff leaves immediately to get me one.

*

We have a small apartment at a funky little rooming house in Phan Thiet near the ocean. It's the least luxurious of all the places we've stayed, and that's because, as Minh says, all the good places were reserved months ago for annual family vacations. Phan Thiet is smaller and less sophisticated than Nha Trang, but the water near the shore is just as polluted with floating garbage. Fortunately, the ocean breezes dissipate potential odor before it has a chance to fester. Geoff is very disturbed by the pollution and has a long conversation with Minh about why the government allows towns to put raw sewage into the ocean.

"It's unsanitary and causes disease, plus it's bad for tourism. People from other countries don't want to see floating garbage near the beaches they swim in."

Minh is unperturbed and simply says, "We have always done it."

Nate calls Geoff around noon and invites us to come for dinner that evening. The story he told his family is that he met a couple of Americans visiting Vietnam, and he'd like us to meet them. It's true. But there's so much more to the story.

When we tell Minh about our plans for the evening, he says it is customary when visiting people during Tet to bring a gift. He suggests we go shopping with him, and he will help us select something. I'm still unsettled about how I feel toward Nate and his conniving mother. Maybe we can buy them a lump of coal for their charcoal burner. I don't dare tell Geoff my uncharitable thought.

At the market, Minh takes us to a stall that sells elaborate arrangements of fruit and flowers all done up in cellophane. Geoff selects the biggest one and pays for it. Minh beams as he says, "You will be welcomed as important guests!"

Yeah, right.

The day is overcast and humid, which adds to my grumpiness. I tell Geoff I just want to take a nap, so they drop me off with the garish gift back at the funky rooming house, and he and Minh go to explore some Buddhist temple up on a mountain or something. Minh's constant smile and Geoff's attempts to cheer me up with his silliness are more than annoying. I stretch out on the lumpy mattress in our stuffy little room and sleep.

*

Fifteen minutes before we are to show up at Nate's family's house, I wait with Geoff, who is holding the enormous arrangement of fruit, on the street outside our rented apartment for Minh to pick us up. Geoff checks me out. "You look lovely this evening," he says.

I roll my eyes. I had awakened from my nap, feeling like I was inside a room full of cotton. My sluggish brain's only sensation was the discomfort of my entire body that was covered in sweat. After a cold shower, I decide to wear my fanciest outfit, an abstract Monet-like sundress and little strappy heels, in hopes of elevating my mood. It wasn't working.

Minh drives us outside the city to an area of rice fields that stretches for miles on both sides of the road. He turns down a bumpy dirt road that eventually becomes shaded by tall bamboo, which gets thicker before it suddenly opens into a clearing. In the center of a packed dirt yard is a rambling house with several thatched-roof outbuildings. A mob of children and three black dogs come running to greet us, scattering a small flock of chickens en route. It is charming in an otherworldly way. I wish I had worn my sneakers.

Nate emerges from one of the doors and walks toward us with graceful, loping strides and a big smile on his face. I have to admit my brother is a good-looking man in spite of his unusual combination of features.

With all the commotion around us, I don't have time to register that I might be standing in the very spot where my father was shot. It's only later in the evening that it occurs to me, and by then I have other issues to deal with.

"Welcome," Nate says and takes the enormous, crinkly gift from Geoff. He turns to Minh and says, "You are welcome to stay for dinner as well. My mother is known for her cooking, and she's made enough to feed an entire village."

Minh declines, saying he has already made other plans.

We walk around the house to the back where there's a patio

all decked out with strings of lights and pots of flowering plants surrounding a banquet-sized table set for serious dining. I remember Geoff telling me that Nate and his mother own two Vietnamese restaurants, so this meal should be pretty good.

Visible from the patio is an open-air kitchen where two women are working. One is younger than the other and looks up, waves, and sends me a beautiful smile. She says something to the other who also looks up, and after a slight double-take, goes right back to work. Eventually, they both come out to be introduced.

Nate gesturers to the older woman first, "This is my mother, Mai," and turns to the other woman, "and her younger sister Kim. They are the chefs for the evening, so prepare yourselves for a treat."

"Welcome," Mai says formally. She must have been pretty at one time with a broad forehead that makes her face look almost heart-shaped. For her age, which I assume is close to my mother's, she is unusually agile, and her small compact body still moves gracefully. But it's her eyes that draw my attention. They appear to see everything, and what she sees when she looks at me is not necessarily good. She stares at me just as I stare at her, then she nods again before returning to her work in the kitchen.

I look at Nate and, with my back to her, say, "Does she know who I am?"

"No," he says. "But Kim does."

CHAPTER 36

Nate

Nate stood opposite his sister, whose high heels made her just slightly shorter than he, and marveled at how beautiful she was. Although she looked like the stereotype of a bubble-headed blonde, there appeared to be more to her. She looked at him now with concern and asked how much his mother knew. She, like he, was worried about how the evening would go.

"Let me show you around," he said, motioning her and Geoff to follow him. When they rounded the corner of the house and were out of sight of the kitchen, he said, "My mother knows nothing, but I've told Aunt Kim everything, and she will be a calming influence on my mother when we discuss the situation after dinner. Let's enjoy the evening and the food as much as we can before the shit hits the fan." Nate took a deep breath. "My mother is predictably unpredictable."

When Nate first told his mother about the couple he wanted to introduce to her, he had said that Geoff was interested in backing their coffee import venture, and it was true. While on the plane to Dalat, he and Geoff had discussed Vietnamese coffee and how it was underrepresented in the US consumer market. Geoff mentioned that he had capital to invest if Nate could persuade him that the market was there. When Mai heard that, she was eager for them to come and offered to cook a meal for them. But she had uncanny intuition. Nate noticed how his mother looked Lindsey over as if she was somebody Mai had met before.

He had a wave of momentary indecision. Maybe all this drama wasn't worth it. But then he reminded himself that it was important they return his father's remains to the States, or at the very least, turn in his dog tags. In addition, from what Kim told him, there was still confusion about what had happened that fateful night. It seemed that Mai and perhaps Tran were the only ones who knew the truth. It was time for the truth to come out.

One of the black dogs came over and sniffed Lindsey. She reached down and rubbed its head, scratched its ears, and had the dog in complete submission within a minute. The other two dogs came over, and soon she, Geoff, and Nate were busy patting all three as they vied for attention, going from one to the other.

Nate finally ended it. "Shoo." He chased the dogs off. "Now we'll need to wash our hands because the dogs roll in the dirt a lot, and we'll be eating in a few minutes." He led them to an outdoor faucet with a small basin underneath it on a stand. "They'll take advantage of you if you let them. I know. They've labeled me a sucker from day one!"

When they returned, the table was set with appetizers and bottles of cold beer. Geoff took a swig of beer and nodded his approval to Nate. "Local?" he asked.

"Yes," said Nate. "Another thing we could import."

Geoff agreed and, when urged, picked up his chopsticks and expertly picked up a crispy fried crab-filled appetizer. Lindsey did as well, and further showed her ability by picking up a steamed dumpling and dipping it into a dark brown sauce.

"This all tastes amazing!" she said. "We've been eating Vietnamese food for over a week now and had nothing as good as this." She caught Mai's eye and said, "Delicious!"

Mai nodded.

Soon, plate after plate of freshly prepared food appeared on the table. Nate noticed that his mother had outdone herself. She took traditional Vietnamese dishes prepared with authentic local ingredients not always available to her in San Jose and somehow took them to a higher level by a creative twist. A whole fish prepared with a sweet and sour sauce had small, delicately fried batter balls edging the plate that added a delicious crunch when dipped into the slightly spicy sauce. The rice was a mix of several varieties cooked in coconut milk.

Nate stood up and went into the lean-to kitchen. He put his arm around his diminutive mother and said, "Magnificent, Mom! Thank you!" He had a twinge of Judas guilt immediately afterwards, knowing what he plotted for later in the evening. But continuing with his very real solicitous feeling of the moment, he said, "Why don't you sit down and join us?"

"Maybe," she said and added another lump of coal to the charcoal brazier. "Kim, you go."

Kim wiped her hands on a nearby towel and came to sit next to Lindsey. She smiled and said in English, "You like?"

"Very much," Lindsey said. "I've never eaten anything so delicious before in my life!"

Kim beamed. Just then, Tran and his wife, An, approached the table. "Sit, sit. Come and join us," Kim said in Vietnamese. "Mai has become a demon in the kitchen today. You need to taste this!"

Nate wondered if word had gotten out through Chien that

there was something special about these guests, and Tran had come from his side of the compound out of curiosity. *So much the better,* Nate thought. *Get all the shit out at once to throw at the fan.*

After Tran and An were seated at the table, Mai brought out the last dish—a whole roast suckling pig with a red tomato in its mouth and garnished with tumbleweeds of wild onion. Everyone applauded. Nate carved the bronzed, crisp skin and carefully assembled equal portions of skin and succulent meat, which he put on each diner's plate.

Kim forced Mai to sit with them, and Geoff poured her a generous portion of rice wine. He toasted her with his bottle of beer. "You are an incredible cook—the best I've ever met!" Mai waved off the compliment dismissively, but Nate noticed a small smile as she took her first sip of the rice wine.

Dusk in the enclave descended earlier than elsewhere and soon the miniature lights around the table were turned on, lending a fairy-like aura to the ravaged platters of food that lined the center of the table.

Geoff refilled Mai's glass of wine. She was noticeably relaxed, as were all the other guests who were sated and seated in silence around the table.

"Ma," Nate began. "Did you ever cook like this for my father?"

"No. In war, food hard to get. But I cook for him what I find."

"I wish he could be with us here now."

Mai, across the table from her son, said, "He is here now. He see us right now."

Everyone at the table froze and looked down at their empty plates.

"Tell me about the last time you saw him alive—here," said

Nate.

"Sad story, very, very sad. Most sad for Tran, right, Tran?" Mai looked at her brother, who understood English, although he rarely spoke it.

Tran rose from the table and rattled off something in Vietnamese that Nate only partially understood. It was something about family loyalty and breaking a promise. His voice rose until he was practically shouting. Mai responded, saying it was about time he admitted to his wrongdoings.

Geoff and Lindsey sat motionless.

"Stop!" Kim stood up and, facing her brother and Mai, said in Vietnamese, "This is Tet and the beginning of a new year. We need to sweep out the old and begin in the new. But we need to do it with sympathy and understanding from all the family. It's time to confess our failings to the ancestor ghosts. We have all failed. We need to confess so that we can face the future without dragging along our sins from the past. I will start. Nate, will you translate for me into English?"

Tran protested. "Perhaps this is something we do within the family, but not in front of strangers!"

Nate got up from his seat, all eyes on him, and went over to Lindsey. He touched her on the shoulder and said, "This woman is family. She is my half-sister."

Mai turned her full attention to Lindsey and stared. "Yes. That is what I saw." She continued to stare. Then, as if gears within her brain meshed and slowly turned, activating areas of memory and feeling long suppressed, she said, "Kim, you are right. The ancestor ghosts need to hear our confessions. You start with your story."

Tran stood abruptly and said to An, "Let's go. We don't have to be a part of this spectacle." An didn't budge. "Come on!"

Very slowly and calmly, An said, "I was there, too, remember? It's time to dig out and remove hidden memories that fester in our brains and make us shudder in our dreams."

"Traitor!" Tran yelled in disgust as he left the table.

Although they couldn't understand the words, Lindsey and Geoff obviously knew that this moment was the one they'd been waiting for. The shit was hitting the fan.

CHAPTER 37

Lindsey

As has happened to me before, my grumpy mood is suddenly gone when my mind becomes occupied with something outside itself. Driving into Nate's family's yard, I am snapped into another mindset that wipes away my self-indulgent funk. I become interested in the place, curious about Nate and his family, and conscious of the fact that my father had been here.

The meal that Mai and Kim prepare is beyond wonderful. By the time the suckling pig appears, I am already so stuffed I have to force myself to taste the final masterpiece of the evening. I marvel at the crispiness of the baby pig's skin while trying not to think of the cute little piglet it used to be.

I notice that Geoff is being very solicitous to Mai and filling up her wine glass. Leave it to Geoff to know how to treat a woman! When the strands of tiny lights come on around the table, it feels like Christmas after a family gathering when everybody is full of food and contentedly tired from too much happiness.

That feeling ends abruptly when Nate starts asking Mai about our father. She answers him in English without hesitation, but it's a little creepy when she says that Steve is there with us. Then she switches to Vietnamese, and soon the yelling starts. Geoff takes my hand and squeezes it. We watch the interchange and follow the emotions but not the words as they pour out of highly charged mouths. Then Nate comes over to me, puts his hand on my shoulder, and says in English, "This woman *is* family. She is my half-sister."

It's as if sound and air are sucked from the space we are occupying and nobody can move. The moment passes, and when I can breathe again, I'm suddenly happy to be related to my tall, calm half-brother.

Mai stares at me, but with curiosity rather than negativity.

There's another interchange between Tran and his wife before he stomps off. Geoff and I look at each other. Soon, Kim is talking, and Nate translates.

"I was just a young girl at that time, no more than fifteen years old, and I took care of grandma here at the house. Mai and Tran were doing important work for the Americans and even though we knew the Americans were finished, they had been good to us. Steve sent us food from the commissary all the time. American food, sometimes cheese that we couldn't eat. But we liked the chocolate! When he brought Mai here one time, Tran became very angry because neighbors saw things and would see that an American drove her to our house, and he said that could be dangerous later. Steve didn't come here again except for that last time."

Kim blinks away tears. "Mai came home very upset. Everything was going wrong. She didn't say exactly what. We heard that all Americans were leaving and the NVA was taking over the country and killing people who helped the Americans. Tran was even more upset. He made An keep baby Lieu inside the house all the time. The night that Steve came, we were hiding in the house. Mai heard him call her and went outside. I heard gunshots, and Mai started screaming. Then her screaming stopped and she was gone, and Steve's body lay in the dirt. An and I dragged him closer to the house and went through his pockets. Tran dug the grave. He couldn't dig it fast enough. We all dragged Steve there and covered him up with dirt before the daylight. Tran said if people came before we had him buried, we should say we were helping to get rid of the Americans for Ho Chi Minh and our new country. And that's all I know."

Mai goes over to her sister and hugs her. She begins talking in Vietnamese between sobs.

Nate translates to us in a low voice. "She's saying she is so sorry to leave her family like that without even saying goodbye. She didn't know what was happening, it all went so fast. All she knew was that Steve was dead, and if she didn't listen to the driver, life was over for her and her baby." His voice breaks.

From the other end of the table, An slowly stands up. Nate translates her halting words. "You all think my husband Tran is a bad man. But he had me and a baby to consider. The war didn't go as he wanted. He made a poor decision to stick with the Americans, and he felt that he failed us. All he wanted to do was protect his family, and that included his two sisters and his old grandmother. He was young. Not even 22 years old." She sat down heavily and put her head in her hands. "And now he thinks I'm betraying him. But we all need to tell the truth. Even him."

"It's my turn." Mai stands up. She takes a breath, then says something in Vietnamese to Nate. Apparently Nate gets the job of translator because he's the only one fluent in both Vietnamese and English. And whatever Mai has to say must be understood by everyone at the table. Nate nods and Mai begins her story in

Vietnamese.

"For over 40 years, I have had a video playing in my brain that I can't turn off. Many nights the gunshots at the end of it wake me up. I hope that now I can turn the machine off and the video will be quiet. For many of those years, I blamed my brother Tran for those gunshots and for making my life go in a crazy direction, not the direction I dreamed of. But now I blame him only for being a coward and not facing us here tonight.

"Yes, Tran shot Steve Nathan. He didn't know who he was. He thought the car that came into our driveway that night was full of NVA soldiers looking for us because we worked for the Americans. Tran's plan was that he would keep watch every night, and I would keep watch during the day."

Mai closes her eyes momentarily. "Yes, it was a mistake. A tragic mistake. Yet Tran is successful with the Communist government now, very successful, and I have had many years to wonder how he did that." She looks directly at An, who meets her eyes but doesn't offer information, probably feeling that she has betrayed her husband enough. I feel bad for her—and strangely enough, I feel bad for Tran. It's hard to know what I would do in a similar situation. Self-preservation is a strong motivator.

Mai looks at me. "Steve told me about your mother." She pauses. "Because tonight we are telling only the truth, I will tell you that I hated her. She had advantages I didn't have. She was a white American. She went to college and lived in a rich country. But mostly I hated her because Steve loved her, and I hated her because I knew I could never be like her. It didn't matter how smart I was, or how hard I worked, or that I was an excellent cook—I could never be like her, and Steve would never love me the way he loved her.

"It's only in my old age that I realize the gift of being myself. People can't change who they are, so the sooner they accept that, the happier they are. And in the end, Steve did love me, after her letters stopped coming."

Letters? My mother wrote him letters?

I grab Geoff's arm, but before we can talk, a voice comes from behind us. It's Tran.

He speaks in Vietnamese but Nate translates softly so Geoff and I can understand.

"You say I am a coward. Well, this coward kept the family alive by working hard and providing for everyone. This coward had to be smart. When the NVA came here to question me, I was ready for them. I took them to the American office and showed them the American secrets. They honored me for that and rewarded me—not like the Americans who left us behind after empty promises.

"And now this coward has lost his family's respect. The family forgets what I did for everyone and listens to Americans again who talk big and do nothing. I will show all of you that I am no coward!"

In the shadowy light, Tran moves an object to his head. The gunshot startles sleeping birds that rise from their nests and go squawking into the night.

EPILOGUE 1: EIGHTEEN MONTHS LATER

October 21

The body of an American serviceman who was missing for over 40 years at the end of the Vietnam War was buried in Arlington National Cemetery today. The body, recently discovered in Phan Thiet, a coastal city east of Ho Chi Minh City, was returned to the US in a white coffin draped with the US flag. After undergoing DNA testing to confirm his identity, Stephen C. Nathan was laid to rest. His younger brother, Mark Nathan, and other family members were in attendance.

Nate

Mai didn't want to attend the burial at Arlington National Cemetery that October. It didn't surprise Nate, but what did surprise him was how docile she had been when they told her they wanted to exhume the body. He half expected her to throw herself protectively on the grave, weeping like she did the first time she saw it.

Something happened to her during the "Tragic Night of the Reveal," as Lindsey and he now called it. It was as if by coming clean with the truth, Mai had made peace with the ghosts of her past.

Rosy also chose not to attend the burial, claiming work responsibilities, but Stevie and Maria, now 16 and almost 13, were excited about visiting Washington and made Nate promise to take them to the White House. They arrived several days before the burial service to visit the Smithsonian and as many Washington attractions as they could squeeze into each day.

After three days, Maria, who had inherited her mother's no-nonsense view of life, liked visiting the Bureau of Engraving and Printing the best because she could watch money being printed. "Money is about now," she said. "The other stuff is old and dusty." She persuaded Nate to buy a sheet of uncut two-dollar bills.

Unlike his sister, Stevie was relaxed and mellow, qualities that helped him coexist peacefully with his spitfire sibling—most of the time. But under his unruffled demeanor was an inquisitive mind that made him pause and read the inscriptions by each display they passed. It stretched Maria's limited patience to the snapping point.

By the end of the three days, Nate was ready to drop the role of tourist father and mediator to two bickering teenagers, but there was one last place he had to take them—the Vietnam Memorial Wall. Lindsey had told him about it, and he felt it would be a good way to introduce his children to their grandfather. He thought back to the rare crumbs of information, growing up, that his mother had given him about his father and realized that he hadn't told his children anything about their deceased grandfather except that they were going to his funeral in Washington. What should he tell them? How much should he tell them? They had met Lindsey, who had been introduced as Aunt Lindsey, without raising even one of their eyebrows.

"Okay, guys," he said, "let's get some ice cream at that food truck across the street and then go to one last place."

Reenergized with sugar that lifted everyone's mood, the three headed across the National Mall toward the Vietnam Memorial Wall. When they arrived, much of the wall space was blocked by groups of people looking for the name of a loved one.

"Let's sit down here for a minute," Nate said and brought his children to a bench under a magnificent maple in full fall colors. There was a slight wind that rustled the leaves overhead and brought with it the scent of hot dogs and popcorn from nearby concession stands.

Nate bit his lip in thought. "You know we're here to bury your grandfather, right?"

They nodded.

"Well, he was my father and I never met him, but I've learned a lot about him in the last couple years. Like he was a hero. If he hadn't been a hero, which cost him his life, you two wouldn't be on this earth."

"What?" Maria scrunched up her face.

"You know about the Vietnam War, right? You've studied it in school?"

"Yes," Stevie said. "My teacher last year said something like what you just said. He's part Vietnamese. He said to a bunch of us in the class who are Vietnamese like him, 'The Vietnam War was the most unpopular war of the century, but if it hadn't happened, you wouldn't be here.'"

"I don't get it," Maria said, kicking at a knob of a tree root that poked out of the ground by the bench.

Nate took a breath. "Hundreds of thousands of Americans went to Vietnam to help the South Vietnamese fight against Communism. While they were there, many of them fell in love with Vietnamese women, like your grandfather who fell in love with Grandma Mai."

"Oh-h-h," Maria said and kicked the root harder.

"So what's the hero part?" Stevie asked.

"It was the end of the war, and the Americans had to leave because the North Vietnamese Army had surrounded Saigon. Grandma Mai was outside Saigon in Phan Thiet, a city about four hours away. Grandpa Steve got a driver to take him to Phan Thiet to bring her back to Saigon so she could escape with him to America. But when he got there, he was shot and killed. The driver took Grandma Mai to Saigon."

"And where were you?" Maria asked.

"I wasn't born yet. Grandma Mai was pregnant with me."

Stevie and Maria sat motionless, as if letting the information sink in.

"Why are they burying him now, after all this time?" Stevie asked.

"Nobody knew where he was, and the US Military considered him missing, not confirmed dead. There was a plus sign next to his name on the wall where most of the others have a small diamond. The diamond means they found the body and the person was confirmed dead. On my last trip to Vietnam, we found grandpa's body buried at Grandma Mai's family's burial plot. It was brought back to the US, and tomorrow we'll have a full military burial for him to honor what he did for his country—and for you and me."

Stevie said slowly, "Most kids get DNA and stuff from their parents and grandparents. But I guess Grandpa Steve gave us even more than his DNA. He risked his life so we could be born in this country, and he died…"

Nate reached over and hugged his son. Maria wriggled in between them, and the three hugged for several minutes.

Finally, Nate said, "Let's go find his name."

*

With Geoff's guidance, Nate had contacted the US military and returned Steve Nathan's dog tags. He and Lindsey, with Uncle Mark as the legitimate family member, requested that the body be exhumed and buried in Arlington National Cemetery. It took more than a year to wade through the red tape and protocol, but finally it was time for the family to gather in Arlington, Virginia, for Steve Nathan's burial.

Lindsey had booked a block of rooms at a local motel not far from the cemetery. She chose it, she said, because it had a large common area where the family could gather and talk.

Uncle Mark, his children, and their spouses were coming, including "sad niece Shelley," whom Lindsey had met but Nate had not. Cousin Sarah from Ridgewood, New Jersey, also was coming and bringing her excitable little dog, which required that they have a dog-friendly motel. Lindsey had been adamant about having the whole family in one place and had even emailed introductory bios of each family member to all attendees to help smooth out potential awkwardness.

Nate was not looking forward to meeting an army of his father's New Jersey relatives. He and the children arrived late at the Arlington motel in a semi-daze after visiting the Wall. Many of the relatives were already in the common area. An elderly woman, smelling oddly of mothballs, squinted up at him as she clutched her dog to her bosom. "So you're the other one," she said.

Shelley immediately appeared from behind and put out her hand. "Nate, I'm Shelley. Welcome to the family."

"The other what?" Maria asked Stevie, who shrugged.

"And this must be the talented Maria!" Shelley said. "I read all about you starring in your school play."

"That was last year," Maria said in a monotone.

*

The day of the burial was one of those perfect fall days where the intense blue of the sky contrasted sharply with white cumulous clouds above, and below with the orange/red/yellow of leaves that had not yet blown off the trees. The air smelled of recently mown grass, a smell that was reinforced by the distant buzz of lawnmowers. It was a magnificent day to be at Arlington National Cemetery.

"Wow!" Stevie said from the front passenger seat of their rental car as they drove into the national cemetery. "Somebody lined up those white stones with a one-millimeter toothpick!"

"There's no such thing!" Maria said from the back seat, and then as they passed row upon row upon row of identical, meticulously placed white marble stones that marched between trees and up and down hills with a precision that flowed and pirouetted like an orchestrated dance, she asked, "How're we gonna find grandpa's?"

"Guess we'll have to check out each one," Nate said.

"Shit, no!"

"Watch your language, son."

"But really! How're we gonna find it?" Stevie persisted.

Just then they passed a caisson drawn by four horses, carrying a flag-draped coffin on its way to a gravesite. The horses clopped by slowly, unfazed by the echoing sound of a 21-gun salute. A line of cars with headlights on in broad daylight trailed behind.

"Is grandpa going in a carriage like that?"

"I don't know," Nate said, trying to remember how to get to the Administration Building where they were to meet.

The arrangements for this burial had been complicated, but once they were given the go-ahead, things had proceeded with typical military exactitude. That and Lindsey's insistence on making it a family reunion gave Nate about as much leeway as a rat in a laboratory. Not that he resented being here, but he was most definitely out of his comfort zone.

At the Administration Building, the family gathered in a room reserved for them. Nate noticed an older man off to the side in dress military attire, talking with Lindsey and Geoff. She motioned him over.

"Nate, this is Willi Henderson, our father's best friend in Vietnam. He has offered to be a casket bearer."

The wiry little man looked Nate over. Then he looked back at Lindsey. "I have something for you two," he said. "It's no big deal, really, but when I look at them, it brings back the day your father and I went to a beach in Vietnam on our day off. He had just arrived in 'Nam and was full of enthusiasm. He was optimistic then, before..."

Willi's voice cracked, and he coughed to cover it up as he pulled a large white handkerchief from his pocket. Inside was a handful of unusual sea shells. He spread them out on a dark, highly polished lamp table where they lay starkly beautiful amid a dusting of fine sand.

"This one," he singled out a ridged spiral with the ridges perfect and uniform on the outside of the shell, "I learned is an epitonium scalare commonly known as a precious wentletrap. These," he pointed to scoops with interiors of iridescence, "are abalone shells. He was going to bring them back to Lindsey's mother."

Willi looked embarrassed for a moment before he recovered himself and asked Nate, "How's *your* mother?"

"She's well. Thanks for asking."

"She was a remarkable woman. Still is, I expect."

Willi looked embarrassed again until Lindsey took his arm and said, "These shells are exquisite. Do we get to pick one?"

"Take them all. I don't need them. I'm sure he'd want you to have them."

Lindsey gave him a hug.

*

An hour later, after following a lead vehicle to the gravesite, Nate and the others assembled around a flag-draped white casket that Willi and five other uniformed men had carried to a designated spot on the lawn. Uncle Mark and his children sat in folding chairs at the front while everybody else stood behind them. Someone, probably a chaplain, read from the Bible and then a trumpet played "Taps." Nate felt Maria's hand grip his.

Two uniformed men with practiced movements began folding the flag that covered the casket until it was a thick triangle. One carried it over to Uncle Mark and said, "On behalf of the President of the United States, the United States Army, and a grateful nation, please accept this flag as a symbol of our appreciation for your loved one's honorable and faithful service."

Tears streamed down Nate's cheeks, released from a deep place inside where for years he had stored conflicting emotions.

*

That evening after a family dinner at a nondescript restaurant that Lindsey chose based on a survey she had sent earlier asking for people's eating preferences, they assembled back at the motel in the large common room.

Nate noticed that Geoff had been very much in the background during the day at this event and was allowing Lindsey to take charge. Nate had no desire to be in charge and had told Lindsey from the beginning that this was her party. But now, back at the motel after the dinner, Geoff took the floor.

"Hi, everyone! This has been an emotional day for me, and

I'm sure you've felt the same way. I believe only two or three of you have actually met Steve Nathan—that would be brother Mark, cousin Sarah, and Mark, did your wife know Steve?"

Mark shook his head no.

"So only two of you were privileged to know Steve. After being with Lindsey the last couple years and sharing her search for her birth father, I've learned a lot about the man. And getting to know Steve's son, Nate, has also given me a feel for him. As Frank Herbert says in his book *Dune*, 'What is the son but an extension of the father?'

"Today we all came to honor Steve Nathan and participate in a ceremony where the United States honored him in an incredibly moving way. It would probably be fitting for us to spend the rest of the evening reminiscing, but unfortunately, I have a different agenda. Sorry, but I have to take advantage of having you all here to talk business."

Nate knew what was coming and had considered leaving his children in the motel room, watching TV or playing games on their iPads while they had this meeting, but decided they were mature enough to attend. And as Steve's only grandchildren, they had a right to be a part of what was coming.

Geoff continued. "Some of you, but perhaps not all of you, know that Steve's death could probably have been avoided. Steve's commanding officer sent him on a death mission on one of the last days Americans were in Vietnam. Some men in Steve's unit thought it was deliberate on the part of his commanding officer because..."

"What kind of a death mission did he send him on?" Cousin Sarah interrupted.

"He was sent out into the countryside that was occupied

by NVA soldiers to retrieve some equipment they didn't want to fall into the hands of the enemy. Steve had wanted to get the equipment located at Phan Thiet much earlier, but his commanding officer, Captain Moseley, didn't see the need for it. Steve proved him wrong about that and on many other occasions made him look bad. It's very possible that Captain Moseley sent Steve out on a death mission, hoping he wouldn't return. The men in Steve's unit complained about Captain Moseley at the end of the war, but it didn't amount to anything. America was tired of the Vietnam War and was recovering from Watergate. There were bigger issues to deal with than an injustice done during an unpopular war.

"But now that you as a family are all together, it is appropriate to talk about what happened to Steve Nathan. Lindsey, Nate, and I have put the pieces together from various sources and have a pretty good idea. We feel you need to know."

"Is this Captain Moseley even alive?" Uncle Mark asked.

"No, Captain Moseley died in 2008."

"I say we kick his butt!" one of Uncle Mark's sons said, "Even if it's a dead butt."

"Well, Captain Moseley was only one piece of the puzzle," Geoff continued in a steady voice. "Apparently Steve had another reason to risk his life to get the equipment. He had recently learned that he was about to become a father, and the mother of his child-to-be was in Phan Thiet, where the equipment was. He might have gone there even without Captain Moseley's order. We've been told that Steve darkened his face, dyed his hair black as a disguise, and found a Vietnamese driver to get him there in a nonmilitary vehicle.

"What happened in Phan Thiet is a tragedy. The truth of it

was kept secret until a year and a half ago when it was told at a family gathering during Tet. What happened at that family gathering was also a tragedy. Like a Shakespeare play, there was intrigue, cover-up, and betrayals by all. At the family gathering, we learned that Nate's Uncle Tran, who had worked at Phan Thiet with Steve, felt the United States was deserting its Vietnamese supporters. US personnel were leaving the country, and the Vietnamese who had supported them were now in danger from the Communist North who was taking over. Tran thought he needed to defend his family, so he guarded the family compound with a rifle. When Steve's car drove in and Steve called for Nate's mother, Mai, Tran shot him, thinking he was someone coming to harm the family."

"Oh, no!" Shelley reached over to touch Nate gently on the shoulder. Nate nodded in acknowledgment but kept his eyes on his two children to gauge their reactions. Maria didn't seem to fully comprehend what was said, but Stevie clenched his fists into balls.

"So," Geoff continued, "it was an accident, a tragic one that was not acknowledged until recently. We filed a formal disclosure to the US military when we requested that the body be exhumed."

"What's exhumed?" Maria whispered.

"Later," Nate said.

"But," Mark's son's said, "what about this Captain Moseley's orders? That was pretty dumb of him to send Steve there at a time like that. Maybe if he hadn't been ordered to go, he wouldn't have gone and he might still be alive today."

Geoff nodded. "That's one of many 'what ifs' we can imagine."

Uncle Mark's other son stood. "You know what this reminds me of? Remember the story in the Bible about King David, who wanted to get rid of one of his generals in the army, Uriah the Hittite, because of, ah, personal reasons. He put Uriah right at the head of a division that was sure to be destroyed. And God punished him severely for that. Isn't this the same thing that Captain Moseley did to my Uncle Steve? And shouldn't he be punished?"

"He's dead, remember?" his brother said.

"I know, but couldn't we convict him and discredit his record or something?"

Lindsey said, "What good would that do? It would embarrass his family, but it wouldn't bring Steve back."

The son, who was still standing, said, "Doesn't God in the Old Testament punish evildoers for generations? Didn't King David's children suffer because of his sin?"

Cousin Sarah said in a loud voice, "'I, the LORD your God, am a jealous God, punishing the children for the sin of the fathers to the third and fourth generation.'"

"Wait, wait, wait a minute here," Uncle Mark now stood and motioned his son to sit down. "There's something most of you are forgetting. I'm one of two people in this room who knew Steve. After listening to all this new information about how he died, my gut feeling is that Steve would have gone through hell and high water to save his son, regardless of whether or not he was ordered to go pick up some equipment. That was the Steve I knew. And sure as hell, if he were alive today, he wouldn't want vengeance on some knuckle-headed officer, especially a dead knuckle-headed officer. I propose we let the matter drop. Steve's gone, and we all miss him even more now that we know how he died. Today we put his remains to rest in a beautiful place. He's home at last. Let's honor him with dignity as a family."

"I second that," Lindsey said.

"And I," Nate stood, "as the son that he risked his life to save, am especially moved by his courage and loyalty. When I think about the consequences of him not saving my mother and me, I realize I'd be in a much worse place than I am now. My life in Vietnam as a mixed breed would have been hell. I am the one who most benefitted from his death mission, and it is a staggering debt I can never repay.

"Yesterday, my children and I stood before his name carved into the Vietnam Memorial Wall. We had just been talking about the fact that if my father hadn't risked his life to save mine, my children would not exist. I wouldn't have come to America and met my wife, Rosy, and we would not have had our three incredible children. That's a pivotal, life-changing realization—my children exist only because of my father's courage."

Nate broke down and couldn't speak. After composing himself, he continued. "Captain Mosely is dead. He did an evil, selfish thing. We don't know if he felt sorry for doing it or whether he rationalized it as within his rights. Bottom line—it's too late to punish Captain Mosely for his action, and to make an issue of it posthumously to embarrass his family does no good. I say we drop it."

He sat down and put one arm around each child. All around him, people sniffed and blew their noses.

Uncle Mark spoke up again. "Well, that does it for me. I say, let sleeping dogs lie, as far as Captain Moseley is concerned. Can we get a feel for this? All who agree, raise their hands."

All hands rose except Cousin Sarah's.

"Majority wants to drop the matter. And now," Uncle Mark continued, "I propose we light into that chocolate cake I brought to celebrate my courageous brother!"

EPILOGUE 2: SIX MONTHS AFTER THAT

Lindsey

Geoff is off on one of his importing trips to Vietnam with Nate when I get a call from my other half-brother Jonathan. He is in the process of moving his family to the Chicago area where he has been transferred, and he calls me frequently to ask if I want yet another of the family heirlooms he doesn't want to take with him.

Before he called, I had been talking to Vivian, who invited me to visit her while Geoff is away. In addition to the travel associated with Geoff's philanthropic work, he is helping Nate set up an importing business, which requires even more travel. I often go with him, and we have been too busy to see Vivian for a couple of months. So when she says she has "fantastic" tickets to a couple Broadway plays and wants my opinion on a redesign she is contemplating for her apartment, I tell her I would be delighted to visit.

When Jonathan calls, I am mentally making a list of things to do, such as contact the dog sitter to watch Bert, our small mutt mix who has the hair of a terrier with German shepherd ears and coloring.

"Lindsey," my half-brother says, "I found something you might be interested in."

Typical Jonathan. He goes right to the point of his call, just like his dad. No time for chitchat or to inquire how I'm doing. He had reacted strangely when he learned that I had another half-brother. "No," he said. "*I'm* your half-brother." It was almost as if he was jealous, yet it wasn't an issue when he found out that we had different fathers.

I love my brother Jonathan because we grew up together and know each other as only siblings growing up in the same household can. But with Nate, I have developed a very special bond. That dramatic night in his family's courtyard in Vietnam drew all of us together—even Mai and me. And the bond only grew when the family gathered together for the burial at Arlington. Geoff and I always spend time with Nate and Mai when we're on the West Coast, and I'm Aunt Lindsey to Nate's children. Strangely, Rosy, like Jonathan, has had a more difficult time accepting that Nate and I are siblings. She usually is away when we visit.

Pulling my mind back to the phone call, I say, "Hi, Jonathan! How's the packing going?"

"It's a nightmare. Listen, Lindsey, I found a box of letters. It was part of the stuff I took from Mom and Dad's house after Dad died. It might have come from the basement or maybe the attic."

"Letters? From who?" I'm trying to decide if I should get the pet sitter we had last time who lost the key and was forced to call a locksmith to get into our house. Everybody makes mistakes, and does this one warrant being fired?

"From a Steve Nathan."

"Who?" My mind doesn't believe what it heard.

"Steve Nathan. I think that was your father's name."

I can't talk.

"Wasn't it?"

"Yes."

"Anyway, there's a whole box of them and a notebook with

what looks like Mom's first draft of her replies to his letters."

I still can't talk.

"Do you want me to bring them over?"

"Yes. Please."

LETTERS

June 25, 1974

Dear Alice,

My tired body is here in the barracks after a 5-mile run, but my mind is floating with memories of our recent two days together. Mind blowing days!

Speaking of floating, I'm glad I decided to "float" on your dad's fishing boat. I saw you selling tickets and I was "sold". It was the start of the best thing that's happened to me in years! I haven't been this happy since my college basketball team won the division title!

Tomorrow I have to go to Vietnam for a year. Major bummer! The good news is that the war is as good as over and I can see the light at the end of my tunnel. The bad news is that I've been assigned to the transition team and security will be tight. You can't call me and I can't make calls either.

You are a beautiful dream and one that I will treasure until I can wake up with you in my arms again.

Please don't forget me.

Love,

Steve Nathan

June 28, 1974

Dear Steve,

I was so happy to get your letter today. I'm hoping that the address on the envelope is the one to use to reach you in Vietnam. When I found your letter in my mailbox, I was just leaving to celebrate my father's 50th birthday with the family. We went to his favorite steakhouse. Figures, him being a fisherman and all! I read your letter before I saw my family, but during the dinner, I'd sneak into the ladies room to read it again. It was too special to share.

Our time together was dynamite, as my fourth grade students would say. I've been in a dream world ever since and my feet haven't touched the ground once! I've never before felt the instant attraction I felt for you and it only got stronger the longer we were together. It's unfair that we met right before you were deployed to Vietnam. We had so little time. I guess we'll have to get to know each other through our letters.

It's late and I have to get up at the crack of dawn to help my father deal with his eager, early-rising summer fishermen.

Stay safe and hurry back!

Love, Alice

July 1, 1974

Dear Alice,

I've arrived in 'Nam and what do you know! I found this typewriter in my office and figured it would help ease your eyes from trying to read my chicken scratch. I hope you got my first letter.

The trip was long and a huge drag. Did I say it was long? No duh! Of course, what did I expect flying over 8800 miles in a military transport! We landed at Tan Son Nhut Airbase, which is (excuse my French) a shithole. Somehow I thought the major airport for the war we've been dumping millions of dollars into for almost 10 years would look more like the airports stateside. But no, the terminal was a small dump of a building, especially next to the huge runways built for our aircraft.

My first impression of Saigon was the unholy humidity. My second was the ungodly smells. Neither was pleasant. But I have a decent room in a hotel along with the other guys in my unit. We have a swimming pool and movies every night and shuttle buses to and from the Embassy where our offices are. The bigwigs are on the 5th and 6th floors. The rest of us peons are in Quonset huts next to the Embassy.

The best thing about being here now in 1974 is that I wasn't here earlier slogging through the jungles like the guys did in the 60's. Soon I'll be back in the US of A and the first thing I'll do is point my car in your direction.

I miss you.

Love,

Steve

July 9, 1974

Dear Steve,

I received your letter written after you arrived in 'Nam and was happy to hear that you arrived safely and have decent accommodations. I, like you, am glad you are there now and not when the war was at its peak. Several of my high school classmates were there earlier and a couple didn't come back. So sad.

We celebrated July 4 as we always do with our family picnic in the backyard where my dad grills burgers and hotdogs and my mom makes her famous potato salad, which you sampled on our picnic. Usually we have about 20 people including aunts, uncles, and cousins. Then we go to the town beach to see the fireworks. It was drizzly this year, so the backyard picnic was indoors and the fireworks were delayed a day.

By the way, my dad remembers you and asked me if I've heard from you. "Nice young man," he said. "And he handled that 20-pound pollock like a pro!"

Next week I'm starting a summer course in Boston that will go towards my Master of Education degree. I'll be commuting and don't look forward to that, but the course sounds interesting. It's Cognitive Psychology where I'll learn about human mental processes such as attention, perception, and problem solving. I think it will come in handy when I go back to my students in the fall.

It's late and I want to finish this so I can put it in the mail tomorrow morning.

Thinking of you and wishing you were here right now!

Love, Alice

July 10, 1974

Dear Alice,

So much has happened since I wrote, but the best thing was getting your letter! It gave me the chance to show the guys the picture we took together. They are all jealous, but they agreed that you are a "hip chick".

The guys in my unit have been here longer than me and are giving me the skinny on things. No surprise--there are politics, not so much governmental, but interdepartmental and interpersonal. Nobody likes our commanding officer, but I won't go into that.

Outside our Americanized hotel, it's a different world. The roads are crammed with bicycles ringing their little bells like they were bullhorns as they swerve around cars and pedestrians. There are cyclos, really oversized tricycles with a driver peddling high in the back over one wheel and a rider in a low seat between the two front wheels. I took one on my day off just to see the city, nice and slow, almost like walking down the middle of the street. I saw men holding hands (it's the custom around here), lots of dirty half-naked kids, and garbage in the streets. People are tired of this supposed truce. The Vietnamese are tired of fighting, and the Americans who are left here are just getting through the day.

And I'm just getting through each day and counting the ones before I can come home again and see you. Only 351 days left. Sigh.

Love,

Steve

July 20, 1974

Dear Steve,

It was great to hear from you and learn more about what a different world you are in. I don't know how I would react to the poor, half-naked children.

I have started my psychology course and love it, just as I expected. The teacher is rather gruff with a carefully trimmed white beard, which a student next to me said looks like Sigmund Freud's. I suppose we all have our idols, ~~who~~ whom we try to emulate. Anyway, I have lots of reading to do and the commute takes time so I can no longer help my dad out with the fishing boat. But I'm glad I was there when you came last month!

We've had an unusually hot, humid stretch of weather and I can't help but think of you there in Saigon with the heat and the smells. It will be wonderful to ~~go back to our special place~~ spend time together again, perhaps out on the water with a cool, refreshing breeze.

It's time to read the chapters for class tomorrow. Stay cool and safe!

Love, Alice

July 21, 1974

Dear Alice,

This morning my friend Willi and I went to a beach where Americans can go on their days off. The beaches here in Vietnam have miles of fine white sand. The locals don't like the sun because it turns their skin darker and they dig lighter skin. I guess everyone wants what they don't have. So needless to say, there weren't many other people on the beach except a few fishermen fully covered in black with coned hats, who were surf fishing or digging for clams.

Willi is an interesting person. He's older than me and this is his second term in Vietnam. He saw some heavy duty stuff on his previous term. Again I'm glad to be here now instead of earlier.

On the beach I found some shells that I'm saving to bring back to you. I've never seen anything like them. They have crazy beautiful shapes and some are pearl-like. We can look them up together when I get home.

The other thing I got from my day at the beach is a major sunburn. The sun here near the equator is stronger than back home. I'll know next time to wear a shirt and a hat. Maybe those fishermen were onto something!

341 days to go.

Love,

Steve

August 3, 1974

Dear Steve,

Your day at the beach sounds idyllic—except for the sunburn! I'm glad you get to do fun things on your days off.

I'm sure you've heard on your news out there about the Watergate scandal. It's all over the news here and everyone is talking about it. There's almost nothing about Vietnam anymore.

~~I've been feeling really sick lately and must have caught a persistent stomach virus.~~

My psychology course is almost over and then I have to prepare for school starting. I'm looking forward to meeting my students this year. Fourth grade is such a rewarding class to teach. The children at that age are becoming little people and are so curious and fun. I've run into some of my students from last year and it's gratifying to see that they remember me and want to talk to me.

A friend from college Mary Lou and I are going to Nova Scotia for a week before school starts. She's also an elementary school teacher and we've vacationed together before, once to Florida during winter break. I think you would like her because she has a quick wit and loves to laugh.

~~I hope you~~ I think of you often. ~~and dream about the day you return~~ Stay safe.

Love, Alice

August 7, 1974

Dear Alice,

This morning I looked at my calendar like I do every morning to see how many days before I can come home. The number was 324. Three hundred and twenty four more @*!* days. Ten months without seeing you. Sometimes I don't think I can stand it.

When I bitched to Willi about it, he said to throw out the @*!* calendar and just let the days slide by, one by one. Before you know it, he said, it's time to go home.

I think I'll try that for a while.

I love you and miss you more than you know.

Love,

Steve

August 17, 1974

Dear Steve,

Your last letter made me very sad, because you are in a strange place waiting for the time to end. I wish I could suggest something to help make the time slide by faster. Sometimes I daydream about things I want to happen and tell myself that those dreams are just around the corner. Like I dream about you walking in the door one day surprising me and it's just the best feeling in the world. Even though I know it didn't happen, I have a small moment of pure happiness while imagining it.

My psychology professor would probably call it escapism, just like drinking or doing drugs. I hope it isn't as bad or addictive. But I need something, just as you do, to help me pass the time waiting.

My class is over and although I enjoyed it, I'm glad I don't have to deal with the commute anymore. Oh, and I'm sure you've heard on the news that President Nixon resigned. It has shocked everyone here. It feels like we are leaderless and vulnerable as a country, but I'm sure Vice President Ford will do a good job.

Next week Mary Lou and I go on our trip to Nova Scotia and after that the school year starts and I'll be crazy busy. If keeping busy makes time fly, I welcome it.

Here's to putting wings on our time apart!

Love, Alice

August 20, 1974

Dear Alice,

This week I drove with my main man Tran to the office in Phan Thiet. Tran is a translator and the head of our office there. We need a place outside the city to send and receive signals from some pretty amazing state-of-the-art equipment. I probably shouldn't be writing you this, but I know you won't tell anybody.

Phan Thiet is a seaside town with amazing beaches like most of the coast of Vietnam. I was psyched to get out of Saigon for a few days. Plus the information we are getting on our equipment is important with serious implications. I came back to Saigon raring to go. Again, please don't say anything to anyone about this.

I hope you have a good trip to Nova Scotia and a good start to your school year.

Love,

Steve

August 31, 1974

Dear Steve,

Other than a flat tire along a country road near Halifax, my trip to Nova Scotia was wonderful. Mary Lou had me flagging down someone to help us change the tire as she rummaged in the trunk of the car looking for the contraption that raises the car. (Excuse my lack of knowledge about this kind of thing.) Eventually, a man stopped and helped us and then tried to talk the both of us into going to his house where he was going to have a party in our honor. We respectfully declined and said we had to get to our friend who would be worried about us if we didn't show up soon and would probably call the police. It was just a little white lie.

When I close my eyes I can still see the rocky beaches in Nova Scotia and the way the fog rolled in off the sea. We stayed in a cottage near the water and took long walks along the beach. I'd love to go there with you someday. Your description of the beaches in Vietnam sounds beautiful as well.

Next week I start the school year with 20 little fourth graders. I've already been to my classroom and decorated the room and organized some of the materials. The school year will occupy me and end just about when you return, so it's like a measuring stick of our time apart.

Be careful and stay safe.

Love, Alice

September 1, 1974

Dear Alice,

This has been one frustrating week for me. I've been going to Phan Thiet at least once a week to get information and when I give it to my commanding officer (we call him the Big Buzz because of his haircut) he ignores it, like I'm an idiot. Willi and the others agree with me, but they don't like putting their necks on the line. They just want to get home in one piece. Not that I don't want to get home in one piece, too, especially to see you again, but when something is obvious and it's critical, you want others to take it seriously.

Enough of my complaining. I've been spending a lot of time with Tran and the other day he brought his little boy Lieu to the office. He's a far out kid who stared at me with big, dark, serious eyes. I don't think he'd seen an American before. Tran's sister also came and wants us to hire her as a translator. She doesn't speak perfect English and is weak on the grammar, but for around here, she's damn good. She brought us all some lunch. I avoid Vietnamese food, but after eating her lunch, I might try more of it.

Last night they showed the movie Alice Doesn't Live Here Anymore and I went because of the name "Alice" in the title. The main character wasn't half as pretty as you, but she made me think of you. I hope you won't ever have the problems that the Alice in the movie had.

I miss you.

Love,

Steve

September 13, 1974

Dear Steve,

There's a little boy in my class named Richard who looks the way I imagine you looked at his age. He's a little blond angel with a bit of the devil in him. too. When he looks at me with his beautiful green eyes, I melt. I have to be careful not to be obvious about it, though. I want to be fair to the other students, who in their own way, are also little angels with tiny horns.

I come home from school each night exhausted. I had forgotten how much energy it takes to keep 20 active little angels happily learning. ~~I'm wondering if perhaps I'm pregnant because~~

I'm so sorry that your commanding officers are ignoring your good work. It must be discouraging and especially when the information is critical. I hope they come to see the truth in what you are giving them.

The days are getting cooler and after the hot summer, it feels good to breathe the cool air. My dad's garden had a bumper crop of zucchini this year so my mom and I had to get creative to find ways to cook it. I'm sure we'll still have some frozen zucchini bread for you to taste when you get back next summer.

Stay safe.

Love, Alice

September 15, 1974

Dear Alice,

Today is my 24th birthday. There was no cake or candles, like my mom had for me as a kid. When I was in college, she'd mail me a care package. Who knows. Maybe I'll get a surprise package from her tomorrow.

Anyway, the guys took me out on the town last night to celebrate. It wasn't the same.

My dad was married to my mom when he was 24 and I was on the way. He had responsibilities that I don't have yet--a wife, a family-to-be, a normal job. These are things I want someday. When I think about what's next after 'Nam, I first want to see you again. You are my anchor, my hope for the future.

The second thing I want is to find a job that does something to make the world a better place. We are so lucky as Americans. I see the way people live here and it makes me sad and mad. Part of their problem is us and the way we threw money and GIs at the war to keep it going on and on before we gave up on it.

I want to come home and settle down. Have a basketball hoop by the garage and shoot baskets with my son. Take my little daughter to ballet lessons or swim lessons or whatever it is she loves to do. If she wants to be a car mechanic or a fisherwoman, that's okay, too.

I'm tired of sweeping up the dust of this unpopular war. I just want to come home to you.

Love,

Steve

September 28, 1974

Dear Steve,

Happy belated birthday! If I had known, I would have sent you a care package. I won't forget your next birthday now that I have it on my calendar!

Your letter made me cry. You sound so discouraged yet noble. The details of basketball hoops and ballet lessons (or whatever) make me feel that you will be a wonderful father.

I, too, am ready to settle down. There's ~~something~~ I haven't told you and very few people know. ~~After two years of college~~ I was married once and divorced. After two years of college, I eloped with my senior boyfriend Will. Not even my parents knew until after it was ~~over and~~ done. They didn't like him, and I knew they would disapprove of our marriage, so we drove to South Carolina over spring break and were married in a quickie ceremony by an unknown justice of the peace. My parents were right about Will ~~and his terrible temper~~. Within six months I knew I had made a big mistake. To add to my problems, I was pregnant. I left him and my parents persuaded me to have an abortion. I have never forgiven myself. I thought that teaching would rid me of guilt and fulfill my need for children, but it hasn't. I want my very own child to cuddle every day, to protect, to watch grow up. And I want a loving husband, one who respects me and whom I respect and love deeply.

So now you know my sordid past. I hope it doesn't change ~~your opinion~~ how you feel about me. Although I want you to love me forever, you can't truly love me without knowing the truth about me.

This was a difficult letter to write. I hope it shows you that I value honesty and will always be honest with you as I hope you are with me.

Love, Alice

October 1, 1974

Dear Alice,

It has been another bummer week. The more I try to convince Big Buzz that my information is critical, the more he ignores me. I've thought of escalating, but Willi tells me that would be a mistake.

What would you do if you knew something was happening but nobody listened? I know I'm the new kid on the block and haven't proven my worth, but it really bugs me that I can't get people to take me seriously. I even requested a one-on-one meeting with my boss and he dismissed me and said to follow protocol. Protocol @**%!

Sorry to vent like this to you. It makes me realize I don't want a career in the military!

I'd better end this stream of misery.

Love,

Steve

October 16, 1974

Dear Alice,

I just received your very honest letter. It makes me love you more because you had the courage to tell me the truth. I hope we can always be that way with each other. My parents have a good marriage and I believe it is because they don't hide stuff from each other.

Things are even more tense at work. Big Buzz avoids me and the last time I went to his office, he said he would charge me with insubordination if I didn't stop bothering him. He ordered me to stay away from Phan Thiet and gave me another assignment. The trouble is nobody else on the team can decipher the code, which changes on a regular basis. Willi says I have Big Buzz between a rock and a hard place.

All this makes me even more ready to come home to you.

Love,

Steve

November 3, 1974

Dear Steve,

~~You letters have been sitting here on my desk waiting to be answered. I could say that I've been extremely busy, which is true, but the real reason is that I have something else to tell you. I've avoided telling you because it puts more pressure on you and it appears you have a lot of pressure already with your job and your difficult boss. So I'm pregnant. Speaking of pressure, I'm having my share of it as well.~~

It has been too long since I wrote. Your last two letters made me feel so badly for you. I can only imagine being in your situation. I happen to have a very understanding boss who has been supportive of me in every way.

It's November so my class has been studying the Pilgrims and the meaning of Thanksgiving. We have fall leaves, real ones that we collected and ironed with wax, decorating the bulletin boards in the room. I've had the children write about what they are most thankful for and some of their stories bring tears to my eyes.

Thanksgiving this year will be at my grandparents' house. It's where my mom and her five siblings grew up and all but one sibling will be there. It will be a huge crowd so all of us are chipping in with the food. I'm bringing two pies, an apple and a pumpkin.

I do hope you have something to be thankful for this Thanksgiving. I'm thankful that I met you and that your time in Vietnam is almost half over.

Love, Alice

November 29, 1974

Dear Alice,

I'm sending this letter through the Vietnam post office. Your last letter to me arrived yesterday and it was obvious that it had been tampered with. I don't trust Big Buzz.

I won't bore you with details, but I think my boss is unfit for his position. Don't know what to do about it. There are rumors that he might be promoted, which blows my mind. If he is, the next in command will be my boss. He's a yes-man and will do whatever Big Buzz says.

But enough of that. We had turkey on Thanksgiving with a side of fish sauce, the Vietnamese national ketchup. Just to be funny, someone brought in a bottle of the stuff and set it on the table. He dared us to dip our turkey in it and most of us did. I'm starting to like the taste, believe it or not.

Of course, we had all the fixings. Our tax payers are unhappily making sure we do. I know everyone wants this fiasco to be over, and I do too, but we've dropped the ball. We're abandoning the South Vietnamese after all these years. It's much more complicated than that, but bottom line, I see what's going to happen and it's a crying shame. We've handed the country over to the Communists because we don't care anymore and don't want to admit what's happening. Sorry to keep harping on this.

Happy Thanksgiving! I'll be more thankful when I can hold you in my arms again.

Love,

Steve

December 27, 1974

Dear Steve,

I just received your Nov. 29 letter. It looks like something chewed it up and spit it out again. It was a visual for its contents. Hope things are better now.

I have waited too long to tell you something that I probably should have mentioned months ago. Now I realize how unfair ~~it was~~ I was to withhold the information, because you had ~~as much a say a~~ right to know and a vote as to what should happen. But now it's too late for your vote and I can only tell you what I have decided to do.

I'm pregnant with our child. My parents urged me to have another abortion, but I couldn't. I'm still haunted by my first and there was no persuading me to do that to our love child. This baby is a part of you and me and will be an amazing person. So I'm quitting my job for the second semester and will give birth to our child who is due the end of March. I will not give our baby up for adoption. Period.

Sorry to spring this news on you so late. I will understand (I think) if it is too much for you to handle. I'm not asking for anything from you. I'm merely letting you know.

I'll be waiting for your response.

Love, Alice

December 29, 1974

Dear Alice,

Christmas has come and gone and I didn't even get a card from you. I know--I didn't send you one either. But it has been a really long time since I heard from you. I hope everything's ok.

It was weird to have Christmas on a humid 95 degree day with a lopsided fake tree in our lobby as the only clue. No one was in the mood.

The one cheery thing this holiday season is that Big Buzz is gone. We now have Little Buzz, his stooge. I haven't had a run-in with him yet, but to tell the truth, I haven't met with him officially. I've started going back to Phan Thiet and the messages are incriminating. I'll present them to Little Buzz next week.

Many of my predictions have already happened. The NVA has aggressively taken over cities north of Saigon and are counting on our inaction. They are also coming at us from the south and will soon surround Saigon.

It won't be long before the joke of a treaty, the Paris Peace Accord, is officially broken and the North Vietnamese will have won the war.

I should look on the bright side. This means I'll be home sooner.

P.S. Just for the heck of it, I'm sending this via Vietnam airmail again.

Love,

Steve

January 31, 1975

Dear Steve,

I finally received your last letter written just after Christmas. Apparently you haven't received my letter with the bombshell news. I've been waiting and hoping to hear that you are happy about being a father.

Your Christmas sounded very depressing and I must admit mine wasn't the best either. My parents are very upset with me so there was a great deal of tension.

I don't know what to say other than I think of you every day and pray you will return to me soon.

Love, Alice

Feb. 1, 1975

Dear Alice,

I haven't gotten a letter from you in over two months.
I can understand if you are tired of waiting. I
sometimes feel that way, too. Maybe you've met someone
else who doesn't write you depressing letters. Maybe
someone like your "understanding boss".

I was hoping we could weather the time and distance
after those two magical days together last summer.
But apparently not.

I wish you the best.

Steve

March 3, 1975

Dear Steve,

Obviously something terrible has happened and you are not receiving my letters. I don't know where else to send them. Yours get to me after 4 or 5 weeks and are all beaten up. Also, I'm hearing on the news about the horrible things that are happening in Vietnam. I worry about you constantly and feel sick that you think I don't care for you anymore.

Our baby is almost ready to be born. I'll send an extra special prayer with this letter so that you get it and know that I still love you as much if not more than I did back in June.

Love, Alice

~ The End ~

ACKNOWLEDGMENTS

I am grateful to so many who have endured this process with me. Thank you, Christy Belvin, for faithfully reading the first draft of everything I've ever written. Thanks to the Wednesday evening writers' group, who critiqued this book in 1200-word segments, and especially to Sara Kelly for doing the final proofreading. Lisa Svenson amazed me with her marathon edit and, among other things, helped me fine-tune dialog to characters' personalities. Jeremy Strozer checked the accuracy of my Vietnam War references, and Jan Frantz met me in Washington DC for the weekend I personally experienced The Wall. Thanks to friends Elaine Gardiner, Carolyn Ekle, and Pat Kerrigan, who slogged through the PDF version.

Thank you, Mark Thomas for designing a great cover and interior, and Hugh Willard for telling me, "It's not a question of 'if' you are published, it's 'when.'" And this wouldn't be complete without acknowledging my wonderful supportive daughter, Elise, and my son, James, who helped me realize that publishing this book was near the top of my bucket list.

ABOUT THE AUTHOR

Mary Marchese has a degree in English Literature and has been a feature writer for a newspaper, a technical writer at IBM, and currently edits a community newsletter. She grew up in Vietnam before the war and recently returned for a two week tour during Tet. She lives in Nashua, New Hampshire, USA.

To contact Mary, please visit her website:

MARYMARCHESE.COM

.

90205484R00195

Made in the USA
Lexington, KY
08 June 2018